Also by Jennifer L. Schiff

A Shell of a Problem

Something Fishy

In the Market for Murder

A Sanibel Island Mystery

Jennifer Lonoff Schiff

Shovel
&Pail
Press

This is a work of fiction. Names, characters, businesses, places, events, and incidents are either the products of the author's imagination or used in a fictitious manner. Any resemblance to actual persons, living or dead, or actual events, is purely coincidental.

IN THE MARKET FOR MURDER: A SANIBEL ISLAND MYSTERY
by Jennifer Lonoff Schiff

Book Three in the Sanibel Island Mystery series

https://www.SanibelIslandMysteries.com

Cover design by Kristin Bryant

Formatting by Polgarus Studio

ISBN: 978-0-692-15416-8

Library of Congress Control Number: 2018909878

My dream is to have a house on the beach, even just a little shack somewhere, so I can wake up, have coffee, look at dolphins, be quiet, and breathe the air.
—Christina Applegate

There's no place like home.
—Dorothy Gale, *The Wizard of Oz*

PROLOGUE

It had been nearly a year since Guin had moved to Sanibel, and she had no desire to move back North. And while she liked her condo, she wanted a place of her own.

Her landlord, a widow from Massachusetts, had moved back there to be with her grandchildren and had rented Guin the condo while she decided what she wanted to do with it. Now she was thinking of selling the place and had asked Guin if she was interested in buying it. Guin thought about it, but what she really wanted was to find a little cottage closer to the beach. So she had politely turned the widow down.

The widow had been disappointed, but she understood, and had agreed to extend Guin's lease through the end of the year and then go month to month. Guin had been a good tenant, and the widow had no idea how quickly she would be able to sell the place. And this way Guin didn't have to worry about moving before the new year.

However, finding that perfect little beach cottage had been much harder than Guin had anticipated. There weren't that many houses up for sale during hurricane season. And the ones that were were either too expensive or required too much work. Then came Hurricane Irma, which, quite literally, put a damper on her house search. The condo had been spared, as had most of the island, but Guin and her real estate agent had agreed it was best to put the house hunt on hold for a couple of weeks. So she had.

Now it was October and the island was as good as new and houses were starting to go back on the market again. And Guin was eager to resume her search and find her beach house—a cozy two bedroom, two bath cottage no more than a twenty-minute walk to the beach. Within her budget.

Guin's real estate agent, Polly Fahnestock, had assured Guin her dream home was out there. But the handful of places Polly had shown her were all nightmares—either total fixers, which Guin didn't have the budget to fix, too expensive, or too far from the beach.

Guin's beau, Ris—Dr. Harrison Hartwick, PhD, to his marine biology students at Florida Gulf Coast University—had suggested (multiple times) that Guin move into his beach cottage in Fort Myers Beach. But Guin wanted a place of her own, on Sanibel.

Guin was beginning to despair that she would never find her dream home when Polly texted her, saying she had a brand-new listing she wanted to show Guin. The place wasn't officially going on the market until the following week, but she had been invited to a private open house for a handful of top real estate agents, and she knew as soon as she saw it that it was perfect for Guin. Was she interested in seeing it that weekend?

What the heck? Guin thought.

She agreed to meet Polly at the cottage that Sunday at two, with Ris. (That morning, like every Sunday between October and May, Guin would be going to the Sanibel Farmers Market, one of her favorite activities.)

Now it was Sunday morning, and Guin was excited and nervous to see this "secret listing," as Polly had referred to it. Could this place be the one? First, however, she needed to get herself dressed, give the cats some food and fresh water, and get over to the farmers market.

CHAPTER 1

It was a beautiful, warm, sunny day on Sanibel. Though to Guin, every day on Sanibel was beautiful. She listened to the jazz station on the radio as she drove to the Sanibel Farmers Market, past the J. N. "Ding" Darling National Wildlife Refuge and the Bailey-Matthews National Shell Museum, feeling grateful to be living in such a special spot.

The market opened at eight, and Guin tried to get there right when it opened, as the parking lots could be full by eight-thirty in season (January through March). However, as it was only October, and most of the snowbirds had yet to arrive, she was able to find a spot relatively easily. She parked and grabbed her cart and insulated bags from the trunk and walked the short distance to the market, passing the Sanibel Police Department on the way.

As she walked past, she looked up, wondering if Detective O'Loughlin would be working today. After working together on a couple of cases over the last six months, she and the detective had formed, if not a friendship, an acquaintanceship. A fellow baseball fan, he had invited Guin to go with him to see his beloved Boston Red Sox play the Tampa Bay Rays over the summer, and Guin had in turn invited the detective to go with her to see her New York Mets play the Miami Marlins.

Guin had enjoyed their outings and thought the detective

had too. Then he had disappeared. She had thought maybe he had skipped town because of the hurricane. Though if anything that would keep him on or near the island. After he had cancelled a coffee date last minute, she had followed up with him to reschedule, but he hadn't written her back, and she felt a bit funny about writing him a second time.

Maybe I should text him again, Guin thought, looking back at the Sanibel Police Department. Invite him out for a coffee to catch up. See how the rest of his summer was. She was just reaching for her phone when it started to buzz. She retrieved it and saw there was a text message from Ris, wishing her a good morning and saying he was looking forward to seeing her later.

Guin smiled and texted him back. Then she put her phone back in her bag and walked briskly to the market.

Guin was a creature of habit and almost always followed the same route through the market. She stopped at Jimmy's Java to get her caffeine fix and purchase beans if she was running low. Then she made her way around the rectangle that formed the market, stopping at the different vendors to pick up this and that.

Ris was coming over to her place that afternoon, to look at the "secret listing" with her, and she said she would make them dinner afterward. As the market sold fresh seafood, right off the boat, she stopped by her favorite seafood vendor and bought a piece of grouper and some shrimp.

She had already bought mushrooms from Mr. Fun Guy. Now she just needed to buy some vegetables.

Her stomach started to growl as she walked by the bagel vendor. So she stopped and bought a half-dozen bagels. She could always freeze what she didn't eat right away. Then she continued on to the cheese vendor, where she bought some sharp cheddar and a lovely semi-soft cheese from France.

Ris hadn't been eating cheese or dairy since he started training for the Florida Ironman, but Guin adored the stuff.

Next she stopped at the meat vendor. Guin had thought it odd to have someone selling meat at a farmers' market, but one bite of Marvelous Meats' steak and she was hooked. She didn't know what they fed their cattle, but whatever it was, it made their meat tender and sweet. And it was supposedly sustainably raised and organic, which made her feel better.

She bought two New York strip steaks and moved on.

She was almost done shopping, but she couldn't resist stopping at the booth belonging to Jean-Luc's, a patisserie/bakery that had opened on the island earlier in the year. Guin had interviewed the owner of the bakery, Jean-Luc, for the paper, just before he had opened. And she had since become a semi-regular customer.

Guin looked around but didn't see Jean-Luc.

"May I help you?" asked a pleasant-looking young man with bright red hair.

"I was just looking for Jean-Luc," said Guin. "Did he run out for a cup of coffee?"

The young man smiled.

"No, Jean-Luc is back at the bakery."

"Ah," said Guin.

She looked at all the delicious looking pastries.

"Can I get you something?" asked the young man.

"A *pain au chocolat*, please," said Guin, "and a mocha eclair. And one of your fruit tartlets," she added.

She knew she shouldn't be buying so many sweets, especially with Ris avoiding sugar, but she couldn't resist. Everything looked so good.

The young man, whose name was Jake, handed Guin her box of pastries and wished her a good day.

Her shopping finished, Guin headed back to her car, a purple Mini Cooper she had driven from New England. She placed her items in the trunk, removing the box of pastries and placing it on the seat next to her. She removed the *pain au chocolat* and took a bite. Crumbs scattered everywhere, but she didn't care.

Oh my God, she thought, closing her eyes and savoring the dark, bittersweet chocolate. Something that good should be illegal. She took one more bite, then hurriedly stuffed the pastry back into the box.

She wiped her hands, then reached into her bag and took out her phone to check her messages. There was nothing urgent, or really anything, it being Sunday morning. She put the phone back in her bag, so as not to be distracted, then started the car.

CHAPTER 2

As Guin started unpacking her grocery bags, her cats, Flora and Fauna, rubbed themselves against her legs.

"I bet you guys smell the fish," she said, taking out the bag containing the grouper and the shrimp and dumping the ice the fishmonger had added to keep the seafood cool into the sink. Though she knew that fresh fish didn't smell.

The cats continued to rub up against her legs and Fauna began to meow.

"What do you want?" Guin asked the black cat.

Fauna continued to meow.

"I'm sorry, but I don't understand cat," replied Guin. "I gave you food already."

"Meow!" repeated Fauna.

"Fine," said Guin, beginning to lose patience. "How about some milk?"

Fauna loved milk, and Guin would give her a little in a special bowl some mornings as she was fixing her coffee. The cat immediately followed Guin to the cabinet where the little bowls were kept and then to the refrigerator, practically tripping Guin in the process.

"Give me a sec, will ya?" said Guin, exasperated.

She placed the bowl on the counter and poured a little milk in.

"Here," she said, placing the bowl on the floor, in front of the black cat.

Fauna immediately dived into the bowl, lapping up the milk.

"Silly cat," said Guin, watching. "And what can I do for you, Flora?" she asked her other cat, a calico-tabby mix. But Flora, who rarely said anything, just rubbed herself against Guin's left leg.

Guin bent down and petted the cat, who purred in response. A minute later, Guin straightened up.

"Okay, team, I need to put the rest of the groceries away and get to the beach before all the day-trippers show up!" she announced to the cats.

She quickly put away the rest of her purchases, then went to the bathroom and applied some sunblock. A few minutes later, her beach bag slung over her shoulder, keys in hand, she was heading out the door.

"You two be good," she called to the cats. "I'll be back before lunch!"

"Hey girl, slow down!" called Guin's friend Shelly.

"Sorry," said Guin. "I just want to get further down the beach, away from the sun worshippers."

Shelly, Guin's best friend on Sanibel, had texted Guin while Guin was getting ready, and they had arranged to meet over at Bowman's Beach, on the west end of the island.

"Okay, but could you slow down a little? I can't run on sand."

Guin stopped and waited for Shelly to catch up.

"Sorry, old habits die hard. I grew up in New York, and if you didn't walk fast there, you were likely to miss the light or get hit by a bike messenger."

"Well, you're on Sanibel now, and if you keep walking

that quickly, you're going to miss all the good shells. Not that I'd mind," said Shelly, grinning.

If shelling were a competition, Shelly, who made beautiful shell jewelry she sold on Etsy, would definitely be in the finals. Her garage was stacked with containers filled with shells, and she visited a beach, whether on Sanibel or Captiva or further south, in Naples or in the Ten Thousand Islands, several times a week looking for new specimens.

Guin slowed down, slightly, and waited until Shelly had caught up.

"So, what's new?" asked Shelly, as she stared down at the sand, looking for shells.

"I'm going to see another house this afternoon," replied Guin, whose eyes were also focused on the sand.

"Where?" asked Shelly, stooping to pick up a bright orange scallop.

"Nice one!" said Guin, looking over. She and Shelly both liked to collect brightly colored scallops. "Over in Gulf Pines."

"It's pretty wild back there," said Shelly, bending down to pick up a glossy brown lettered olive shell.

"Wild?" asked Guin.

"You know, rugged, untouched."

"Ah," said Guin, who had never been in Gulf Pines, one of the many communities that made up Sanibel.

"You have pictures?"

"No, it hasn't officially come on the market yet," she replied, stooping to pick up a small orange horse conch.

"Cute!" said Shelly, glancing over. "I hope it works out. Take some photos and send them to me if the place is decent."

"Will do," replied Guin.

They continued to walk westward along the beach, stooping to pick up shells.

Guin felt her phone vibrating in her back pocket and took it out. It was a text from Polly, confirming their appointment at two. Guin quickly texted her back.

"Everything okay?" asked Shelly, stopping.

"Oh yeah. That was just Polly confirming our appointment."

"Why the frown?"

Guin hadn't realized she was frowning.

"Nothing," said Guin. "I'm just tired of house hunting. I thought it would be a lot easier."

"Yeah, well…" said Shelly, looking back down at the sand.

They walked in silence for several minutes.

"So, how's work?"

Guin was a reporter for the *Sanibel-Captiva Sun-Times*, the local paper, known as the *San-Cap Sun-Times* for short.

"Okay," said Guin. "Ginny wants to make sure we post a few articles on the website every day, and we still have the print edition that comes out on Friday. So I've been keeping busy."

Ginny was Ginny Prescott, the editor and publisher of the *San-Cap Sun-Times*.

"Working on anything interesting?"

"I'm doing a piece on Halloween activities on Sanibel and Captiva."

"That sounds like fun," said Shelly, who wasn't really paying attention. (Her two kids were long past the age for trick-or-treating.)

"Hey," said Guin, stopping. "You mind if we turn around? I want to get back home and shower before Ris shows up."

They had nearly reached the end of the beach.

"No problem," said Shelly, looking up. "I'm not in the mood to wade thigh deep in the water today anyway," she said, looking over to the next strip of beach.

The next beach over, Silver Key, was just a little way away, but the tide was too high to cross over without getting wet up to your thighs.

They turned around and headed back down the beach, toward the parking lot.

"So, any news to report on your end?" asked Guin. "Justin still seeing that girl?"

Shelly's son, Justin, who had just started his junior year of college, had been dating an attractive blonde Political Science major from California, who bore a striking resemblance to Shelly and who Shelly didn't particularly like.

Shelly made a face.

"I don't know what he sees in her," she said.

Guin tried to hide her grin. She knew exactly what Justin saw in the young woman.

"Does that mean he's still seeing her?"

Shelly made another face.

"Yes, and he says he's bringing her home for Thanksgiving!"

"Well, that will be nice, to have him home for Thanksgiving," said Guin.

Shelly grumbled.

"And how is Lizzy liking her new job at Disney?"

Lizzy, short for Elizabeth, was Shelly's daughter.

"She loves it!" said Shelly. "Steve and I are going to go visit her, and she said she'd give us a behind-the-scenes tour."

"That sounds like fun," said Guin.

"And how does Ris feel about you getting a place on Sanibel?" Shelly asked.

Guin sighed.

"He's supportive, I guess."

"You guess?" asked Shelly.

"He doesn't understand why I don't just move into his

place. But as I've explained to him, I want my own place, and I don't want to live in Fort Myers Beach."

"Honey, if a man as good looking and smart and nice as Ris asked me to come live with him, I'd say, 'I'll be right over' and move in the next day."

Guin laughed.

"Well, I admit, I've thought about it, especially after seeing what I can get here on my budget. But I'm not ready to move in with him just yet. Who knows? Maybe Polly's 'secret listing' is the one."

"And maybe you're just afraid of commitment," said Shelly.

Guin didn't reply. Instead she continued to look down at the shoreline, trying to spy a gaudy nautica, or an alphabet cone, or a Scotch bonnet, or a king's crown conch, or maybe, just maybe, a junonia. But the tide was already coming in, and there weren't that many shells of any kind to be had that morning, except for the usual suspects (arks, pen shells, clams and cockles, and a few other shells that didn't interest most conchologists, at least the ones who lived on or regularly visited Sanibel).

They walked in silence the rest of the way, until they reached the entrance to the beach.

"Well, that wasn't very fruitful," said Shelly, looking into her bucket, which had only a handful of shells in it.

"True," said Guin, "but you have more than enough shells in that garage of yours and in your crafting room to make enough shell jewelry to outfit everyone attending next year's Shell Festival."

"True," said Shelly. "But I have to keep replenishing my stock. Christmas is just around the corner, and if sales are as good as last year, I've got to get going."

"Speaking of getting going…" said Guin.

"What time's Harry Heartthrob coming over?" asked Shelly.

Guin made a face. She hated when Shelly called Ris that. A few years back, one of the local lifestyle magazines had nicknamed him that, or had picked up the nickname, and used it in their profile of him, and it had stuck.

"Noon," said Guin. "We're going to go have lunch and then meet Polly."

"Well, have fun. And don't forget to send me pictures!"

"Only if the place is worth photographing," said Guin.

They made their way to the parking lot, rinsing off at the foot showers on route.

"Well, I'll be seeing you," said Shelly, when they got to the parking lot.

"Have a good afternoon," said Guin.

They exchanged hugs and kisses and headed off to their cars.

CHAPTER 3

Ris showed up promptly at Guin's at noon. Then they biked over to the Sunset Grill for lunch. Guin had wanted to drive over, as she had just taken a shower. But since Ris was training for the Ironman, he insisted they bike. Guin thought about objecting, as it was hot and humid, but she kept her mouth shut. At least she would burn or sweat off most of what she ate.

As it turned out, it wasn't so bad. There was a breeze blowing off the Gulf, and Sanibel being flat, the ride was pretty easy. Though Ris immediately zoomed ahead of her and Guin struggled to keep up. But she was proud of herself for making it to the restaurant just a couple of minutes after him. Of course, while she looked like she had been biking for miles (her shirt was clinging to her back), Ris looked fresh as a daisy.

"What's wrong?" Ris asked, looking over at her. "You're making that face."

"What face?" asked Guin, trying not to look annoyed.

"That face you make when you're annoyed or frustrated," said Ris, smiling at her.

She scowled at him.

"That face," he said, continuing to smile at her.

Guin sighed.

"I'm just annoyed that you look like that," she said,

waving a hand at him, "and I look like this," she said, pulling her damp shirt away from her body.

"I love how you look," Ris replied.

Guin rolled her eyes.

"Let's go eat. All that biking made me hungry."

Ris gestured for her to lead, and they made their way into the restaurant.

It was too hot, in Guin's opinion, to sit outside, so they sat by the window, under the fan. Guin, as usual, ordered an Arnold Palmer, and Ris ordered water, no ice.

"So, tell me about this house we're going to see this afternoon."

"I don't really know much about it," said Guin. "But Polly insists I will love it."

"You know you don't have to do this, Guin," he began, reaching across the table and placing a hand on top of hers.

Guin knew what was coming.

"I know what you are going to say, Ris, and I appreciate you inviting me to live with you, but…"

Now it was Ris's turn to look annoyed.

"I'm not inviting you to live with me because I feel an obligation, Guin. I want you to live with me because I care about you, and I think you care about me, and I'd like us to live together."

Guin didn't know what to say. She looked into his gray-green eyes and wanted to tell him she'd move in with him, but she just couldn't. She cared about him. Enjoyed spending time with him. And she loved his little beach cottage. But the idea of living with him full time made her uneasy. She had been divorced for just over a year and was enjoying living on her own and having her own place. Why couldn't he understand and just be happy with the way things were?

She was about to say something to that effect when their drinks arrived.

"Are you two ready to order?" asked the server.

"Yes!" Guin practically shouted.

Ris looked bemused.

"I will have the fried green tomato sandwich, please, with some of your homemade potato chips."

Ris ordered a salad with grilled shrimp.

"So," said Guin, eager to change the subject. "Are you ready for the big race?"

The Florida Ironman was November 4th, just a couple of weeks away.

Ris gave her a look that indicated he knew what she was doing but was willing to play along, for now.

"As ready as I'll ever be. I wish you'd reconsider and come with me."

Ris had asked Guin to drive with him to Panama City and attend the race, but she had declined.

"Would I even see you? How long does it take to complete an Ironman?"

"I'm hoping to complete the race in under twelve hours, but I'd be okay if it was a bit over that."

Guin couldn't imagine swimming over two miles, then biking over a hundred miles, then running a marathon in one day, or even a month.

"Won't you be exhausted?"

"No doubt. But I figured we could spend Sunday together."

Guin hesitated. She wanted to support Ris, did support him. But the idea of driving to Panama City, nearly eight hours away, then hanging out someplace unfamiliar while Ris swam, biked, and ran all day was not her idea of a romantic weekend.

She was about to say something when the server came over with their food.

"Just think about it," said Ris, touching her hand.

Guin nodded her head, happy to have the distraction of food.

They biked back to Guin's condo after lunch. Upon arriving, Guin announced she needed to shower (again). Ris, who had hardly broken a sweat, told her to go ahead. He would hang out in the living room with the cats.

"Thanks," said Guin, annoyed that he never seemed to sweat or smell. "I'll be out in a few."

She emerged a short while later, attired in a pretty sundress.

"Ready?"

Ris stood up and walked over to Guin.

"Come here," he said.

She took a couple steps toward him and he pulled her into an embrace, kissing her.

"What was that for?" asked Guin, when they finally broke off. She felt a bit lightheaded, but Ris often had that effect on her.

"No reason," he said, grinning down at her.

Guin eyed him suspiciously.

"You just want me to forget all about house hunting."

"Maybe," he replied. "Is it working?"

"No," stated Guin. "But feel free to keep trying."

He laughed and followed her to the front door, the cats trotting after him.

"We'll be back soon," she told the cats. "Do me a favor and don't throw up or scratch anything while we're gone, okay?"

Flora and Fauna gazed up at her.

"I don't think they understood," said Ris.

Guin sighed.

"Yeah, well. Couldn't hurt."

A few minutes later, they were in Ris's vintage red Alfa Romeo convertible, heading down Sanibel-Captiva Road to Gulf Pines.

They arrived at the cottage to find Polly there waiting for them.

The cottage looked cute from the outside, though it could use a coat of paint and some landscaping, Guin thought.

"Nice wheels," said Polly, admiring Ris's car. And nice chauffeur she thought, gazing up at Ris. (At around six-foot-two, he towered over both Guin and Polly.)

Ris smiled at her and extended his hand.

"Harrison Hartwick. Nice to meet you."

"Polly Fahnestock, and I know who you are. A pleasure," she said, shaking his hand and continuing to smile at him.

Guin watched, amused. Ris, who was tall and lean, with dark wavy hair that was just starting to turn gray, and smiling green-gray eyes, looked more like someone you would see in *Men's Health* than a professor lecturing college students. And women were constantly flirting with him.

"Shall we go see the house?" asked Guin, interrupting.

Polly turned to her and smiled.

"Let's go! I think you're really going to love this one, Guin. It needs a little work, but it has good bones—and it's less than a fifteen-minute walk to the beach."

Guin took a deep breath and released it.

"Okay, let's go see it."

They followed Polly up the stairs to the front door. There was a lock box on it, which Polly opened using an app on her phone.

"That's cool," said Guin. "Haven't seen that before."

"Yeah, it's a new thing some of the real estate agents are trying out."

Interesting, thought Guin.

Polly took the keys out of the lock box and opened the door. Guin walked in and stopped to look around.

The layout was open concept, with the kitchen just to the right of the front door and a small but bright and airy living area in front of them. Just beyond was the lanai, with a view of a little lake. Guin walked around, moving slowly from the kitchen around the living-dining area. As Polly had warned, the place needed work, but it had charm.

Guin pulled out her phone and took a few pictures.

"Shall we go see the master?" Polly asked.

Guin followed Polly past the kitchen, down a short hallway. To the right were a little laundry room and a closet; to the left were the master bedroom and bathroom.

Guin looked around the room. There was a king-sized bed, with a nightstand on either side, a lamp topping each table, and a chest of drawers with a television on top across from the bed. It wasn't quite as large as her bedroom at the condo, but it was still a good size, and there were sliders leading out to the lanai and a view of the lake.

"It needs some work," said Guin, looking at the marked-up walls and the dated furniture, "but it's a nice size, and I like the view."

She took a few photos, then put her phone back in her pocket.

There was a walk-in closet on one side of the room and next to it a door leading to the master bathroom. Guin walked in and was pleasantly surprised to find that the bathroom looked like it had been updated in the last decade.

"It's actually pretty nice," she said, snapping a couple photos.

"According to the listing agent, the bathroom was recently updated."

Guin walked into the closet. Like the bedroom and bathroom, it was a good size.

"Let me show you the guest bedroom," said Polly. "And I have a surprise for you!" she added, leading them to the other side of the cottage.

They walked past the kitchen and the living area down another short hallway. In front of them was the guest bathroom, which looked like it had also been updated relatively recently. To the left was the guest bedroom, which was small but fit two twin beds.

"And here," said Polly, opening the other door, "is the surprise!"

Guin took a step forward and peered into the room. There were some book shelves, and a desk and chair, and there on the floor…

"Oh my God!" she said, her hand flying up to cover her nose and mouth.

There on the floor, lying mostly face down, was the body of a woman.

CHAPTER 4

"I'm guessing this was not the surprise," said Ris, bending down over the woman and feeling for a pulse.

"Is she dead?" asked Polly, watching wide eyed as Ris gently lifted the woman's right wrist, which was adorned with a charm bracelet. Though from the smell in the room, it was safe to say the woman wasn't sleeping.

He shook his head.

"I'm calling the police," said Guin.

She pulled out her phone and pressed 9-1-1.

"This is Guin Jones," she told the 911 operator. "I just found a dead body at…" She gave her the address. "They're on their way," she said, after ending the call.

Polly walked over to the body and had bent down to examine it when Guin admonished her not to touch anything, though it took all her willpower not to turn the woman over herself, so she could at least see her face. Instead, she took several photos.

"Any idea who she is?" asked Ris.

Polly looked down at the corpse. The woman's head was turned sideways, her shoulder-length blonde hair covering most of her face. She was probably around five-foot-six, in good shape. From her attire, she looked young, probably in her twenties.

Polly shook her head.

"She doesn't look familiar."

"Any idea how she got in here?" asked Ris.

"No," said Polly. "The owners are an older couple who just moved to an assisted living community on the other side of the Causeway. I know the family. They have a granddaughter, but she lives off-island and is a brunette."

"So, no idea who it could be?" asked Guin.

"None," said Polly.

"Shall we go wait in the living room?" asked Ris.

"Good idea," said Guin.

They didn't have long to wait.

"Detective O'Loughlin," said Guin, eyeing the detective.

They had heard the police siren and had gone outside.

"Ms. Jones," replied the detective. "Why am I not surprised to find you here?"

"Detective," said Ris, taking a step forward, as if protecting Guin.

"Dr. Hartwick," said the detective, giving Ris a brief nod.

"I'm Polly Fahnestock, with Sanibel Homes," said Polly, taking a step forward and extending a hand, which the detective did not take. "I was showing Ms. Jones and Dr. Hartwick here the home when we, uh…"

"Which one of you found the body?" asked the detective.

"I did," said Guin.

"But we were all together," added Ris.

The detective looked from Guin to Ris.

"And how long ago was this?" asked the detective.

"Less than thirty minutes," replied Guin.

"And what brought you here?" asked the detective.

"I've been looking to buy a place. Polly—she's my broker—was showing us around."

"It's a brand-new listing," explained Polly. "Not even

officially on the market until tomorrow."

The detective looked from Guin to Polly.

"So you met Ms. Jones and Dr. Hartwick here at the house?" asked the detective.

"I did," said Polly.

"And when did you arrive?"

"A couple of minutes before two. I know because I remember looking at the clock on my dashboard, and it said 1:58."

"And did you enter the house before Ms. Jones and Dr. Hartwick arrived?"

"I did not," said Polly. "Like I said, I got here just a couple minutes before they did."

"And do you have any idea who the deceased is?"

"No," said Polly. "I don't even know how she could have gotten in. The place was supposed to be locked up, and only a handful of real estate agents had the code to the lock box."

"Did either of you recognize the victim?" the detective asked Guin and Ris.

"Never seen her before," said Ris.

"You could barely see her face," added Guin. "Maybe if I had gotten a better look at her…"

The detective finished writing in his little notebook and put it away.

"All right then. Officer Rayburn and I are going to go in."

Guin started to follow them back inside the house when the detective stopped her.

"Sorry, Ms. Jones. I know how you find crime scenes irresistible, but I need you and your friends to stay outside."

Guin made a face.

"Will your friend Mike be joining us?" she asked.

Mike Gilbertie was a Lee County medical examiner who Guin had met the last time she found a dead body. He was also a fishing buddy of the detective's.

The detective smiled, or it could have been a smirk. On the detective, it was hard to tell.

"I'm not sure if he's on call today," replied the detective. "But someone from the medical examiner's office should be here shortly."

"Can we get back in, after you're done?"

The detective gave her a look.

"Is that a yes or a no?"

The detective sighed.

"Don't you have some other houses to look at?" asked the detective, looking from Guin to Ris and Polly.

"No," said Guin, before Polly could answer. (She had been hoping to show Guin another place.)

The detective and Guin stared at each other.

The detective blinked.

"Fine. But it could be a while," said the detective.

"I'm fine waiting," said Guin, though Polly and Ris didn't seem nearly so eager.

The detective scowled and signaled for Officer Rayburn to go in. He followed him a minute later. Soon after, a van from the medical examiner's office pulled into the driveway and a woman and two men got out. Guin introduced herself and told them where they could find the body and the detective.

"Are you sure I can't show you a couple of other houses, Guin?" asked Polly, as they waited outside. "There's a real cute one just around the corner. We could go see it and then come back."

Guin had been pacing around the driveway, trying to reach her boss at the paper, but she was having no luck.

"Where is she?" Guin asked, looking down at her phone.

"It *is* Sunday, Guin," said Ris. "Maybe she's out on a boat somewhere."

"But why isn't she answering her phone?" Guin replied, not really listening.

Ris sighed and looked at Polly.

"Guin, be reasonable," said Ris. Which was absolutely the wrong thing to say to Guin, as he realized the second after he said it.

"Reasonable? Is it reasonable to go look at houses when there's a dead body just a few feet away?"

Guin looked from Ris to Polly.

"I'm going back in," she announced.

"Do you think that's wise, Guin?" Polly asked. "You heard what the detective said."

Guin stopped.

"They've been in there forever."

It was an exaggeration, which Guin knew, but she hated to be kept waiting. She wanted another look at the body and the room.

She started to climb the stairs when a member of the medical examiner's team emerged.

"Are you all done in there?" Guin asked. "Can I go in?"

"You'll have to ask Detective O'Loughlin about that," said the man. "I'm just getting something from the van."

"Can you at least tell me how the victim died?" asked Guin.

"Again, you'll have to ask the detective."

Guin stood there, not sure what to do.

"If you'll excuse me," said the man.

Guin stepped aside to let the man pass. Then she went up the stairs and knocked on the door. A few seconds later Officer Rayburn, who was wearing crime scene gloves, appeared.

"Yes, can I help you, miss?"

"Ms. Jones," said Guin, trying not to sound as irritated as she felt. "Please tell Detective O'Loughlin I would like to see him."

"He's kind of busy, Ms. Jones."

"Look, Officer…"

"Rayburn."

"Look, Officer Rayburn, I'm the one who found the body, and…" She wasn't sure what to say. "And I'd really appreciate finding out what happened. I know the detective, personally, and I'm sure he'd understand. Could you please just go tell him Ms. Jones would like a word with him?"

She gave Officer Rayburn a pleading look, not caring if she was humiliating herself. She just wanted in, before the body was carted away.

"Fine," said the officer, with a sigh. "Let me go ask him if it's okay to let you in."

He went inside, and, as he did, the man from the medical examiner's office ran up the steps and gently squeezed past Guin into the house. Guin decided to follow him in.

She stood just inside the door. A minute later the detective appeared. He did not look happy to see her.

"Well?" she asked, as he walked toward her.

The detective stood and looked at her.

"Do the words 'crime scene' mean nothing to you, Ms. Jones?"

Guin ignored him.

"So what was the cause of death? Any idea who she is, or was?"

"To answer your first question, it looks like she was strangled," said the detective. "But the medical examiner has ordered an autopsy to be sure. As to your second question, not yet. We found no ID on her or anywhere in the home."

"But surely someone must know who she is," said Guin. "Certainly the murderer did."

"Not necessarily," replied the detective. "She could have been in the house and startled a burglar."

Guin made a face. It was possible the woman had a legitimate reason to be in the house and had startled a burglar, but her intuition told her that was not the case.

"May I take a look around?" asked Guin.

"Only if you promise not to touch anything," said the detective.

"Well, we were already in the house, touching stuff," Guin pointed out. "No doubt our fingerprints are on all the doorknobs."

"Well, try not to touch anything else," said the detective.

"May I see her?" asked Guin.

The detective eyed Guin, as if trying to come to a decision. Guin stared back at him.

"Fine. Come with me. But again, don't touch anything."

Guin followed him to the office. Officer Rayburn was there, standing guard as the medical examiner made some notes, her two assistants standing by her side.

"She's younger than I thought," said Guin, squatting down and looking at the woman's face, which was now visible. "Early twenties?"

"Most likely," said the medical examiner, a woman who looked to be in her late fifties or early sixties.

The young woman was wearing a sundress, with a cardigan over it. Pretty girl, thought Guin. Or she was.

"How long has she been dead?"

"Less than twenty-four hours," said the medical examiner, "though I could be off by an hour or two."

"And you said you couldn't find any ID, no wallet or purse?" Guin asked the detective.

"Nope, nothing," said the detective.

"Any identifying marks, tattoos, or piercings?"

"Actually…" said the detective.

Guin waited.

"There's a small tattoo just over her heart," said the medical examiner.

Guin raised her eyebrows, then looked down at the body. She was itching to check out the tattoo, but she restrained herself.

"It's a heart with initials inside, but someone covered up the initials with a permanent marker."

Guin looked from the young woman to the detective.

"The murderer?"

"Possibly. Or she could have done it herself," he replied.

Guin was about to ask why, if the woman no longer wanted the tattoo, she didn't just have it removed. Then she recalled reading somewhere that tattoo removal was expensive and painful. Maybe the young woman figured this would be the quickest way to remove the offending mark, or maybe she had done it in a fit of pique.

As Guin was musing, the medical examiner spoke again.

"I'm all set here, detective. Okay if we remove the body?"

"You get those photos?" the detective asked Officer Rayburn.

"Yes, sir," he replied.

"She's all yours," said the detective.

"Go get the stretcher," commanded the medical examiner.

Her two assistants left and returned a few minutes later with the stretcher. They carefully placed the young woman's body on it and covered her up.

Guin watched as they made their way out of the room. She remained behind with the detective.

"You okay?" he asked. "You don't look so good."

"I'm fine," she replied. Though she didn't feel fine. Something about seeing someone so young dead made her feel her own mortality.

"So, she was strangled," she said, looking down at the spot on the floor where she had found the dead woman just a short time before.

"There were marks on her neck consistent with strangulation," said the detective. "We'll have to wait for the medical examiner's report to confirm that was the cause of death, though. Could have been drugs or something else."

Guin unconsciously placed a hand around her neck and shivered.

"Ahem," came a male voice. "Are you done here, Guin?"

"Oh my God, Ris!," said Guin, turning to face her beau. She had totally forgotten about him, and Polly. Her face turned a bright pink. "Have you been waiting long? Is Polly still there?"

"She left," Ris replied. "I hope that was okay, detective?"

The detective regarded Ris.

"I'll follow up with her tomorrow."

"May we go now?" asked Ris.

Guin wasn't sure if he was asking her or the detective.

"Be my guest," said the detective.

"But—" began Guin, looking at the detective.

He raised an eyebrow.

Guin sighed.

"Fine, but I want to know the results of the autopsy and take a look around the house."

"Call me tomorrow," replied the detective.

Guin was about to say something about the detective not returning her calls or messages, but Ris interrupted her.

"Guin, let's go. You heard the detective. You can follow up with him tomorrow."

"Fine," Guin said again. "But if you don't take my call, I'm coming down to the police department," she said, giving the detective her I-mean-business look.

"Good afternoon, Ms. Jones, Dr. Hartwick," said the

detective, taking out his notebook and turning away from them.

"Guin," said Ris, taking hold of her arm.

He led her out of the house and down the steps to his Alfa Romeo. He opened the passenger side door and waited for her to get in, closing the door after her. Then he made his way around to the driver's side and got in.

Guin's mind raced as they drove back to the condo. Who was the young woman and what was she doing at the cottage? Who would want to kill her and leave her there? And whose initials were on that tattoo?

"I'm not going to even ask what you're thinking about," said Ris, glancing over at Guin.

"Is it that obvious?" asked Guin.

Ris gave her a smile. Guin sighed.

"Sorry."

"Nothing to be sorry about," he replied. "I get it. I just hope you won't let it interfere with the rest of our time together. I feel like I haven't seen you in ages."

Between Ris's Ironman training schedule and his work at FGCU and the Shell Museum, where he was acting science director, he hadn't had a lot of free time lately, but Guin didn't want to point that out. She had kept herself busy and had enjoyed whatever time they had together. But she did feel bad that their day together had been spoiled.

She placed a hand gently on Ris's right arm.

"I promise to try not to think about work for the rest of the day," Guin began, "but I really need to text Ginny."

Ris glanced over at her.

"Go ahead," he sighed. "Then can we please not talk about work or dead bodies?"

"Deal."

Guin then reached into her bag and pulled out her phone.

CHAPTER 5

"Nope, no idea who the dead woman is."

Ginny had called Guin seconds after she and Ris had walked into the condo, demanding details.

"I told you, Ginny, the detective would barely let me back in, let alone look around the place. But I'm hoping to go back there tomorrow. I told O'Loughlin I'd call him in the morning."

"Good. If I know my star reporter, she'll figure out a way to get back in there."

"I thought Craig was your star reporter," said Guin.

Craig was Craig Jeffers, an award-winning crime reporter from Chicago who had retired to Sanibel to spend his days fishing. Ginny had lured him out of retirement by offering him the fishing beat, and then sweet-talked him into covering local crimes, explaining that they rarely occurred on Sanibel and Captiva.

"You're both stars," Ginny replied.

"Uh-huh," said Guin.

Guin knew that Ginny valued her work, and she was a great boss, giving Guin free rein to pretty much cover whatever she wanted.

"Just find out what you can about the woman. The sooner the better. I don't want us to be scooped."

"I'm on it."

She paused.

"What about Craig?"

"What about him?" asked Ginny.

"You want me to work with him? I know he typically covers crime on the island, but…"

On the last two murder cases Guin had been involved with, Ginny had insisted that Craig, as an experienced crime reporter, be in charge. But Guin felt she had earned the opportunity to take the lead this time.

Guin could practically hear Ginny thinking on the other end of the line.

"It would be nice if my two best reporters could work together on this," she replied.

"Fine," said Guin. "But I want to take the lead on this one."

"Fine," said Ginny. "But don't try to do everything yourself. There's a killer out there. And Craig has a lot more experience dealing with these kinds of things."

"I know, and he's a *guy*, so…"

"That has nothing to do with it, Guinivere," said Ginny. "I don't care what gender my reporters are as long as they get me a good story and can write. Craig's just been at this longer than you, and he has connections."

Guin felt chastised, and rightly so. Though it wasn't like she was some kid, just starting out. She was over forty and had worked as a reporter for years in New England before moving down to Sanibel. True, she had mostly covered business and human interest stories, but she had now successfully covered and helped solve two local murder cases.

"You still there, Guinivere?"

"Yeah. Sorry Ginny."

"No need to be sorry. Just get me that story." She paused. "Will I see you this week?"

Guin usually stopped by the office, located just off Periwinkle, on Tuesdays, after the print edition went to press, to discuss story ideas and hear the latest island gossip.

"I was planning on it," said Guin.

"Good," said Ginny. "Just send me a text to make sure I'm available before you drive over."

"Will do."

Guin ended the call, then phoned Craig. His voicemail picked up, so she left a brief message, asking him to call her back.

"Everything okay?" asked Ris, who had been texting with his daughter Fiona, who was away at college.

"Yup, all good. Ginny gave me the go ahead to work on the story for the paper, and I was just leaving a message for Craig."

"So, what do you want to do?"

Just then Guin's phone rang. It was Craig, calling her back.

"Craig," she said, giving Ris an apologetic look.

She excused herself and went into the bedroom to speak with him.

A short time later Guin emerged from her bedroom, which doubled as her office, expecting to find Ris hanging out in the living room or on the lanai. But he was nowhere to be found.

"Ris?" Guin called, knocking on the door of the half bath.

No answer.

She walked into the kitchen, though he was obviously not there either. Where could he be? She then spied the notepad she kept near the fridge. Ris had left her a note. "Gone for a run. Be back by 6." Guin stared at it. She felt badly. She had barely seen Ris the last few months and now when she finally did she got distracted by work. Well, at least he could get his Ironman training in, she told herself.

She looked up at the clock on the microwave. It was a little after five o'clock. She still hadn't looked at the photos she had taken at the crime scene, and she still had to edit her Halloween article. Might as well get some work done while Ris was out.

As she was standing there, Fauna brushed against her leg.

"Meow," said the black cat, looking up at her.

"Let me guess," said Guin. "You want food."

"Meow," repeated Fauna, still looking up at her.

"Fine," replied Guin. She walked over to the pantry and got out the bag of cat food. "But just a little bit," she told the cat.

Fauna followed her as she made her way to the cat bowls. As the dry food hit the bowl, she heard Flora come trotting down the hall.

"Here you go, team," said Guin, taking a step back. "But no more food until bedtime."

As usual, the cats ignored her, focusing on their food instead.

Guin smiled and put away the bag of cat food, making sure to clip it and put it where the cats could not get at it. Then she went back down the hall to her bedroom/office.

The sound of the doorbell startled Guin. Who can that be? she thought. Then she remembered, Ris. She hurriedly got up and went to the front door. It was, indeed, Ris, a very sweaty Ris. (Good to know he could actually sweat, she thought.) She opened the door and let him in, keeping her distance.

"You have a good run?" she asked. He was positively

drenched, but he had a big smile on his face.

"I did. I love running on Sanibel," he said.

"Where'd you go?"

"I ran down to Captiva and back," he replied.

"All the way to South Seas?" asked Guin, wide eyed. "How fast were you running?"

"Not that fast. It's only around seven miles from here to South Seas," he said.

Guin stared at him. Back in the day, when she was into running, she would regularly run five miles or so, but 14 miles? No way.

"You want to take a shower?" Guin asked, watching the sweat roll down his neck and arms.

"Probably a good idea," he said, smiling.

"You know the way," Guin said.

"Thanks," said Ris. "I'll just be a few minutes."

"Take your time," said Guin. "Just one question: What do you want for dinner?"

"What are my choices?"

"I got a nice piece of grouper at the farmers market, which I can roast with some veg, or we can have steak. I picked up a couple of juicy looking New York strip steaks, in case you were craving meat. And I have some fingerling potatoes, mushrooms, carrots, and Brussels sprouts."

"Tough choice," said Ris. "Can I think about it while I'm in the shower and get back to you?"

"Sure. No problem," said Guin. "I'll be at my desk, working."

"Just promise me, no more working tonight, okay? We were supposed to take a break from work today, remember?"

For the second time that afternoon, Guin felt badly. She had promised Ris no more talking about or doing work, and here she was breaking her promise.

"Deal," said Guin, mentally crossing her fingers.

Ris gave her a look, and Guin gave him a sheepish smile.

"Come here," he said, reaching for her.

"No!" she squealed, leaping out of the way. He was very sweaty, though she was tempted. Ris took great care of his body, and it showed.

"Go take a shower!" she ordered, pointing toward the bathroom.

"Fine," he said.

He headed back to the bathroom, whistling something as he went. Guin smiled and shook her head.

Guin wound up roasting the grouper, along with a bunch of vegetables, and they spent the rest of the evening cuddling on Guin's couch, with the cats, watching a documentary about the world's oceans that Ris had been wanting to see.

"Doesn't this count as work?" asked Guin, since Ris was a marine biologist.

"Only if I test you on it," said Ris, smiling at her.

She snuggled closer to him.

"I'd probably fail."

"Aren't you in training to become a Shell Ambassador?"

Guin was, in fact, in training to become a Shell Ambassador, a designation given to amateur shell enthusiasts (also known as conchologists) who attended a day-long class and passed a series of tests administered by the Bailey-Matthews National Shell Museum. But the actual class and test weren't for several weeks yet.

"Yes, but they don't test you on the salinity of the ocean," she replied.

"It's approximately 3.5 percent or 35 parts per thousand," said Ris, grinning down at her. "In case anyone asks."

She punched him in the arm.

"Ow," he replied, though Guin knew she hadn't hurt him.

"Wise guy."

They watched the rest of the documentary in near silence, with Guin occasionally asking Ris a question. Then Guin insisted they watch an episode of *Island Life* on HGTV. Which reminded Guin, she should really call Polly to apologize.

CHAPTER 6

Ris had gone for another run early the next morning, and Guin decided to go for a walk on the beach while he was out. She was trying to decide which beach to go to, Blind Pass, Bowman's, or West Gulf Drive. (Lighthouse Beach was too far on a day when she had a lot of work to do.) She looked down at the cats, who were nestled next to her on the bed.

"Should I go to Blind Pass, Bowman's, or West Gulf to look for shells today?" she asked them.

Flora looked up at her, lazily, then closed her eyes again.

"You two are no help."

She sighed and got out of bed, then went into her walk-in closet and pulled on a pair of shorts and a t-shirt. Next she went into the bathroom. She pulled her hair into a ponytail, gave her teeth a quick brushing, and slathered 50 SPF sunblock on her face and all visible body parts, even though the sun had not yet risen. Then she went into the kitchen, poured herself a glass of water, gave the cats some food and fresh water, grabbed her fanny pack, keys, and beach bag and was out the door.

The sun was just rising as Guin made her way onto the beach along West Gulf Drive. There were only a few people out, mainly dog walkers and runners, as West Gulf Drive at that point was mostly residential and you needed a Sanibel resident sticker on your car to park at the handful of access points.

Guin had parked at Beach Access #4, near Mitchell's Sandcastles, a low-key resort that harked back to what Guin imagined Sanibel looked like 40 or 50 years before, with small cottages set back behind the dunes, a small swimming pool, and old-fashioned bicycles that were available for guests to ride.

She stopped at the water's edge and gazed east, watching as the sun made its debut. Then she started heading west, toward Captiva. She looked down at the sand, hoping to find some good shells. But there were just the usual suspects: little tellins and coquinas, some clams and cockles, arks and turkey wings, and bits and pieces of other shells. She sighed and looked out at the Gulf.

"Hey Neptune!" she called. "A little help here?"

She waited, but there was no reply, just some brown pelicans flying overhead. She looked up at the sky, which was pink and red and orange in the dawn light, and smiled. Another crummy day in paradise. Then she turned back and continued walking down the beach.

Guin had been so busy looking for shells that she forgot about the time, until her phone started vibrating. It was a reminder for her to call the detective. She looked at the time and let out a curse. Ris would probably be back by now and would wonder where she was. So much for spending quality time together, she sighed. Hopefully, after he was done with the Ironman, things would go back to normal.

She hurried back down the beach, not pausing to look for shells, though occasionally something would catch her eye and she would glance down. She finally got back to her car and saw that it was just past eight-thirty. Ugh. It would take at least 15 minutes to get back to the condo. She paused to send Ris a text, telling him she was on her way back from the beach and to please wait for her. Then she put the car in drive and headed home, trying to drive no more than 37 mph, so she wouldn't be stopped for speeding (as the island speed limit was 35 mph and cops were known to wait for speeders over by the school, which was on her way home).

She ran up the stairs and flung open the door.

"Ris?" she called. She stopped and listened. She could hear the shower running.

She breathed a sigh of relief. At least she hadn't missed him.

She walked into the kitchen and saw that there was some coffee warming in the coffee pot on the counter. She smiled. She got down the box of Cheerios and poured some into a bowl. Then she grabbed the milk from the fridge. She ate standing up, by the counter, checking her messages as she did so.

She scanned for an email or text from the detective, hoping he had messaged her, but, as usual, there was nothing. She made a face.

"Bad news?" asked Ris, who was standing a few feet away in just a towel.

"Not really," said Guin, looking up at him and smiling. She loved how his dark wavy hair curled when it was wet. "You planning on wearing that to work?" she asked, teasingly.

"Yeah," he replied, grinning down at her. "Whatcha think?"

"I think you should go get dressed," replied Guin.

He walked over to Guin and put his hands on her shoulders, then gently caressed her face. Next thing she knew, they were kissing. If they kept it up much longer, he'd never make it to the museum.

"Go get dressed," she said, pulling away from him.

"Is something wrong?" he asked.

"No. I just don't want you to be late for work."

"I have plenty of time."

He moved to kiss her again. Guin hesitated for a moment then gave in, only stopping as they tumbled onto the bed.

"Is something wrong?" he asked her again. "I feel like we haven't been connecting lately."

Guin looked over at him. (They were both lying on the bed.) She wanted to say, "Well, maybe if you weren't so busy." But she held her tongue.

"I know my Ironman training hasn't helped things," he said, as if reading her mind. "But as soon as the race is over, how about you and I go away for a long weekend?" he said, gently placing a hand on her face.

"Are you sure you can get away?" Guin asked.

Between his teaching schedule and office hours at FGCU and his commitment to the museum, he didn't have a lot of free time. And he also had two college-age children he tried to see at least once a month.

"I'll figure something out," he said. "Maybe you can come with me on one of my college visits."

Not Guin's idea of a romantic weekend getaway.

"Go get dressed," she repeated, sitting up. "I need to make a few calls and have work to do."

"Okay," he said, getting up and heading back into the bathroom.

He emerged a few minutes later, fully clothed.

"I'm just going to get some coffee, then head out."

Guin glanced at him and mumbled something, not really paying attention. A few minutes later, when she had finished editing her story and had gone into the kitchen to get more coffee, she realized he was gone.

It was nearly nine-thirty and she was eager to speak with the detective, but she wanted to speak with Craig first. They had spoken only briefly the night before, and she had said she'd ring him back the next morning.

"So none of you had any idea who this young woman was?" asked Craig.

"Nope," said Guin.

"Any chance Polly could have been lying?"

Guin thought about that. But why would Polly lie? She seemed just as surprised as they were at finding the body, which she told Craig.

"Hmm…" he said. "So you're planning on speaking with the detective?"

"As soon as I get off the phone with you. Any suggestions?"

Craig chuckled.

"You seem to be doing just fine."

"What if he won't let me back into the house?"

"You could always ask your real estate agent."

"I thought about that, but I'm pretty sure the police are going to have someone patrolling the place."

"Well, let me know what the detective says. I may have a way of getting us in."

Guin raised her eyebrows but didn't say anything.

"Okay. I'll let you know what he says. Talk to you later."

She got off the phone with Craig and immediately called the number for the Sanibel Police Department and asked to speak with Detective O'Loughlin.

"Who should I say is calling?" asked the woman.

"Tell him Guinivere Jones."

"Will he know what this is in regard to?" asked the woman.

"He should," said Guin.

"Just a moment, please."

Several minutes later the woman came back on the line.

"I'm sorry, the detective is busy."

I bet he is, thought Guin.

"Would you like to leave a message?"

"Just put me through to his voicemail," Guin said with a sigh.

The woman connected her and Guin left a message, telling the detective it was urgent she speak with him.

While she waited for the detective to call her back, Guin looked over her Halloween article one more time, then she sent it off to Ginny. That done she opened the photos app on her computer and looked at the pictures she had taken at the beach cottage.

It was a nice place. But was it her forever home? There was also the matter of that dead body.

She looked closely at the images of the girl on the floor. She didn't see anything unusual, which in itself was unusual. It was almost as if she had decided to take a nap on the floor. Nothing in the room was disturbed. There was no blood. Guin sighed.

She glanced at the clock on her monitor. It was nearly twelve-thirty. She picked up her phone, willing the detective to call her back.

"Screw it," she said, getting up. She marched into the living area, grabbed her purse and her car keys, told the cats that she would be back in a little while (not that they listened or cared), and headed down to the garage. A few minutes later, she was in her purple Mini Cooper, driving down Sanibel-Captiva Road to the Sanibel Police Department.

CHAPTER 7

"I'm here to see Detective O'Loughlin," Guin announced.

"Is he expecting you?" asked the officer manning the window.

Guin debated what to say. Then she smiled.

"Tell him Ms. Jones is here. We have a lunch date."

The officer, someone Guin hadn't seen before, looked at her a bit suspiciously.

Guin continued to smile. "I can wait."

The officer gave Guin a look, then he turned and picked up the desk phone and rang the detective's extension.

Guin watched as the officer spoke with the detective. At least she assumed he was speaking with the detective. A minute later he returned to the window.

"Detective O'Loughlin said he'd be with you in a few minutes. He's just finishing up something."

"Excellent," said Guin, beaming at the officer. "I'll just wait for him outside."

Guin exited the police department and stood against the railing, looking out at the trees. It was shady there, and she felt a slight breeze. She closed her eyes.

"Lunch date, eh?"

Guin opened her eyes and turned around to see the detective smiling at her, or what passed for a smile on him. She smiled back.

"I thought it was rather inspired. Besides, you owe me."

"I owe you?" asked the detective.

"For canceling on me," replied Guin.

"Canceling on you?"

He looked genuinely confused.

Guin sighed.

"Never mind."

"So, shall we?"

"Shall we?" said Guin. Now she was confused.

"Go have lunch," said the detective, the right side of his mouth curling into a grin. "You did say we had a lunch date, though I didn't seem to have it written down on my calendar. Funny that."

Guin felt herself blushing.

"Right!" said Guin. "Where would you like to go?"

"It's your date, you tell me," replied the detective.

"Doc Ford's?" asked Guin.

"Fine. I'll drive," replied the detective.

Of course you will, thought Guin. But still she was happy that he had agreed to meet with her. She had been wondering for the last couple of months if she had done something to annoy the detective—something more annoying than usual. But standing there looking at him, he seemed happy to see her.

"Lead on," said Guin.

She followed him down the stairs to the parking area. When they got to his car, he came around the passenger side and opened the door for her.

"Thank you," she said, getting in. She thought about teasing him, that she could open a door herself, but thought better of it. If I want to get information about the case, best to be gracious, she thought.

The detective got in and started the car.

Guin looked over at the detective as he drove to the

restaurant. She had always thought him ruggedly good looking, with his square jaw and boxer's physique. Not handsome, per se, but there was something very masculine and confident about him that she found attractive. And she liked his tawny eyes, which matched his hair.

"What?" he asked, catching her looking at him.

"Nothing," Guin replied. She turned away and looked out the window.

A few minutes later, they had arrived at Doc Ford's.

"So, have you discovered who the young woman was?" asked Guin, after they had been seated and ordered.

"Not yet," said the detective.

"Any ideas?" asked Guin.

"Ms. Jones, you found the body less than 24 hours ago, and the woman had no ID on her."

"What about that tattoo you mentioned, the heart with the initials?"

"Like I told you, someone had covered up the initials with a permanent marker."

"Surely, someone in the medical examiner's office could remove the ink and see what was there?" she asked.

"They're working on it."

"What about a picture? You must have taken a photograph of the woman, probably several. Do you have a good one of her face? If you send it to me, I could ask around. Save you some time."

Guin was surprised when the detective took out his phone.

"There," he said, a minute later, putting his phone away.

Guin heard a soft ping, indicating she had a message. She took out her phone and saw there was a text from the detective. She opened it. There was a photo of the girl, her blonde hair forming a kind of halo around her face, her blue eyes open in surprise.

"Sad," said Guin, looking at the photo and shaking her head. There was something about the girl that seemed familiar, but she couldn't place her. "So, any word from the medical examiner?"

"No. We're still waiting for the autopsy report."

The server came over with their drinks: an Arnold Palmer for Guin and a Diet Coke for the detective.

"Thanks," said Guin.

"Do you think she could have been raped? What about drugs?" asked Guin.

"Don't know yet," said the detective, taking a sip of his Diet Coke.

Guin took a sip of her drink. Then she looked directly at the detective.

"I need to get back into the cottage."

"Why?"

"I'm covering the story for the paper."

"Of course you are," replied the detective.

"So, can you let me take a look around?"

She waited for him to say something.

"Well?"

"I don't know what you're expecting to find. We swept the place. It was clean."

"So it's okay for me to go take a look?"

The detective eyed Guin.

"Fine. We can go over there after lunch."

Guin couldn't believe her luck.

"Don't you have work to do?" she asked.

"Solving this case is my work, Ms. Jones. And I was planning on going back over there later anyway."

Guin took another sip of her Arnold Palmer.

"And you don't mind spending all this time with me?"

The detective gave her a look.

"Am I missing something?"

"Well, you cancelled our last get together and you stopped returning my messages."

The detective rubbed his face.

"I've been busy," he replied.

Guin wanted to say something, to call him out. Instead she took another sip of her drink.

They sat there for several seconds, not saying anything, when finally the server came over with their food.

"Here you go!" she said. "Can I get you anything else?"

"I'm good," said Guin. "Detective?"

"I'm good, too," he replied.

"Well, enjoy!" said the young woman.

Guin watched as the young woman, who was blonde, moved to the next table.

"I wonder…" said Guin. She got up and stopped.

"Would you excuse me for a minute?" Guin asked the detective. "I'll be right back."

The detective waved his hand and Guin smiled and headed to the hostess stand.

"Excuse me," she said to one of the women standing there.

"Yes?" said the woman.

"I was hoping you could help me," said Guin. She pulled out her phone and pulled up the photo the detective had just sent her. "Do you happen to know or recognize this woman?" she asked, placing her phone in front of the hostess.

The hostess took Guin's phone and looked at the photo.

"I don't know her." She turned to the other hostess. "Hey Maggie, this chick look familiar to you?"

Maggie looked at the photo. She paused.

"Do you know her?" asked Guin, watching the woman's face.

"She looks kind of familiar," said Maggie, "but I can't say why. I don't think she worked here, but maybe she hung out here. She looks kinda odd. What's this about?"

Guin looked around. The place wasn't crowded, but there were still people coming in, and she didn't want to be overheard. Guin indicated for Maggie to step away from the hostess stand.

"The young woman in the photo? Her body was found not too far from here yesterday. I'm helping the police ID her."

"You a cop?" Maggie asked.

"No, I'm a reporter with the *San-Cap Sun-Times*," replied Guin, "but I'm working with the police."

She looked over toward their table, where the detective was eating his burger.

"You should speak with the manager, Vic," said Maggie. "She knows everyone."

"Thanks," said Guin, pocketing her phone. "Is Vic around?"

"I'll go check," said Maggie.

"Thanks. I'm going back to my table," she said. "If you could have Vic stop by…"

Maggie said she would, and Guin headed back to join the detective.

"What was that about?" asked the detective.

"I was just checking to see if one of the hostesses recognized the woman. I thought maybe she worked here."

She took a bite of her salad.

"And did they?"

She finished chewing and swallowed.

"One of them, Maggie, thought the woman looked familiar. But she didn't think she worked here."

Guin took another bite of her salad.

"What?" she said, noticing the detective watching her.

"Anything else, Nancy Drew?"

Guin couldn't decide if she was annoyed at the nickname or found it endearing. When she was a girl she loved reading Nancy Drew and Hardy Boys mysteries and had identified with the titian-haired girl sleuth. But coming from the detective, it didn't sound like a compliment.

"Maggie suggested I speak to the manager, Vic."

The detective continued to regard her.

"What?" she said, somewhat exasperated.

The detective downed the last bite of his burger and drained his Diet Coke.

"Tell you what," he said, getting up. "Why don't you finish your salad and I'll go speak with Vic?"

Guin wanted to tell him that she had already asked Maggie to have Vic stop by their table, but her mouth was full of salad, and before she could swallow it the detective had gone off in search of the manager. She thought about following him, but she didn't want the server to think they had run off without paying.

She looked around the room, trying to spy their server. Finally, she located her and signaled for her to come over.

"Yes?" said the young woman.

"Could you do me a favor?" asked Guin.

"Shoot," said the server.

"Two favors, actually. Can you tell me where I can find Vic, the manager, and can you watch our table? I'll be back in a few minutes."

"Everything okay?" asked the young woman.

"Everything's fine," said Guin, smiling. "I just need to ask Vic a question. Then I'll be right back. Promise."

"Okay," said the young woman. "Vic should be upstairs, in her office."

The server gave Guin directions and told her she'd keep an eye on the table.

"Thanks!" said Guin. "I'll be back in a few. Don't let them clear."

Guin practically ran up the stairs. When she got to the office she found the detective already there.

"Ah, Ms. Jones. How nice of you to join us," said the detective, as if he had been expecting her, which he had.

"Well?" asked Guin, looking from the detective to a woman she assumed was Vic.

"Ms. Morales here believes the woman in the photo could be Veronica Swales."

"Veronica Swales?" asked Guin, looking at Vic.

"She came around here looking for work a few months ago," explained Vic. "I told her summer wasn't a great time and to come back in November if she hadn't found anything."

"And you're pretty sure this is the same young woman? How can you tell?" asked Guin.

"The detective mentioned she had a heart tattoo just underneath her collarbone," said Vic. "I may not remember everyone's face, but tattoos I remember," she said.

Guin looked more closely at Vic Morales and noticed she had several tattoos.

"You wouldn't happen to recall anything about the tattoo, like any initials?" asked Guin.

Vic smiled. "I'm good, but not that good."

The detective made a noise, sort of like he was clearing his throat.

"I'll go get you that resume," Vic said, getting up and walking over to a set of filing cabinets. She opened a drawer and came back with a single sheet of paper, which she handed to the detective.

"Thank you," said the detective.

"No problem," said Vic. "Not like it's of any use to me."

The detective got up.

"One more thing," asked Guin. "Did she ever come back?"

Vic smiled at her.

"Not for a job, but I used to see her hanging out at the bar."

"Do you recall who she was with?" asked Guin.

"Just some other kids. I don't really remember. A lot of the twentysomethings who work on the island come in here after work for the three-dollar beer."

"Well, thanks for your help," said Guin.

"No problem," said Vic.

The detective held the door open for Guin, and they headed back downstairs to their table.

Guin looked down at her salad. There was still a lot left, but she wasn't hungry. The detective's phone buzzed. He looked at it and made a face.

"Everything okay?" she asked him.

"I need to get back to the office."

"What about going back over to the cottage?" asked Guin.

"Sorry, that will have to wait," replied the detective.

Guin opened her mouth to say something but quickly shut it. The detective signaled for the server.

"Just the check," he said when the server arrived. He turned to Guin. "You want to take your salad home?"

"Sure," she replied.

The server took Guin's salad and said she'd be back in a minute with the check. As usual, the detective insisted on paying, even though Guin pointed out she was the one who had invited him out to lunch.

A few minutes later, they were back in the detective's car, on their way to the police department.

"Thanks for lunch, Ms. Jones," said the detective, after they had gotten out of his car. Guin opened her mouth to speak, but the detective cut her off. "Just, next time, let me know in advance, so I can put it on my calendar."

He grinned at her then turned and headed up the stairs.

Guin felt herself coloring.

"So will you let me know if the dead woman is actually this Veronica Swales?" Guin called after him.

She waited for the detective to reply, but he continued up the stairs, as if he hadn't heard her. "And let me know what the medical examiner found out!" she added, but the detective had already gone inside.

Guin stood there for several seconds, her eyes pinned to the door to the police department, willing the detective to come back out. But it remained closed. Fine, she said to herself. If you don't want to help me, I'll just do a little digging on my own.

CHAPTER 8

"Pretty girl," said Craig.

Guin had forwarded Craig the photo the detective had sent her, then called him from her car. He was at home, having just had lunch with his wife, Betty, and invited her to swing by.

"So you say the manager at Doc Ford's didn't know her, but that she thought she saw the girl at the bar a couple of times?"

"That's what she said. And she gave the detective the girl's resume."

"You get a copy of it?"

Damn. How could Guin have been so stupid? The detective had taken it, and Guin should have asked him for a copy or just taken a picture of it with her phone.

"Hold on a sec," said Guin. She quickly sent the detective a text, asking if he could take a picture of the girl's resume and send it to her.

"Texting the detective?" said Craig, with a smile.

"How did you know?" asked Guin.

Craig gave her a look.

"Right," said Guin. "Of course, knowing the detective, I will probably have to follow up."

"I can also ask my contacts."

"In the meantime, I figured I could ask around town

about the girl, go visit the resorts and restaurants, see if anyone recognizes her."

"Are we sure she worked on Sanibel?" asked Craig.

"No, but considering her body was found on Sanibel and she was seen having drinks with some other young people at Doc Ford's, there's a good chance she did."

Craig scratched his head. "There're a whole lot of restaurants and resorts on the island…"

"You have a better idea?" asked Guin.

"What about social media?"

"What about it?" asked Guin.

"Aren't people your age always on Instagram and Facebook?"

"Actually, that's not a bad idea," said Guin. "Maybe I should post the photo the detective sent me on Facebook, in the Sanibel group, and see if anyone recognizes her."

"You may want to Photoshop it a bit, so she doesn't look quite so…"

"Dead?" said Guin. "Good idea. I'll see if I can touch it up a bit. Thanks."

Craig smiled. "Happy to help. And while you are doing that, I'll reach out to my contact in the medical examiner's office."

"Is there any place you don't have a contact?" Guin asked.

Craig grinned.

"You need to take up fishing."

Even though he was a seasoned crime reporter, most of Craig's information and contacts came through fishing. As an avid fisherman and the paper's fishing reporter, he knew all the local fishermen and charter boat captains, as well as the best places to fish and when.

"Clearly," said Guin.

"Any time you want to go out, Captain Al and I are

happy to take you," he replied.

"One of these days, I'll to take you up on that offer." Though the idea of spending all day, or even half a day, just sitting around on a boat, hoping some poor fish would take your bait, sounded incredibly boring to Guin.

"What about that boyfriend of yours? Does he fish?"

"He's strictly into mollusks," said Guin. "And besides, he has no time. He's been training for the Ironman up in Panama City."

Craig whistled.

"Fishing is about the only sport I can handle these days—and walking with Betty."

"Yeah, well, I could use some more exercise, but for right now, I have a murder that needs solving."

"Technically that is the detective's job," said Craig.

"Yeah, yeah, yeah," said Guin. "You know what I mean."

Craig looked again at the photographs of the dead woman Guin had sent him.

"I was supposed to go with the detective back over to the cottage after lunch, but something came up and he had to get back to the office," said Guin.

"Have you asked your real estate agent if she could get you back in?"

Guin had not and still owed Polly a call.

"You okay if I ring her right now?"

"Be my guest," said Craig.

Guin pulled out her phone and entered Polly's number. She waited as the phone rang.

"Polly Fahnestock," came the familiar voice. "Please leave a message after the beep."

"Hey Poll, it's Guin. Sorry about the other day. I was wondering, could you get me back into that cottage? I'd like to see it again. Call me back as soon as you get this."

Guin ended the call and turned to Craig.

"I gather she wasn't there," he said.

"No, but knowing Polly, I'll hear back from her within the hour."

"Ah yes, real estate agents," said Craig.

"So what are you working on?" asked Guin.

"The usual," said Craig. "But Ginny told me this was top priority—and to help you in whatever way I could."

Guin had been worried that Ginny wouldn't mention to Craig that she was the lead on this piece, or that Craig would bristle about Guin calling the shots. But he seemed okay with it.

"Thanks Craig. I really appreciate it. I'm going to post that photo on Facebook, and maybe Instagram, too, like you suggested, and see what I come up with. And I'll go back over to Doc Ford's during happy hour and see if any of the bartenders recognize her. If she had drinks there after work regularly, chances are one of them will remember her, maybe even know where she worked."

"Good idea," said Craig. "And I'll check with my contacts and see what I turn up."

"Great," said Guin. "Let me know what you find out. And I'll do the same."

"And let me know if Polly gets back to you. I'd like to take a look at that cottage."

"You and Betty thinking of moving?" asked Guin, teasingly.

"Betty and I have been living in this house for over ten years now, and we have no desire to move," he replied.

"Just be careful. You know how persuasive these real estate agents can be," said Guin.

Craig was making a face.

Guin went over to him and gave him a quick kiss on the cheek. He reminded her so much of her Uncle Lou, a bit of a curmudgeon whom she had adored as a kid.

"I'll check in with you later. Say hi to Betty for me."

Craig walked her to the door and watched as she made her way to her purple Mini. She turned and waved goodbye.

Once in the car, she quickly checked her messages. There was a text from Shelly, asking her what she was up to.

"How would you like to go to happy hour at Doc Ford's with me tonight?"

"I'm in!" Shelly wrote back. "What time?"

Guin thought for a few seconds.

"5:30?"

"Sounds good!" Shelly replied. "See you then!"

CHAPTER 9

Guin arrived at Doc Ford's promptly at 5:30. She went inside and checked out the two bar areas, to see if Shelly had beaten her there. No sign of her. She went back outside to wait. A few minutes later, Guin saw Shelly's car pull into the parking lot.

"So, what's up?" asked Shelly, climbing the steps. "You never go to happy hour."

Guin took Shelly aside. "I'm doing research."

Shelly grinned. "About happy hours? I can definitely help you with that."

"No, not about happy hours. I'm looking for information about someone, someone who's been a regular at the happy hour here."

"Sounds intriguing. So why do you need my help?"

"You know I'm not a big drinker."

"And I am?"

"No, that's not what I meant," said Guin. "You're just better around people than I am."

"So you want me to be your wing man?"

"Something like that."

"So, what, or who, am I looking for?" asked Shelly.

Guin debated how much to tell Shelly. She'd probably find out anyway. And better for it to come from her than for Shelly to read or hear about it elsewhere.

"So yesterday when I was looking at that beach cottage Polly told me about, we found a dead body."

"What?!" said Shelly.

"Shh!" said Guin.

"You found a dead body?! Whose was it?"

"I don't know. That's why we're here."

"I don't understand."

"The dead body belonged to a girl, a young woman, probably in her twenties. She had no ID on her, and Polly had no idea who she was, though when I saw her picture, she seemed kind of familiar. Anyway, I was having lunch here with the detective—"

"You were having lunch with the detective?" interrupted Shelly, staring at Guin.

"Will you let me finish? As I was saying, I was having lunch here with the detective, and I thought maybe someone at Doc Ford's would recognize the woman. So I showed her picture to the two hostesses, and one of them said she looked kind of familiar, but that I should talk with the manager. So I did. Or rather the detective did. Turns out the woman had applied for a job here, but they didn't need anyone at the time, so they didn't hire her."

Shelly opened her mouth to say something, but Guin again cut her off.

"But Vic, she's the manager, said she saw the girl here a couple of times, during happy hour. Apparently it's a popular spot with the local twentysomethings."

"So you thought you'd come here during happy hour and show people her picture and someone might recognize her."

"Exactly," said Guin. "So, shall we?"

"Is the paper picking up the tab?" asked Shelly.

Guin chuckled. "I don't think so, but I can ask Ginny."

Shelly looked disappointed.

"Well, I think I can ante up for one drink."

"My treat," said Guin.

"Well, in that case, what are we waiting for?" said Shelly, smiling again.

Guin grinned at her friend and held the door open for her.

"Let's start at the downstairs bar," said Guin, after they had entered the restaurant. "Then we can check out the one upstairs."

"Whatever you say," said Shelly.

They found two seats in the middle of the bar and sat down.

"What can I get you ladies?" asked the bartender, a good-looking young man probably in his late twenties or early thirties.

"I'll have a margarita, no salt," said Guin.

"And I'll have a Sanibel Sunset," said Shelly.

"Coming right up," said the bartender.

"So, who do we ask first?" whispered Shelly.

Guin looked around. The bar was busy but not too crowded, but there wasn't a group of twentysomethings. Mostly it was older men, probably stopping off to have a beer on their way home from work or fishing. Then again, a pretty young blonde would probably have stood out in that crowd.

The bartender brought over their drinks.

"Thanks," said Guin. "May I ask you something?"

"Shoot," said the bartender.

"Have you seen this young woman?"

Guin showed him the photo the detective had sent her.

The bartender took Guin's phone and looked at the photo.

"She looks kind of funny," he said.

"That's because she's dead," said Guin.

"How'd she die?" he asked.

"We're not sure," she replied. "Right now we're trying to figure out who she is, or was."

"You a cop?" asked the bartender.

"No, a reporter," said Guin.

"Well, she doesn't look familiar to me, but I don't usually work weekdays. Let me ask Sam." He called over to the other bartender. "Hey Sam, you got a sec?"

Sam, who was balding and looked to be in his fifties, came over.

"What's up, Pete?"

"May I?" asked Pete, gesturing with Guin's phone.

"Go right ahead," said Guin.

"You see this girl?"

He handed the phone to Sam, who moved it forward and back.

"Hold on a sec."

He reached into his pocket and pulled out a pair of reading glasses, then put them on.

"Yeah, I've seen her here a few times," said Sam. "She usually comes here Thursdays, with that group that works on the island."

"Do you know who she is?" asked Guin.

"Why do you want to know?" asked Sam, eyeing Guin suspiciously.

"She was found dead yesterday, not far from here, and she didn't have any ID on her."

"You a cop?" Sam asked.

"No, a reporter," Guin replied. She reached into her bag and pulled out her card case. "Here's my card."

"Guinivere Jones. That's an interesting name. Who's your husband, King Arthur?" Sam chuckled. Clearly, he was enjoying the joke.

If he only knew, thought Guin. She forced a smile.

"So, can you help me, Sam?"

Sam looked thoughtful. Guin waited. Then she decided to help things along.

"By any chance did you overhear anyone use the name Veronica?"

Sam scrunched his face. "Veronica…" he said.

Suddenly he snapped his fingers.

"Yeah, that was it. Though her friends called her Ronnie."

"You sure?" asked Guin.

Sam looked thoughtful again. "Yeah, pretty sure."

"Hey, Jimbo!" called Sam to a man a couple of barstools away, who was nursing a beer. "You remember a pretty blonde chick, in her twenties, used to come here for happy hour with her friends?"

"Lots of pretty blondes here," said Jimbo, smiling. "It's Southwest Florida."

"Here, take a look," said Sam, thrusting the phone in front of Jimbo.

Jimbo looked at the image on the phone. Guin watched him. Was that recognition or something else? Something about Jimbo's expression as he looked at the photo set off something in Guin's brain.

"I need to go," he said, suddenly getting up.

He handed Sam the phone, then reached into his pocket and threw some money on the bar.

"But you haven't finished your beer!" said Sam.

But Jimbo was already making his way to the door.

Sam shook his head, then gave the phone back to Guin.

"What was that all about?" asked Guin, staring after Jimbo.

"Beats me," said Sam.

"So about the girl, any idea where she worked?" Guin asked Sam.

"Nope. Come back Thursday."

"Why Thursday?" asked Guin.

"That's when all the twentysomethings come in, for three-dollar Thursday. You can get up to three beers for three dollars apiece."

"Ah," said Guin. "Thanks."

However, Thursday was several days away, and Guin needed to know who the young woman was now. She sighed and took another sip of her margarita. She had thought about posting the photo of Veronica, if that was in fact her name, on social media before she left for happy hour, but had decided to wait until around eight, when she figured more millennials would be online.

"You look bummed," said Shelly.

"Yeah, well…"

She took another sip of her drink. Shelly was nearly done with hers.

They sat at the bar a few more minutes, chatting about this and that. Then Guin asked for the check and paid.

"Hope you find whoever killed that girl," said Pete.

"Me too," said Guin.

She left a tip on the counter, then she and Shelly made their way to the door.

Guin walked with Shelly to her car.

"Thanks for meeting me."

"Any time. You know I love a good happy hour," said Shelly, smiling at her.

Guin smiled back.

"I'm just sorry you didn't get what you were hoping for."

"I'll just have to keep looking," said Guin.

She leaned over and gave Shelly a hug.

"Thanks again for coming."

"No problem," said Shelly. "Just keep me in the loop, and let me know if you need any help."

"Will do," said Guin.

"So, we going shelling later this week?"

"I hope so," said Guin. "Can I text you later?"

"Whenever. You know how to find me. Though I'm working on my new collection. Gotta get ready for Christmas!"

"That's nearly two months away."

"And it's going to be here before you know it. Which is why I need to get going. Need to make sure I have plenty of stuff before Thanksgiving."

They said their goodbyes, then Guin headed back to her Mini. She got in and checked her messages. Nothing from the detective. But Polly had gotten back to her. They had an appointment to go back to the cottage the next day at noon, providing the police let them in.

Guin was about to put her key in the ignition when she picked up her phone and dialed the detective's mobile. He picked up after a few rings.

"Yes?" he replied.

"This is Guin, Ms. Jones," said Guin, who was a little tipsy, she realized, from her margarita.

"I know," said the detective.

"I asked you to send me Veronica Swales's resume."

"I've been busy."

"Are you busy now?"

The detective sighed.

"So you'll send it me?" asked Guin.

"Fine."

"Oh and did you get the report from the medical examiner?"

"I should have it tomorrow," replied the detective.

"Will you let me see it?"

Again there was silence.

"Detective?"

"Remind me tomorrow."

"Fine, I'll text you tomorrow. But if I don't hear back from you, I'm coming to the police department, and I won't leave until I see it."

She realized she was wagging her finger.

"Good evening, Ms. Jones."

"Good evening, detective."

The detective ended the call, and Guin put her phone back in her bag. She started the car and then realized she was hungry. She checked the clock. It was just past six-thirty. I should pick up something to eat, she thought. But what she really craved was ice cream, specifically frozen custard.

She got out of the car, locking it behind her, and headed across the street to Joey's Custard. She walked in and said hello to the young woman working behind the counter.

"May I help you?" asked the young woman.

Guin looked at the menu.

"I'll have a small Lion's Paw."

"Coming right up!" said the young woman.

A minute later she presented Guin with a cup of soft serve vanilla custard mixed with chocolate-covered pretzels and caramel sauce. Guin paid and thanked the woman.

She moved away from the counter and took a bite of the Lion's Paw, closing her eyes in ecstasy. She took another bite, then wandered around the shop. Hanging on a wall around the corner was a big bulletin board filled with photos of happy customers eating custard (or ice cream). Guin stopped to take a look. Then stared. There, off to the right, was a photo of an attractive blonde with shoulder-length hair, flanked by two attractive young men, big smiles on their faces, holding ice-cream cones. Guin took a closer look. The blonde in the photo was the dead girl. She was sure of it. She looked at the young men. The one on the left, a red-head, looked familiar, but she couldn't quite place him.

CHAPTER 10

Guin glanced around. Then, not seeing anyone around her, she removed the thumbtack from the wall and took the photo, surreptitiously placing it in her bag. She then moved a couple of photos to hide where the photo had been and left.

She walked briskly across the parking lot, back across the street, clutching her cup of custard. She didn't really think the young woman in the ice cream shop would come after her, but she wasn't taking any chances. She stopped next to the Mini and ate several spoonfuls of her now soupy treat. There was no place to throw the half-empty cup, so she placed it in her cupholder, taking one more bite. Then she started the car.

She drove as fast as she dared (39 mph) to the condo, parked the Mini in her garage, then raced up the stairs. When she was safely inside, she pulled out the photo of the girl and her two friends and compared it to the photos the detective had sent her. It was definitely the same girl.

She took a picture of the photo, then edited it on her computer. Then she opened Facebook and clicked on the Sanibel Island group. She wanted to post the photo there, to see if anyone recognized the girl or knew her, but what should she type? She finally settled on "MISSING: Have you seen this young woman? If so, leave a comment or DM me

— or contact the Sanibel Police Department." It was brief and to the point. She held her breath and hit "Post." Who knows if anyone would even recognize the girl? After all, she was much younger than most people in the group. But it was worth a shot.

Next she sent the photo to Craig, telling him that she had just posted it in the Sanibel Island Facebook group. Then she sent the photo to the detective.

Seconds later, her phone began to ring. It was the detective.

"Detective," said Guin, "to what do I owe this honor?"

Though she knew why the detective was calling.

"Where did you get that photo?"

"I found it," Guin replied.

"Where?" asked the detective.

"At Joey's Custard. It was on the wall of happy customers. I was getting some ice cream, technically custard, and I happened to see it. You're not going to arrest me for stealing it are you?"

"Don't tempt me," said the detective. "Do you have the original?"

"Are you going to arrest me?"

Guin could almost hear the detective gritting his teeth.

"Only if you don't answer the question," he replied.

"I have it," said Guin.

"Bring it to the police department first thing tomorrow."

"Can I get back into the cottage?"

Guin could practically see the detective rubbing his face, trying to contain his annoyance.

"Fine. Meet me at the cottage tomorrow morning at eight and bring the photo."

"I'll be there."

The detective mumbled something then hung up.

Guin looked at the photo and smiled. The evening had

proven to be more productive than she had hoped, though she still hadn't confirmed the girl's name or learned anything about her. But she was one step closer to doing so.

She sent Polly a text, cancelling their appointment for noon the next day.

Guin checked Facebook several times before she turned off her phone at ten. Several people had commented that they hoped Guin found the young woman or how sad they were that she was missing. But no one had yet identified her or the two men in the photo. She took another look at the picture, which she had brought with her to bed and had placed on her nightstand.

Suddenly it came to her, why the young man on the left looked familiar. It was the young man who had waited on her at Jean-Luc's booth at the farmers market Sunday. What was his name again? Jake! At least she was pretty sure it was Jake.

She yawned and took another look at the photo. Now that she thought about it, the girl definitely looked familiar, but she couldn't say why. She would have to stop by Jean-Luc's bakery the next day and have a little chat with Jake. But right now she needed to get some sleep.

She turned off the light and tried to fall asleep, but her mind was still fixated on the photo and the dead girl. She turned the light back on and picked up the book she had been reading, about the history of Florida. It was an interesting book, but after a few pages, Guin felt herself nodding off. She shut off her light, told the cats not to wake her up at 3 a.m., then rolled over.

That night she dreamed that she and Ris were back at the cottage, in the master bedroom. There was no dead body anywhere. It was just the two of them.

Ris was smiling down at her and she was smiling up at

him. There was music playing in the background and Ris had put his arms around her and was starting to kiss her. At first it was nice. Then the kisses started to get rougher and Ris was squeezing her arm.

"Take it easy!" she said. She tried to push Ris away, but his grip only got tighter and rougher. Guin suddenly felt scared. She tried to push Ris away, but he only laughed at her.

"Stop!" she begged him as he forced her onto the bed. She could feel herself start to cry. "Please!" she sobbed. But the Ris in her nightmare wouldn't.

Guin bolted awake and sat upright. She turned on the light and could feel herself breathing heavily. Get a grip, she told herself. It was only a dream. That wasn't the real Ris. Still, she could feel her heart pounding inside her chest. It had felt so real.

She looked over at her clock. It was 3 a.m. Great, she thought. She desperately wanted to go back to sleep, but she was terrified the nightmare would pick up where it left off.

She felt something furry brush against her arm. Fauna.

"Hey girl," she said, petting the cat.

Fauna climbed into her lap and rubbed her face against Guin's, purring. Guin continued to pet her, feeling some of the tension melt away. She concentrated on her breath and inhaled to the count of eight, then exhaled slowly. She continued to do so until she started to feel sleepy again.

She lay back down, and Fauna curled up next to her, continuing to purr softly.

"You're a good cat," Guin said, continuing to stroke her. "Mostly."

A few minutes later, Guin was asleep, and when she woke up again a few hours later, she didn't remember what else she dreamed, though she remembered her nightmare.

"Good morning, detective!" Guin said.

She had arrived at the cottage a few minutes after eight, having slept until almost seven-thirty. Seeing the time, she had sprung out of bed, started brewing some coffee, then hurriedly got dressed and brushed her teeth. She grabbed the photo and her phone, not bothering to check her messages, and thrust them in her bag. She poured the coffee into a to-go mug and was about to leave when the cats came running up to her, meowing.

"Right. Food," she said.

She put down her bag and walked quickly into the kitchen. She went into the pantry and grabbed the bag of cat food, pouring some food into each bowl. Then she grabbed the water bowl and filled it with fresh water.

"There you go!" she said, placing the water down next to the food bowls. "Please try not to throw up your food this morning, Flora, okay?"

Flora ignored her and made for the food bowl.

Guin sighed and left.

The detective was about to say something when a car pulled into the cottage's driveway and parked behind Guin's Mini. Guin watched as Polly and another woman emerged.

"What are they doing here?" Guin asked the detective, lowering her voice.

"Ms. Campbell, the listing agent, kindly offered to let us in."

"Surely you didn't need her to let us in?" asked Guin in a hushed voice. "The police must have a set of keys."

"I have a few questions for her," the detective replied.

Polly and the listing agent headed toward them. Guin regarded them. Ann Campbell was easily a head taller than Polly, at least five-foot-ten, Guin reckoned. And she was solidly built. Could she have killed the young woman? Guin wondered. She certainly looked capable of it. Even though the woman had gray hair, Guin figured she was no more than seventy and still in good shape.

"Well, let's get this over with," said Ann, not stopping to say hello or introduce herself.

"After you," said the detective, gesturing toward the house.

Guin watched as Ann walked up the stairs, went over to the lock box, took out her phone, and got the keys out. She certainly had opportunity, Guin thought. I wonder if she had motive?

"You coming?" Ann asked.

Guin looked at Polly. But Polly just held out her hand, indicating Guin should go ahead of her.

Guin had texted Polly to apologize about the other day, and Polly had told her not to worry about it, she understood.

"Have the police figured out who the girl is?" asked Polly, her voice pitched low, as they headed toward the house.

"Not yet, or if they have, they haven't told me," replied Guin, quietly.

That reminded Guin, she hadn't turned her phone on or checked her Facebook messages.

Ann had opened the door and was waiting for the two of them, the detective having already entered.

"You two coming in? I'm not a doorman, you know."

"Sorry!" said Guin, as she jogged up the stairs, Polly right behind her.

"Is she always like that?" Guin whispered to Polly as they walked into the kitchen.

"No, sometimes she's kind of crotchety," said Polly, smiling.

Guin looked at her.

"How does she sell any houses?"

"Oh, she's perfectly nice to her clients," replied Polly.

"She just doesn't like people she feels are wasting her time."

"And she thinks trying to find out why there was a dead girl in her listing is a waste of time?" asked Guin, still whispering.

Polly was about to answer when Ann spoke up, her voice practically booming.

"Go ahead. Have a look around. Though I don't know what you expect to find. Your boys gave this place a pretty thorough going over already, from what I understand."

"Thank you," said Guin, even though she knew Ann and had been addressing the detective. "This shouldn't take too long."

"I hope not," said Ann.

Guin walked around the kitchen, examining the counters and the appliances. She opened the fridge, but there was nothing inside. She made a face.

"Were you hoping to find something?" asked the detective.

"I don't know," said Guin. "Maybe the woman came here with someone, thinking the place was empty, and had a picnic or something."

The detective looked at Guin.

"A picnic?"

"You know what I mean," said Guin.

"If people had eaten or drunk something here, we would have found some evidence of it," said the detective.

Guin ignored him and opened the cabinet beneath the sink. Inside were two bins, one for garbage and one for recycling. She looked inside each, but there was nothing in either one.

"You find anything?" the detective asked.

"I'm going to look around the rest of the place, if that's all right with you, detective," she said.

"Be my guest. You don't mind if I join you, do you?"

Guin did mind, but she didn't feel she was in a position to tell him to bug off.

Polly and Ann were in the living area, discussing something.

"I don't think we've been formally introduced," said Guin, going over to Ann and extending her hand. "Guin Jones."

The listing agent looked down at Guin's hand, then back up at Guin's face.

"I was the one who found the body," Guin added.

Ann continued to look down at her, not shaking her hand.

"I know who you are, Ms. Jones."

"Any idea who the young woman was?" asked Guin.

"None," said Ann.

"And you have no interest in finding out who she was and what she was doing here?"

Ann continued to look down at Guin.

"Ms. Jones, I'm sure you mean well, but I have a bad back, a sick husband, and a half-dozen houses I'm trying to sell, and better things to do than try to play detective."

Guin clenched her teeth and smiled politely. The listing agent continued.

"I agreed to let you back in here and told the detective I'd answer any questions he had. But unless you intend to buy this house, I have nothing more to say to you."

Wow, thought Guin, someone sure woke up on the wrong side of the bed this morning. She glanced over at Polly, who was shaking her head, trying to signal Guin to just leave it alone.

"Well, thank you for letting me look around," Guin said.

She waited for a response from Ann, but the woman was busy checking her phone.

"Shall we, detective?" asked Guin, gesturing toward the master bedroom.

The detective looked as though he was trying his best not to laugh.

"What's so funny?" hissed Guin, as they entered the master bedroom.

"Nothing," said the detective, suppressing a grin.

Guin began to look around the master. She went over to the bed and looked closely at the quilt. Then she eyed the pillows. Finally she looked down at the floor. She got on her hands and knees and looked under the bed and the nightstands. It was clear the place had been cleaned recently.

"What exactly are you hoping to find, Ms. Jones?" asked the detective.

"I don't know. Something," she replied, still on her hands and knees.

She looked over at the detective.

"You say your team found nothing in the house?"

Guin thought she saw a slight twitch.

"You did find something!" said Guin. "What?"

"Just some hairs," replied the detective.

"The girl's?"

"Possibly. We found several strands of hair. Pretty common in most houses."

Guin continued to look around the bed. She had reached the other nightstand and was about to stand up when she thought she saw something hidden underneath, something shiny. She reached her hand under the nightstand and felt something. She grabbed it and slowly stood up. In her hand was a small heart-shaped locket on a delicate gold chain.

She was about to open the locket when the detective stopped her.

"Don't touch that," said the detective.

"I already did," replied Guin.

The detective reached into his pocket and pulled out a small plastic baggie.

"Gently place it in the bag," he ordered her.

"Don't you want to see what's inside?" she said, lowering it into the bag.

The detective felt around in his pockets and sighed.

"Let me go down to my car and get a pair of gloves, in case you make any more discoveries."

CHAPTER 11

The detective returned a few minutes later with a pair of disposable gloves. He donned them and gently removed the locket from the plastic bag. Then he opened it. Guin moved closer to get a better look. Inside, on the left, was a photo of the girl, and on the right was a photo of a boy.

"I know him!" Guin blurted, looking at the tiny photo.

"Oh?" said the detective.

"It's the boy from the photo, the one I took from Joey's Custard. Or one of the boys. There were two of them."

The detective looked at the photos inside the locket. Guin peered over his shoulder. She was sure the young man in the locket was the same one she had seen in the photo with the dead girl. Not Jake, but the other young man. Just to be sure, though, she reached into her bag, pulled out her phone, and turned it on. It started buzzing wildly.

"Oh my!" she exclaimed, seeing all the Facebook messages she had.

She had forgotten about her Facebook post. She opened the app and was amazed to see dozens of comments on her photo. She quickly started going through them.

The detective cleared his throat.

"Sorry, just checking Facebook," she said, not looking up at him.

"Seriously?" said the detective.

Guin looked up. She knew that expression.

"It's not what you think," she said. "I posted that photo I sent you, of the girl with the two young men, in the Sanibel Island group and asked if anyone knew who she was or had seen her."

"You did what?" asked the detective.

"I posted the photo on Facebook, in the Sanibel group," Guin repeated.

"Maybe I should have you arrested," said the detective.

"Since when is posting on Facebook a crime?" Guin retorted. "You said yourself she had no ID on her. It's not like I said she had been murdered and the police were looking for her killer. I just said she was missing and asked if anyone had seen her or knew who she was."

The detective sighed and rubbed his face.

"I also wrote that anyone with information should contact the Sanibel Police Department," she added, smiling at the detective.

The detective grunted. "So, anyone ID her?"

"I was just checking."

Guin continued to scroll through the comments.

"Wait, I have something!"

"Not sure who the girl is, but the guy on the right is Billy Simms," Guin read aloud.

The detective looked over Guin's shoulder.

"Here, you can take a look," she said, handing the detective her phone.

The detective squinted down at the phone.

"I hate these damn things."

Guin wasn't sure if he was referring to Facebook or smartphones. Probably both.

"If you're having trouble reading on that little screen, you could come back to my place when we're done here and look at it on my big monitor."

Guin didn't know what possessed her to say that.

The detective thought for a minute.

"Fine. You done here, or did you want to snoop some more?"

"I'm not snooping, detective. I'm just doing my job."

"Whatever you say, Nancy Drew. Just let me know when you're done."

"Just give me a few more minutes. I want to check out the bathroom and then the office and the guest bedroom."

"Fine, just don't take too long."

"Didn't you say you needed to ask the listing agent some questions? Why don't you go speak with her while I look around?"

"You mean you don't want to listen in?" asked the detective.

Guin looked at him. Was that a smirk?

"You'd let me?" she asked.

The detective shrugged.

"Just give me a few minutes to finish up," Guin said.

She quickly searched the master bathroom but didn't see or notice anything unusual.

"You find anything?" asked Polly, as Guin entered the living area.

Guin looked over at the detective, who was shaking his head.

"No," she replied.

She looked around.

"Where'd Ann go?"

"She went outside to make some calls," Polly replied. "You need me to go get her?"

"I'll go find her," said the detective.

Guin watched as the detective stepped outside. Then she turned back to Polly.

"Hey, Poll, does the name 'Billy Simms' ring a bell?"

"You're kidding, right?"

Guin looked confused.

"Billy Simms, the quarterback for the UCF Knights?"

Guin still looked confused.

"Don't you follow college football?"

"A little?" Guin said.

Polly sighed.

"Billy Simms was the Knights' star quarterback the last two seasons. Most game-winning QB in the team's recent history. He's a hero around here. As a matter of fact, this is his grandparents' cottage, though I probably shouldn't be telling you that," she said, lowering her voice.

Guin stared at Polly.

"What?" asked Polly. "You have a funny look on your face."

Guin pulled out her phone and showed Polly the photo she had posted on Facebook.

"Is that guy on the right Billy Simms, the Knights' quarterback?" asked Guin.

Polly took Guin's phone and enlarged the photo. She looked closer. Then she looked at Guin.

"Please don't tell me you think Billy Simms killed that girl."

"I don't know what to think," said Guin.

"Ann is not going to be happy about this," said Polly, glancing toward the front door.

"I'm going to finish looking around," said Guin. "Please don't say anything to Ann."

"Are you kidding? My lips are sealed," said Polly, making a zipping motion with her fingers.

The detective reentered the house.

"You done?" he asked.

"Almost," said Guin. "I still need to check out the office and the guest bedroom. Hey, did you know that Billy Simms was the star quarterback for the UCF Knights?"

"You didn't?" asked the detective.

Guin sighed.

"I'm going to check out the office and the guest bedroom," she said.

The detective followed her to the other side of the house.

"What? You don't trust me, detective?"

He gave her a look.

"Fine."

Guin went into the guest bedroom. She searched around the bed. Nothing. She sighed and got up, then went over to the chest of drawers, opening each one. Empty.

"Not having any luck?" asked the detective.

Guin scowled.

She opened the closet and looked inside. Just a lot of empty hangers.

"I'm going to check out the guest bath and the office," she announced.

The detective indicated for her to lead on.

She walked into the guest bathroom and examined the shower. It was dry. The detective watched in silence.

"Not finding what you were looking for?"

"I don't know what I was looking for," said Guin, feeling frustrated. "Something."

"You don't think the Sanibel Police Department went over this place with a fine-tooth comb?"

"I just wanted to see it for myself. I'm going to check out the office, then we can go."

"I still need to speak with Ms. Campbell."

"I thought that's why you went outside."

"She was on the phone."

"Okay," said Guin. "Just give me a minute."

The detective followed Guin into the office, where she had found the young woman.

"This would have made a great office," she sighed, eyeing the desk and chair and the window with a nice view of palm trees.

She opened the desk drawers and closed them. Then she got down on all fours and hunted around the floor. Nothing. She stood up and walked over to the closet. Again, nothing. She sighed.

"I don't think I've ever seen a place this empty or so clean. No personal effects. And barely a speck of dust. It doesn't seem natural."

Had the place been this clean before, or had the killer tidied up to hide any possible evidence? Guin wondered.

"Let's go talk to Ann Campbell," said Guin, moving toward the door.

"Just do me a favor and let me ask the questions, okay?" said the detective.

"Of course, detective," Guin replied, turning and smiling at him.

They headed back into the living area. Ann was back, discussing something or other with Polly.

"You all done here, detective?" Ann asked.

She seemed somewhat less grumpy, thought Guin. Maybe she got some good news. Though the news about the owners' grandson, if the young man in the photos was in fact Billy Simms, would probably put her in a bad mood again.

"Almost," said the detective. "Ms. Jones, do you have that photo?"

Guin had forgotten about the photo.

"It's in my bag," she replied.

"Could you bring it over here?"

Guin reached into her bag and pulled out the photo. She handed it to the detective, who held it up for Ann.

"You recognize any of the people in this photo?"

She squinted at the photo.

"May I?" asked Ann, reaching for the picture.

The detective nodded and handed her the photo. She held it up and then moved it away.

"Need my readers."

She walked over to her bag and pulled out a pair of reading glasses. She placed them on her face, then examined the photo again.

"Not sure who the other two are. They look a bit familiar. But that's Billy Simms on the right. Why?"

She handed the photo back to the detective.

"I understand this cottage belongs to his grandparents," said the detective.

Guin regarded the detective. Clearly he knew more than he had let on.

"That's right," said Ann. "What about it?"

"Billy come here often?" asked the detective.

"You should ask his grandparents that," said Ann.

"But I'm asking you," said the detective, looking at Ann, who was about the same height as the detective.

"Mmph," said Ann.

The detective, and Guin, waited.

"Look here, detective, I'm the listing agent for this house, not the owner."

"But you know the owners," said the detective.

"I do, but not that well. Do I think Billy visited them here? Sure. Why not? But you should ask his grandparents, like I said, or the neighbors. Why do you care anyway?"

"We found a locket with a photo of Billy in the bedroom," said the detective, his face neutral.

"His grandmother must have forgotten it," said Ann. "If you give it to me, I'll see that she gets it back."

"I don't think it belonged to his grandmother," said the detective.

"Oh? What makes you say that?" Ann asked.

"We think it belonged to the dead girl. It's her photo in the other half of that locket," said Guin, looking at Ann.

Ann looked from Guin to the detective.

"Can you tell me if anyone else knew about the house being for sale?" asked the detective.

"Besides nearly every real estate agent on the island?" asked Ann, giving the detective a condescending look.

The detective did not reply.

Just then Polly came in from the lanai, where she had gone to return a call. She looked from Guin to the detective to Ann.

"Is everything okay?"

"I was just telling the detective here that lots of folks knew the house was up for sale," said Ann.

"That's true, detective," said Polly.

"And did everyone know the Simmses were no longer in residence?" asked Guin.

"The neighbors probably knew," said Ann. "Kind of hard to hide a moving truck."

"Did Billy know?" asked Guin.

Ann regarded her as though she was an idiot.

"Thank you for your time, Ms. Campbell," interjected the detective. "I'll call you if I have any additional questions. Ms. Jones?" he said, giving Guin a look.

"This mean you're done?" asked Ann.

"For now," said the detective. "Thank you for your time."

"Here's my card," said Ann, reaching into her pocket and pulling out a business card. "Let me know if you're ever looking for a place."

"Thank you," said the detective. "I'll be in touch. Ladies?"

He indicated that they should all go, and they filed out

the door. Ann locked the front door behind them. Then she placed the keys back in the lock box.

"This place is off limits," said the detective. "No showings until this matter has been resolved."

Ann made a face.

"I'll text you," Guin whispered to Polly.

They exchanged air kisses, then Polly followed Ann back to her car. Guin and the detective watched as they pulled out.

"So, you want to come back to my place and see what those Facebook people had to say about the dead girl?" Guin asked the detective.

He looked at his watch.

"I should get back to the office."

"It's only ten minutes away. And I'll make a fresh pot of coffee," Guin said, smiling.

She knew how much the detective liked a good cup of coffee.

"Fine," said the detective. "But I need to make it quick."

"You remember how to get there?" asked Guin.

The detective gave her a look.

"Alrighty then," said Guin. "I'll see you there in a few."

She unlocked the Mini and got in. A few minutes later, she was driving down San-Cap Road, the detective following close behind her.

CHAPTER 12

"First, coffee," said Guin, bustling about the kitchen.

The detective watched as she ground some fresh beans, then placed several large scoops in her coffee maker. She poured in the water, then pressed "start."

"I'll go boot up my computer while the coffee is brewing. Be back in a sec."

She headed back to her office/bedroom, where both cats were asleep on the bed, and turned on her computer. She entered her password at the prompt, then headed back into the kitchen.

"All set," she said.

A minute later, the coffee was ready.

"How do you take it?" she asked, taking down two mugs.

"I can fix it myself," said the detective. "You got some milk and sugar?"

"I do," said Guin.

She reached into the fridge and pulled out a container of two-percent milk. Then she reached into a cabinet and grabbed the sugar.

"Help yourself."

The detective poured some coffee into the mug Guin had set out for him, then he stirred in a spoonful of sugar and some milk. Guin watched, then poured some coffee into her mug.

"Okay then. Shall we?" she asked, picking up her mug.

She headed down the hall to her office/bedroom, the detective following behind. She entered the room and was about to sit at her desk when she realized the detective hadn't followed her. She turned around to see the detective standing in the hallway, just outside her door.

"Is there a problem?" asked Guin. "Oh, right, I should get you a chair."

She walked quickly past him to the front hall closet and pulled out a folding chair.

"I know it's not ideal, but it's what I've got," she said as she passed him.

She placed the chair next to her office chair and turned around.

"Come on then. Have a seat," she said, patting the chair.

The detective remained in the doorway, holding his mug of coffee.

"Come on, detective. I won't bite you," she said. Though a little part of her thought it might be fun to bite the detective.

"Can't we view the photos someplace else?" he asked.

"This is where my big monitor is," she replied.

"Let's go sit at your dining table."

"Seriously?" said Guin.

She got up and moved to the doorway, where the detective was standing.

"Is it because my office is in the bedroom?"

The detective didn't reply.

Guin rolled her eyes.

"You afraid I'm going to sexually assault you?" she said, looking up at him.

The detective was a good six inches taller than Guin and probably outweighed her by at least 50 pounds, most of it muscle. He opened his mouth to say something, then shut it.

"Fine," he said, walking over and seating himself on the folding chair.

Guin glanced over at him. He looked distinctly uncomfortable, but she didn't care. She was just relieved she had decided to make the bed that morning, even though she had been running late.

"Now let's take a look at Facebook," she said.

She quickly brought up the website and saw that her post had over 60 comments.

"Wow," she said. "Okay, let's see if anyone posted anything useful."

She clicked on the post and started scrolling through the comments. Many of the commentators, as they had the night before, simply expressed their hope that the girl was found. She kept scrolling.

"Here! Take a look at this one," said Guin, pointing to the screen.

"Pretty sure that's Ronnie Swales," said the commentator, a man Guin didn't know.

Guin looked over at the detective, but his face was unreadable. She continued to scroll.

"Here's another one," she said, stopping. "'Pretty sure that's Ronnie Swales, and isn't that Billy Simms with her? Love that guy! Hope she's okay,'" Guin read aloud. The comment came from another man.

Again, she looked over at the detective.

"Keep going," said the detective, staring at the screen.

She continued to scroll. Several more people identified the woman as Ronnie Swales and the man to her right as Billy Simms, the football player, or former football player. Guin made a mental note to find out what Billy was doing now.

She got to the last comment and stopped.

"So it would seem as though Vic was right and the girl

was, in fact, Veronica Swales," said Guin, turning to look at the detective.

"So it would seem," said the detective.

"Now we just need to find out where she was working and living. Though you have that resume she gave to Vic, which you said you would send to me."

Guin waited for the detective to say something, but he was staring at the screen.

"Well, I'm just going to ask some of these people who identified her if they can provide some additional information," said Guin, turning back to the computer.

The detective put a hand on top of Guin's. It felt warm. Guin turned and looked at the detective.

"You sure that's a good idea?" he asked her.

Guin thought for a minute. The detective's hand still rested on top of hers. She looked down at it, then up at the detective. His face was hard to read, especially with the coffee mug in front of it.

"I'll be careful," said Guin.

The detective removed his hand.

Guin regarded him for another minute. He was powerfully built, with a face that revealed nothing, and soulful eyes. He had the air of a boxer, or former boxer (the human kind, not the dog, though now that she thought about it…). His skin was fair, like hers, though it had a weathered look and was covered with freckles. His eyes were tawny, just slightly browner than his auburn hair, which he kept cut short, though it would probably be quite wavy or curly if he let it grow out. Guin had guessed he was in his early fifties, though he could be older or younger.

"Well, I should get going," said the detective, getting up.

"Okay," said Guin, also rising.

The detective walked quickly out of Guin's bedroom, heading to the kitchen. He left his mug in the sink, then headed to the front door.

"So, will you let me know what you find out, about the girl?" she asked him. "You said you'd be getting the medical examiner's report…"

"I have a busy day ahead of me, Ms. Jones," he said, looking at her. "You going to let me out?"

Guin was blocking the door.

"Only if you promise to tell me what the medical examiner found and where Ronnie Swales was working."

"Fine," said the detective. "Now will you let me out?"

"You'll email me the moment you get the report?"

The detective ran a hand over his face. Guin knew that meant he was losing his patience. She stepped back and opened the door.

"Thanks for stopping by, detective," she said, sweetly, as he made his way out the door and down the stairs.

The detective did not reply.

Guin closed the door and smiled. Then she hurried back to her computer.

CHAPTER 13

Guin sat down and opened the Facebook post again.

"Thanks for your help!" she replied to the first commentator who had identified Ronnie. "When did you last see her? Do you happen to know where she was working or living?"

She copied the comment and pasted it into several more replies, to those who had commented that the girl in the photo was Ronnie Swales. Then she did a Facebook search for "Ronnie Swales." She quickly found her, but due to Ronnie's privacy settings, she was only able to see her profile picture and her cover photo, neither of which was very helpful.

Next Guin checked out Instagram.

"Aha!" she said, finding what she was pretty sure was Ronnie's Instagram account, as it had the same photo she had found at Joey's Custard, along with several selfies of Ronnie. Billy Simms was featured in several photos, as was Jake from the bakery, and a bunch of young women who looked to be about Ronnie's age. Guin kept scrolling, hoping to find something that would show a place of employment, but Ronnie's feed was mostly made up of selfies and photos of her and her friends.

Then she found it.

There amongst the selfies and photos of Ronnie with attractive young men and women and beach scenes was a photo of a bunch of pastries, with the caption "Best pastries ever!" and the hashtag #JeanLucsBakery.

She looked at the date on the photo. It was posted in September. So was Ronnie a customer or did she work there? She would go to the bakery and find out.

"I could stop there on my way to see Ginny," Guin said aloud to the cats, who were still asleep on the bed.

Flora opened her eyes to regard Guin, then shut them again.

Guin turned back to the computer to type an email to Craig, letting him know what she had found out about the dead girl. As she wasn't that into college football and knew Craig was, she asked him what he knew about Billy Simms and if he could do a little bit of snooping, though she hated to use that word. "You know," she wrote, "find out what he's been up to since graduation, where he's been living, maybe ask him about Ronnie."

Of course, she could just Google Billy Simms. She had already done a quick search, which turned up lots of stories and photos of Billy from UCF, but she hadn't seen anything super recent. Besides, Craig would probably get more information out of him in person, provided he knew how to find him. But as Craig was an old hand at reporting, and seemed to know everyone on the island, he should have no problem digging up information, Guin reasoned.

She read over the email to Craig, then hit "send."

"Alrighty then," she said, getting up. "You guys be good. I'm going to Jean-Luc's and then to the office. Be back later."

The cats, as usual, ignored her and continued to nap.

Guin walked into Jean-Luc's on Periwinkle and was immediately hit by the smell of freshly baked bread. She closed her eyes and inhaled. Oh my God, it smelled good in there. She opened her eyes to see a middle-aged woman smiling at her, Jean-Luc's Irish wife, Christina.

"May I help you?" asked Christina, who everyone referred to as Madame Fournier.

"I'll take one of everything," said Guin, eyeing the pastry case. Everything looked so good, and Guin had a weakness for French pastries.

Madame Fournier laughed.

"Actually," said Guin, tearing her eyes away from the pastries, "I'm here to ask about one of your employees."

"Oh?" said Madame Fournier.

"Actually, two of them."

"Have they done something wrong?" asked Madame Fournier, looking concerned.

"Oh no!" Guin quickly asserted.

"I'm sorry, I should have introduced myself. Guin Jones," she said, extending her card across the counter. "I'm with the *Sanibel-Captiva Sun-Times*. I interviewed your husband just before the place opened, and I've been in several times since."

Madame Fournier took Guin's card and looked at it.

"I thought you looked familiar," she said. "That article you wrote did a world of good for us."

"I'm so glad," said Guin. "I love your pastries. And I saw you have a stall at the Sanibel Farmers Market."

"Yes, we do."

"And the young man I saw there, Jake, he works here at the bakery?"

"He does," said Madame Fournier.

"Has he been working here long?" asked Guin.

"Since shortly after we opened."

"And does a young woman named Veronica Swales also work here?"

Madame Fournier's face went from sunny to overcast.

"Why do you ask?"

"She's been reported missing," Guin replied, not wanting to tell the woman she had found Ronnie's dead body.

"No surprise there."

"Oh?" said Guin.

"Always making excuses and showing up late for work," said Madame Fournier, her Irish accent becoming more noticeable.

Guin regarded Madame Fournier. She was in her late forties or early fifties, heavyset with graying hair and muscular-looking arms, a true baker's wife.

"Anything else you could tell me about her?"

"She was always flirting with the customers."

"So she worked for you, here at the bakery?" asked Guin.

"She did," replied Madame Fournier. "Though to say she 'worked' here is being charitable."

"Oh?" asked Guin.

"Like I said, she was always arriving late and chatting with the customers. I told Jean-Luc he needed to talk to her, but…"

Was Madame Fournier jealous of the attractive young woman?

"So if she wasn't a good worker, why didn't you fire her?"

"Jean-Luc had a soft spot for the girl," replied Madame Fournier. "And it's hard finding help."

"Do you know where she was living?" asked Guin.

As her employer, Madame Fournier would have her address. Whether she was willing to give it to Guin was another matter.

The woman eyed Guin suspiciously.

"Why all the questions? Has she done something?"

"Like I said, she's gone missing," said Guin. "I'm just

trying to help the police track her down."

"She probably ran off with some fellow. Found herself a new sugar daddy."

Guin raised her eyebrows. What did Madame Fournier mean?

"Was she seeing someone?"

"I wouldn't be surprised if she was sleeping with half the town," snorted Madame Fournier.

It was clear the woman had no love for Veronica Swales.

"What about Jake?"

"Jake?" asked Madame Fournier.

"The young man in charge of your stall at the farmers market."

"Oh, Jake," said Madame Fournier, smiling. "He's a good lad. I don't know what he ever saw in her. He's the reason why we hired her. Said she was in desperate need of a job."

"Were the two of them dating?" asked Guin.

"I don't rightly know," said Madame Fournier. "I don't think so. Heaven help him if he was. You can ask him yourself, though. He should be back any minute."

"So do you know where Ms. Swales was living?" Guin asked again.

"Ask Jake," said Madame Fournier.

Guin was going to ask if she could just check her files, but she decided to leave it alone, for now.

"Just a couple more questions, Madame Fournier."

"Go on," she replied.

"Do you know if Ms. Swales was in any kind of trouble?"

The baker's wife let out a peal of laughter.

Guin was taken aback.

"I'm sorry," said Madame Fournier, wiping an eye. "It's just that if you knew Veronica like I did… Well, trouble could have been her middle name."

Guin was about to ask her if she knew of anyone who might wish Ronnie any harm when the front door opened and Jake walked in.

"I'm back, Madame!" he cheerily said to her. "Got everything you asked for."

"There's a good boy," said Madame Fournier, smiling at him.

Clearly, she had no trouble with Jake.

"I'll just put everything in the back," he said.

"And then come talk to this lady," said Madame Fournier. "She has some questions about Veronica."

At the mention of Veronica's name, Jake stopped.

"Is Ronnie okay?" he asked. "I've been trying to reach her, but she hasn't answered her phone or returned my texts."

Guin could see the concern on his face.

"Run along and put those packages in the back, then you and the lady can talk," said Madame Fournier.

"Yes, Madame," said Jake, dashing into the back of the shop. He came back out a few minutes later.

"So, you know something about Ronnie?"

"Why don't we step outside," suggested Guin.

Jake looked over at Madame Fournier.

"It's okay, Jake. Just don't be long."

Guin opened the door and the two of them stepped outside.

"So, do you know where Ronnie is?" asked Jake, his eyes hopeful.

"I do," replied Guin.

Jake waited for her to say more.

"Her body is at the Lee Country Medical Examiner's Office."

"Oh my God," said Jake, his face going pale.

"I'm sorry, Jake."

"I don't understand," he said.

"Her body was found Sunday morning."

"Where?"

"In a house not too far from here."

Guin watched Jake, gauging his reaction.

"When did you last see her?" asked Guin.

"Are you a cop?" he asked.

"No, I'm a reporter with the *San-Cap Sun-Times*. I'm also the one who found her body."

"I saw her Friday, here at the bakery."

"Were you and Ronnie close?"

"You could say so."

"Were you dating?"

Jake looked momentarily wistful.

"We dated, briefly, back in college. But things didn't work out. We remained close, though. She was my wing woman."

"Wing woman?" asked Guin.

"You know, she helped me pick up girls, let me know which ones I should go out with and which ones were just using me."

"Ah," said Guin. "What about Billy Simms?"

"What about him?" asked Jake.

"Were he and Ronnie dating?"

"Like now?"

Guin was confused.

Jake sighed and ran a hand through his hair.

"Ronnie and Billy were kind of an item at UCF. Total cliché: the quarterback and the head cheerleader. Ronnie followed Billy here after graduation. His family owns the Island Trust Company. Been here for generations. Billy's the only son and was expected to go into the family business.

"Things seemed fine when Ronnie first got here, but then they had some big blow-up. I don't know what happened. They refused to talk about it. It seemed like they had broken things off, but…"

"But?" asked Guin.

"You know," said Jake, giving her a look.

"I don't know," said Guin. "Maybe you could enlighten me?"

"You know, they still got together."

"Ah," said Guin, finally getting it. So they were still sleeping together, though there was probably little sleeping involved.

"And how did you know Billy? Were you at UCF too?"

"Yup," said Jake. "We were fraternity brothers. I've actually known Billy since high school."

"And you both dated Ronnie," said Guin.

Jake gave her a sheepish grin and ran a hand through his hair again. He was a nice-looking young man.

"We did, though Billy was the better man."

"Were you jealous of Billy and Ronnie?" asked Guin.

"Jealous?" asked Jake. "Nah. Ronnie and I had broken up by the time Billy started dating her. We were better off being friends."

Guin wanted to believe him.

"And do you know where Ronnie was living? Did she have a place here on the island?"

"She was living with a couple of other girls in a rental, not too far from here," he said.

"Do you know these girls?" asked Guin.

"Sure," said Jake.

"Could you put me in touch with them? I'd like to ask them a few questions."

"No problem," said Jake.

Guin fished in her bag and brought out her card case.

"Here's my card. Let me know how to get in touch with Ronnie's housemates."

"Sure, no problem," repeated Jake.

"And what's the best way to get in touch with you, Jake, in case I have more questions?"

He gave her his mobile number and told Guin she could text him.

"And what's your last name?"

"Longley," he replied.

"Thanks," said Guin, smiling at him.

He smiled back at her.

"No problem. Happy to help." His expression became downcast. "I just can't believe Ronnie's dead."

"I know," replied Guin. "But I'm hoping we can find whoever killed her."

Guin paused.

"Any idea who'd want to hurt her?"

Jake looked back at the bakery. He could see Madame Fournier staring out the window.

"I need to get back to work," he said.

Guin followed his gaze.

They headed back into the bakery and Guin picked out half a dozen pastries to take to the office. Then she thanked Madame Fournier for her help and left.

CHAPTER 14

"Oh my God, this mocha eclair is amazing!" said Ginny, swallowing a bite of the French pastry. "So much for my diet."

She took another bite, then put the eclair down. Guin smiled at her.

"Glad you like it."

"Like it? Honey, if I wasn't already taken, I'd marry it. You say you got these from Jean-Luc's?"

"Yup, on my way here," replied Guin.

Ginny eyed the box of pastries sitting on her desk.

"Take them away," she ordered Guin. "Offer them to Jasmine [the head designer] or Mark [the paper's copy editor] or Phoebe [the head of sales], she said waving the box away. "I will eat them all if they remain here."

"You sure?" asked Guin. "You could always take them home and—"

Ginny cut her off.

"Go."

Guin got up and headed to the front area, where most of the staff worked.

"Who wants pastries?" she announced.

Immediately several heads appeared.

Guin smiled.

"I'll just leave them here on the table. Whoever wants one can have one."

Like bees to honey, a small swarm of workers appeared, hovering over the pastry box.

"I call dibs on the fruit tart!" said Jasmine, making a grab for it.

"What's that?" asked Mark, pointing to something green and mousse-like.

"It's a white chocolate matcha mousse," said Guin.

"I'm game," said Mark, taking it.

"Is that opera cake?" asked Phoebe, looking at Guin.

"It is," said Guin.

"I love opera cake!" she said, picking it up and grinning. "Thanks Guin."

"My pleasure," Guin replied.

A young man Guin didn't recognize was hovering nearby.

"Meet our new intern," said Jasmine. "Colin here is a student at FGCU."

"Nice to meet you, Colin."

"Guin here is one of our star reporters," said Jasmine, smiling at Guin.

"I don't know about 'star,'" said Guin.

She caught Colin looking down at the pastry box, which contained a chocolate eclair and a Napoleon.

"Go ahead and take one," said Guin, smiling at the young man.

"You sure it's okay?" he asked, looking around.

"Go ahead!" said Jasmine. "You're probably the only one of us who can afford it," she said with a chuckle.

"Thank you," said Colin, taking the eclair.

"Well, I should be getting back to Ginny," said Guin. "Enjoy!"

She made her way back to Ginny's office.

"All gone," she said.

Ginny looked momentarily wistful. Then her face took on a serious expression.

"So, what have you found out?"

Guin then relayed what she knew about the dead girl, Veronica Swales.

Ginny listened patiently until Guin had finished. Then she leaned forward.

"So Craig's going to talk with Billy?"

"Yes," said Guin.

"Good. And you're going to follow up with the detective?"

"Right after I'm done here," said Guin.

"Okay then. Keep working on this," said Ginny. "I know a bunch of other papers are going to want to cover this, especially if they think Billy Simms is involved. But I want us to be the ones to break the story."

"What about the two profiles I'm doing?" asked Guin.

Guin's main beat was covering local businesses and profiling the owners or events they participated in.

"What about them?" asked Ginny.

"Should I postpone them?"

Ginny looked at her. Guin knew that expression well.

"You can't do both?"

Guin sighed. She probably could. She would just prefer to devote all her energy to finding out who killed Ronnie Swales.

"Fine, but I may need a few extra days."

"You know when we go to press," said Ginny. "Just make sure you get me at least one of those profiles by next Tuesday."

"Yes ma'am!" said Guin, getting up.

"And don't be a smart ass," said Ginny, looking up at her.

Guin made to leave Ginny's office.

"And keep me posted," Ginny called, having turned her attention back to her computer.

"Will do," said Guin.

Guin made her way back down the hall. She stopped by Jasmine's work area to say goodbye and to pet Jasmine's dog, Peanut, a friendly miniature labradoodle.

"Thanks again for the pastries," said Jasmine.

"No problem," replied Guin. "Everything good with you?"

"No complaints," said Jasmine.

Guin always admired Jasmine's laid-back attitude. She smiled and said her goodbyes to the rest of the staff, then left.

Guin leaned against her Mini, checking her messages. There was a text from Ris, which made her smile, as well as a text from Shelly. No word from the detective. Typical. She sighed and quickly checked her email. Nothing that required her attention right away. She would check in with Craig later.

She got in her car and her mind immediately went back to her earlier conversation at the bakery. She hoped that Jake would speak with Ronnie's housemates sooner rather than later and put them in touch with her. But if she didn't hear from him by the next afternoon, she would follow up with him.

She also thought about Madame Fournier's reaction to the girl. Clearly, there was no love lost there. Was she just jealous of her, or was something else going on? Guin hadn't noticed Jean-Luc at the bakery. Maybe he was more objective than his wife. Guin made a mental note to revisit the bakery and speak with him.

So where to now? She was tempted to stop by the police department, which was on her way home. "I'll call him first, make sure he's there," she said aloud.

She called the number for the police department and a woman picked up.

"Detective O'Loughlin, please."

"Who should I say is calling?" asked the woman.

"Tell him Guinivere Jones."

"Oh hey, Ms. Jones," said the female voice. "It's Officer Rodriguez."

"Hi officer," said Guin, smiling. Guin had worked with Officer Rodriguez on the Matenopoulos murder. "How's it going?"

"You know," she said. "So, what do you want to speak with the detective about?" She paused. "Is it about that dead girl? I heard you were the one who found the body."

"Yes, it is. Is he around?"

"Let me check. Can I put you on hold?"

"Sure," said Guin.

She waited while Officer Rodriguez rang the detective. It seemed to be taking a while. Had Officer Rodriguez forgotten about her? She was about to hang up and call back when the officer picked up.

"Sorry about that," said Officer Rodriguez.

"So, is the detective available?" asked Guin.

"He's on his way out," replied Officer Rodriguez.

"Did you tell him I need to speak with him?"

"I did," she replied. "He said he would be in touch. Sorry, Ms. Jones."

Guin made a face.

"Do you happen to know if he received the autopsy report?"

"I'm sorry, I don't," replied Officer Rodriguez.

Guin sighed.

"Well, thanks for your help," she said. "Could you please let the detective know I need to speak with him?"

"Will do," said the officer.

"Thanks," said Guin.

She ended the call and stared down at her phone. Where

had the detective gone? She continued to stare at her phone, but nothing came to her. Then her phone began to ring. Could it be the detective?

It was Polly.

"Hey, Polly. What's up?"

"I just found out about another house that's about to come on the market later this week, and I wanted to know if you wanted to take a look."

"Any dead bodies in this one?" asked Guin.

"Ha ha," replied Polly, who was clearly not amused.

"Sorry," said Guin. "Where is it? Can you send me some details?"

"It's around the corner from the Simms place. Very similar: two bedrooms with another little room that could be used as an office, two bathrooms, decent kitchen."

Guin asked her how much. Polly told her and Guin whistled.

"Aren't there any affordable homes on this island?" Guin asked.

"Hey, in another month, they'll be asking more," replied Polly.

"So why are they putting it on the market now?"

"Husband is ill. They're moving to an assisted living community and they need to raise some cash. But you didn't hear it from me."

It was a common refrain on the island. Many people moved to or wintered on Sanibel starting in their early sixties and wound up moving away again in their late seventies or early eighties, when they could no longer take care of themselves or a loved one.

"Well, no harm in taking a look," said Guin. "Let me know when you can get me in there."

"Excellent," said Polly.

"So Poll, what do you know about Billy Simms?"

"What about him?"

"Is he close to his grandparents?"

"I don't know. Why?"

"Well, apparently, he was dating the dead girl."

Polly whistled.

"And I was thinking, maybe he was using his grandparents' place as a love nest."

Polly didn't say anything.

"Hello?"

"Sorry. Can't help you there."

"So what can you tell me about Billy? I know he played football at UCF. Was he a partier? Did he get into any trouble?"

"I can only tell you the rumors."

"Yes?" asked Guin.

"Well, rumor had it he hung out with a kind of wild crowd when he first got to college, though that's not that unusual. But I never heard of him getting into any actual trouble, like getting arrested. And he was supposedly a good student. Graduated with honors. Works for his parents now."

"So do you think it's possible he had access to his grandparents' place?"

"It's possible," said Polly.

She paused.

"You don't think Billy killed that girl?"

"I don't know what to think, but..."

She trailed off.

"His parents are not going to be happy," said Polly.

"Speaking of his parents, they live here on the island, yes?"

"Oh yeah, they own Island Trust and have a big place over on West Gulf. Killer views." Polly caught herself. "Oops. Bad choice of words."

"Don't sweat it," said Guin. "Do you happen to know how I could reach them?"

"Just call or go over to Island Trust."

"Thanks Poll. I'll do that. Well, I gotta run. Let me know when you want me to check out the other place. Just send me a text."

"Will do," said Polly. "And good luck with your story."

They hung up and Guin started the car. She was dying to know if the detective had received that autopsy report and, if so, what it revealed. But she figured she should give him until at least the end of the day to get back to her.

She put the Mini into gear and slowly backed out.

CHAPTER 15

The next morning Guin got up and immediately checked her phone. She hadn't heard back from the detective, or Jake, or received an update from Craig by the time she had turned it off at nine-thirty, and she was hoping that they had gotten back to her overnight. No such luck.

She sighed, then got up and opened the shades. It was still dark out, but it didn't seem like it was raining. May as well go for a walk on the beach, she thought. She checked the weather on her phone. No chance of rain until the afternoon. Though the weather forecast was often wrong. Still.

She went into the bathroom and splashed some cold water on her face. Then she combed her hair and forced it into a ponytail. That accomplished, she went into her closet and threw on a pair of shorts and a t-shirt.

"Ready," she announced.

She glanced over at the bed, where Flora and Fauna were still sleeping, or pretending to. Then she headed to the kitchen. She turned to see the cats following her down the hall.

"I thought you two were sleeping?" she said, looking down at them.

They followed her into the kitchen and sat in the middle of the floor.

"Who wants Friskies?" she asked.

Immediately Fauna started meowing. Guin smiled.

"I'll take that as a yes," she said.

She opened the door to the pantry and Fauna ran inside.

"Hold your horses," said Guin, grabbing a can of cat food.

Fauna started to meow. Guin ignored her, or tried to, as she opened the can. She grabbed a fork and started to scoop the contents into the bowls. Immediately, the cats lunged for the food.

"Man," she said, shaking her head.

She picked up their water bowl and refilled it.

"I'm heading to the beach," she announced, after she had placed the water bowl back down, but the cats ignored her. "Fine. I'll see you two later."

She grabbed her fanny pack and her keys and headed out. She thought about going to Blind Pass or Bowman's Beach but decided to head over to West Gulf Drive instead. Maybe I'll run into Billy Simms, she thought. He seemed like the type to go running on the beach first thing in the morning. (Guin often saw fit young men running down West Gulf Drive beach.)

She backed out of the garage. Fifteen minutes later, she was parked at Beach Access #4, just as the sun started its ascent over the horizon.

Guin stood on the beach, watching as the sun rose above the palm trees. She loved sunrise. Most people who came to Sanibel came to watch the sun set, but Guin's favorite time of day was dawn, when you could see the sun rise and the world looked pink and fresh and new.

She took a deep breath and brought her hands up over her head, closing her eyes. Then she slowly lowered them, opening her eyes again. She looked out over the sea and called out, "Hey, Neptune! How about you toss me a junonia? Or maybe you could spare a gaudy nautica or a king's crown conch?"

She paused, then looked down. She saw some shells tumbled by the tide but nothing worth placing in her bag. She sighed and began to head west.

It was a beautiful morning, and the beach was nearly deserted. That was one of the things she loved about shoulder season. That and the cooler temperatures.

She made her way down the beach, her eyes firmly planted on the sand, looking for shells. She walked a little way. Then she stopped and turned to look at the houses rising up just behind the dunes.

I wonder which one belongs to the Simmses, she thought.

One of her favorite games to play on her beach walks was to pick out the houses she could see herself living in and imagine what it would be like. There were several houses along West Gulf and just beyond she could easily picture herself in, assuming she had a few million dollars to spare.

As she was staring at the beach houses, she suddenly heard her name being called.

"Guin!" came the female voice.

Guin turned to see her friend, Bonnie, the treasurer of the Sanibel-Captiva Shell Club, who volunteered at the Bailey-Matthews National Shell Museum, walking towards her.

"Hey Bonnie," said Guin. "You find anything good?"

"Just some lettered olives and lightning whelks," she replied. "I was actually hoping to find some wentletraps."

"Here?" asked Guin. "I thought you could only find them down at Lighthouse Beach."

Bonnie grinned.

"That's what people want you to think, but I've found a bunch here. Come, I'll show you."

Guin dutifully followed Bonnie down the beach, until they reached the place marked by a leaning palm tree, where the land jutted out.

"Right around here," said Bonnie, sweeping with her hand.

Guin looked down.

"You have to get down real low to find them," said Bonnie. "Look for bubble shells. The wentles are often right next to them."

Guin watched as Bonnie squatted down and ran her hand over a pile of tiny shells and seaweed.

"Found one, no, wait, two!" Bonnie crowed.

Guin looked down.

"Two nice angulate wentletraps," said Bonnie, showing them to Guin.

"Well, what do you know?" said Guin.

"Come on, Guin, you'll find some. Just get down real low and squint, like this."

Bonnie demonstrated her wentletrap technique.

Guin squatted down a few feet from Bonnie and began to scan for the tiny white shells that looked a bit like vanilla soft serve ice cream, but she was having no luck. A few minutes later, she gave up and took out her phone. It was nearly eight-thirty. Where had the time gone?

"Hey Bonnie," she called over. "I've gotta roll. Good luck with the wentletrap hunting."

Bonnie got up.

"Thanks. Nice seeing you, Guin. Don't worry, you'll find some. Just come back here at low tide one morning and look just above the shoreline, where you see bits of dark seaweed."

"Sure," said Guin, not feeling very confident.

They said their goodbyes, then Guin walked quickly back down the beach, towards where she had parked her car. She glanced at some of the big houses, then back down at the sand, hoping Neptune would deposit some fabulous shell at her feet, but no such luck.

It was nine o'clock by the time she got in the Mini. She checked her phone again. Still no word from the detective, or Jake, or Craig.

Guess I'm going to have to follow up with everyone, she sighed. Then she had an idea. She smiled and started the car.

"Good morning, Jean-Luc!" Guin called cheerily to the owner and head baker at Jean-Luc's.

"*Bonjour, Mademoiselle Guin*," replied Jean-Luc, a smile on his face. "I'm sorry I missed you the other day."

"No worries," said Guin. "If you have some time later, I have a few questions to ask you, but right now I'd like to pick out some breakfast pastries and get a couple of coffees to go."

"*Bien sûr*," said Jean-Luc. "What can I get for you this morning?"

"I will have two *pains au chocolat*, two of those raisin pastries, and two regular croissants, *s'il vous plait*."

"*Bon*," said Jean-Luc, boxing up her order. "Anything else?"

"Two cappuccinos, please," said Guin.

"I will fix them for you myself," he replied.

Guin looked around.

"Is Jake working today?"

"He's out making deliveries," replied Jean-Luc. "Why?"

"He was going to send me some information."

"Well, if he said he would send you something, I'm sure he will," said Jean-Luc, handing Guin her box of pastries and the two cappuccinos.

Guin handed him her credit card and he rang her up.

"So what time would be a good time to chat? Will you be around later?"

"Come by whenever. If I'm not out front, just ask for me."

"Okay, I'll do that. Thanks, Jean-Luc."

"*Mon plaisir*," said Jean-Luc, smiling at her once more.

Guin smiled back at him and waved goodbye. Madame Fournier was a very lucky woman.

Guin looked at the Mini, then down at her hands, which were full. Hmm…

She gently placed the cappuccinos, which were in one of those recyclable trays, carefully on the roof of the car, along with the box of pastries. Then she unlocked the car, opened the door, placed the box on the passenger seat, and arranged the cappuccinos in her cupholders.

"Now to see the detective," she said aloud.

She arrived a few minutes later at the Sanibel Police Department, carrying the box of pastries and the cappuccinos. Fortunately, there was someone else about to enter, who held the door open for her.

"Thank you," she said.

She went up to the window and saw a familiar face.

"Good morning, Officer Pettit," Guin said.

Guin had first met Officer Pettit a little over six months back, during the Sanibel Shell Festival in early March, when the star attraction, the Golden Junonia, had gone missing. Since then she had encountered the young policeman, who looked like he was barely out of high school, several times. Though thankfully not because she had done anything wrong. And he was always friendly and polite to her.

"Good morning, Ms. Jones," Officer Pettit replied, smiling back at her. "You bring me breakfast?"

"That depends," said Guin. "Is Detective O'Loughlin available?"

"Do you have an appointment?"

"Let's just say he's expecting me," said Guin. She had shot the detective a text right before she left the bakery, saying she had something important to share with him and she'd be right over.

"All right, I'll just call his extension and let him know you're here."

"Thank you," said Guin.

She rested the pastry box and the coffees on the little ledge outside the reception window while Officer Pettit rang the detective. A minute later he returned to the window.

"He said to tell you, 'This better be good,' and to let you go back to his office."

"Thank you, Officer Pettit," said Guin. "I'll be sure the detective saves you a pastry."

Officer Pettit smiled and buzzed her in.

The detective's door was ajar, so Guin let herself in. As she entered, the detective looked up and took in the box and the coffee cups.

"You bearing gifts?"

Guin placed the box of pastries and the coffees on his desk.

"Yes, but I'm not Greek, so you have nothing to worry about."

Guin was pretty sure she saw the detective trying to suppress a smile.

"I got you some breakfast pastries and a cappuccino," she said, removing one of the coffees and placing it in front of the detective. "You may need to heat this up in the microwave, though."

She opened the box of pastries.

"Pick your poison," she said.

The detective looked inside the box, then up at Guin.

"What are these?"

"Those are *pains au chocolat*," said Guin, pointing to the two *pains au chocolat*. "Basically chocolate-filled croissants. Those are raisin pastries. I forget what they are called in French. And those are croissants."

Guin looked around the detective's office, which was covered with Boston Red Sox paraphernalia and stacks of papers and files.

"You have any plates or napkins stashed around here?"

He reached into a drawer and pulled out a roll of paper towels.

"Will this do?" he asked.

"Fine by me," Guin replied.

The detective took a sip of the cappuccino.

"I'm going to go heat this up. You want me to heat up yours?"

"Please," said Guin.

She followed him down the hall to a small kitchen.

"I've never been back here," she said. "It's nice."

The detective placed the two cappuccinos in the microwave. Thirty seconds later he removed them.

They made their way back down the hall to his office. He closed the door after Guin, then helped himself to a raisin danish. He took a couple of bites, then looked up at Guin.

"So, what brings you to my little corner of the world?" he asked.

Guin had helped herself to the other raisin danish.

"Did you receive the autopsy report?"

The detective took another bite of his danish and drank his cappuccino.

"This is good. You get it from Jean-Luc's?"

"I did," said Guin. "The autopsy report?"

"Death was caused by strangulation."

"Could it have been suicide?"

"Possible, but unlikely. There was no suicide note at the scene, nor evidence that she hung herself there."

"And unless she was a zombie, dead people can't walk."

"So, any idea what she was strangled with or who strangled her?"

"The medical examiner thinks it was some kind of cotton cloth."

"Hmm…" said Guin, taking another sip of her cappuccino. "Any drugs in her system?"

"Not on the initial screen. They're still waiting for the results on some tests."

"What about sex?"

"Female," replied the detective.

"Ha ha," said Guin. "You know what I meant. Had she been…"

"Raped? There was no indication of forced entry or bruising."

"You speak with Billy Simms?" asked Guin.

"Billy Simms?" asked the detective, taking another bite of his danish.

"Come on, detective. I know the dead girl was seeing him."

The detective took a sip of his cappuccino.

"What about the girl's housemates? You talk to them?" asked Guin.

The detective wiped his hands then looked up at Guin.

"Officer Pettit said you had something important to share."

"Yes, those pastries," Guin replied.

The detective looked stone faced.

"Well, I have a murder to solve and work to do. So, if

there's nothing else," he said.

There was a lot else Guin wanted to ask him, but she could tell she wouldn't get any answers.

"No, nothing else, for now," she said with a sigh, getting up. She turned and headed toward the door.

"Aren't you forgetting something, Ms. Jones?"

She stopped and turned around. The detective inclined his head toward the box of pastries.

"Keep them," said Guin. "Just save a *pain au chocolat* for Officer Pettit."

She smiled, then exited his office, closing the door behind her.

Well, at least I found out the cause of death, Guin consoled herself.

CHAPTER 16

Guin sat in the Mini and thought about next steps. The detective was pretty much a dead end, though she knew if she pestered him enough, he'd probably throw her a crumb or two. Speaking of crumbs…

She put the car in gear and headed back over to the bakery. When she got there, she found Jake behind the counter.

"Just the man I wanted to see," she said, smiling.

"Oh, hey, Ms. Jones," said Jake, returning her smile. "What can I do for you?"

"Were you able to get in touch with Veronica's housemates?" asked Guin.

"Right!" said Jake, looking sheepish. "I did ask them if it would be okay for you to contact them."

"And?" said Guin.

"They said, 'Sure, no problem.'"

Guin waited.

"Aren't you forgetting something, Jake?"

Jake looked confused.

"Their names and contact information?"

"Oh right!" he said, giving her another sheepish grin. "Sorry, I'm a bit sleep deprived. Jean-Luc has me getting up way earlier than I ever had to in college, and I haven't learned how to fall asleep before midnight."

"I'd keep working on that if I were you," said Guin. "You need sleep."

"Tell me about it," said Jake.

"So, that contact info? Can you write it down for me?"

"Oh yeah, sure," said Jake, coloring slightly. "Let me just go into the back. Jean-Luc doesn't let me keep my phone up front."

"I'll wait," said Guin. "Say Jake," she called, as he was about to disappear.

"Yes?" he said, pausing.

"Is Jean-Luc back there? If so, could you tell him I'd like to speak with him?"

"Sure, but he may be baking," replied Jake.

"If that's the case, ask him when would be a good time to chat."

"Will do," said Jake. He then disappeared into the back.

He came out a couple minutes later and handed Guin a piece of paper.

"Here you go," he said. "Hope you can read my handwriting."

Guin looked over the piece of paper.

"Thanks."

"And is Jean-Luc available?"

"Oh right. He said he should be done in a few minutes, if you're okay waiting," replied Jake.

"I can wait," said Guin.

"Can I get you something?"

"No thanks. I already had one of your raisin pastries earlier," she replied.

"They're my favorite," said Jake. "Though I also really like the Napoleons and the chocolate mousse," he added, grinning.

A few minutes later, Jean-Luc appeared.

"Jake said you wanted to see me?"

"Is there someplace private we can talk?" asked Guin.

"Let's step outside," said Jean-Luc. "There's a table we can sit at."

He turned to Jake.

"Let me know if a customer needs me."

"Yes, chef," Jake replied.

Guin followed Jean-Luc outside and to a little area where there were a couple of tables and chairs set up, next to a little garden.

"This is charming!" exclaimed Guin. "I had no idea this was here."

Jean-Luc grinned.

"We just set this up a few days ago, in preparation for all the snowbirds returning. We wanted to create a little sanctuary, where they could come and eat pastry, sip their *café au lait*, and read the paper."

"Of course, you know that once people find out about this, you'll never get rid of them," Guin said, smiling.

"I'm sure they'll leave when it gets too hot. Madame Fournier insisted we not put up umbrellas for that reason," he said, chuckling.

Guin laughed.

"Probably smart of Madame Fournier."

"Would you like to sit?"

"Thank you," said Guin, taking a seat.

"So, what have you come to ask me?" said Jean-Luc.

"It's about Veronica Swales," said Guin.

Jean-Luc frowned.

"Such a shame," he said.

"Your wife didn't seem to think so," said Guin.

"Oof," remarked Jean-Luc, waving a hand in the air. "Madame Fournier doesn't like anyone younger and prettier than she is."

"So you found Veronica attractive?" asked Guin.

"I am a man, no?" he replied. "I have eyes in my head, yes?"

Guin waited for him to continue.

Jean-Luc sighed.

"She was a very attractive young woman. You would have to be blind not to notice her. My male customers, they noticed. They would come in just to see her, to exchange a few words, then they would walk out with a big box of pastries."

He grinned.

"And you got along with her?"

"*Bien sûr*," said Jean-Luc, as if it were a silly question. "Everyone loved Veronica!"

Everyone except Jean-Luc's wife, thought Guin.

"Any idea why anyone would want to kill her?"

Guin assumed the police had spoken with the Fourniers by now and informed them that Veronica was dead.

"*Non*," said Jean-Luc. "Like I said, everyone loved Veronica."

"What about a boyfriend? I heard she was seeing Billy Simms, the former football player."

Jean-Luc scowled.

"Pff. Billy Simms."

He waved a hand in the air, as if dismissing him.

"Did you know if she was seeing him at the time of her death? I had heard they had broken up but may have gotten back together."

"I do not involve myself in my employees' love lives."

Guin regarded Jean-Luc. There was something about his expression and his body language that made her wonder if he was hiding something.

"Now, if you don't have any more questions for me," he said, getting up. "I must get back to work."

Guin got up.

"No, that's it for now. Thank you, Jean-Luc."

"*Enchantée*, Mademoiselle Jones," he said, smiling at her and clasping her hand.

Guin smiled back. He was a good-looking man. No longer young, but not old. She could imagine many women being attracted to him. Had Ronnie?

They walked back to the front of the bakery.

"Can I get you anything?" asked Jean-Luc, gesturing toward the pastry case.

"Thank you, but I'm good," said Guin.

"Very good then. *Au revoir*, Miss Jones."

He turned and went back to the kitchen. Guin then said goodbye to Jake and left.

She sat in the Mini, staring out the windshield, turning on the engine when it started to get too hot. What had happened to Veronica Swales? Could she have been having an affair with Jean-Luc? Is that why his wife didn't like her? Or maybe she had gotten back together with Billy Simms and Jean-Luc was jealous? Guin sighed. It was all conjecture.

I need to speak with Billy Simms and Veronica's housemates, she said to herself.

She got out her phone and called Craig. He picked up after a few rings.

"What's up?" asked Craig.

"You interview Billy Simms yet?"

"Later today," said Craig. "He's been out of town. Just got back last night."

"Oh?" said Guin. "When did he leave?"

"Saturday," replied Craig.

"Where was he?" asked Guin.

"In Orlando. Supposedly meeting up with some of his college buddies, then doing some business."

"Ah," said Guin. "So he was out of town when Ronnie was killed."

"Allegedly," said Craig.

"You think he did it?" asked Guin.

"I don't know. I did a little digging. Back when he was a

freshman at UCF, a girl accused him of groping her at some frat party," Craig replied. "Said he took advantage of her when she had had too much to drink."

"Did he rape her?" asked Guin.

"He stopped before it went that far."

"Were formal charges filed against him?"

"No," Craig replied.

"What happened to the girl?" asked Guin.

"She transferred."

"And Billy?"

"Probably just had his wrist slapped," said Craig.

"So he wasn't suspended or punished?"

Craig snorted.

"He may not have been the starting quarterback yet, but he was on the football team, and he denied the charges, which were dropped."

Guin was disgusted.

"So when and where are you meeting him?"

"Over at Island Trust at four."

"Any chance—"

Craig cut her off.

"No."

"How do you even know what I was going to ask?"

"You were going to ask if you could sit in," Craig replied.

That was exactly what Guin was going to ask.

"And I don't think it's a good idea."

"How come?" asked Guin, miffed.

"Just trust me on this one, Guin."

"It's because I'm a woman, isn't it?"

Craig sighed.

"What was the Knights' record last year? How many touchdowns did Billy make? What was his passing yardage?"

"I can look all that stuff up," said Guin, annoyed. "Besides, what has that to do with Ronnie Swales's death?"

"Just let me handle this one, Guin. I promise I'll give you a transcript of the conversation if you want me to."

Guin was annoyed, but she realized that Craig would probably have a better shot at getting information out of Billy than she would.

"Fine," she said. "Just let me know what you find out."

"Of course," said Craig. "How are things on your end?"

"Okay. I met with the detective. Death was by strangulation, but you probably knew that. And I spoke with Jean-Luc Fournier. I have a feeling he knows more about Ronnie than he's telling me. And I got the names and contact information for Ronnie's housemates. I'm going to reach out to them, see what they know."

"Anything else?"

"Not really," said Guin.

"Tell you what, why don't you come over for dinner tonight? Betty would love to see you, and I can tell you all about my interview with Billy Simms."

"Can I get back to you on that?" asked Guin. "Ris and I had talked about maybe getting together later."

"Bring him along. Betty loves him. Always tries to attend his lectures at the Shell Museum. If I was younger, or she was, I'd probably be jealous."

Guin laughed. Ris had that effect on women. That's how he had earned the nickname "Harry Heartthrob." Women positively swooned over him. What he was doing with her, Guin didn't know.

"I'll text you in a bit."

"That's fine," said Craig.

They said their goodbyes, then Guin headed back to the condo and her computer. She had work to do.

CHAPTER 17

Guin arrived at Craig and Betty's at 6:30. She had invited Ris to join her, but he had declined, citing work and his training. She walked up the front steps and rang the bell.

"Coming!" called two cheery voices.

Guin smiled.

"So glad you could make it, Guinivere," said Betty, hustling her inside.

"Thank you for inviting me," said Guin.

She followed Betty into the living area.

"Can I help with anything?" Guin asked her.

"Oh no. You're the guest!" Betty replied.

They walked over to the dining table, which was already set. Craig pulled out a chair for Guin.

"Thank you," said Guin, taking a seat. "You sure I can't help?"

"We've got this," said Craig, winking at her.

A minute later Craig and Betty had placed a platter of roast chicken and another with roasted vegetables on the table, along with a basket of multigrain rolls.

"Dinner is served," Craig announced.

He and Betty sat and poured some ice water for themselves. (Guin had already helped herself to some water from the pitcher on the table.)

"Thank you for joining us," said Betty, smiling at Guin.

"My pleasure," said Guin.

They made small talk for the next fifteen minutes or so while they ate the chicken and vegetables. (Betty had gotten very into nutrition and exercise after Craig had had a heart scare a year earlier and had insisted they eat a healthier diet, at least at home, and walk and lift weights regularly.)

"That was delicious, Betty," said Guin, placing her napkin on the table. "May I help you clear?"

"I've got it, Guinivere. You go chat with Craig. I know the two of you are dying to discuss what happened to that poor girl."

Guin started to protest, but Betty made a shooing motion with her hand.

Craig stood up and began clearing the table, but Betty shooed him away too.

"Why don't you two go out onto the lanai?" she suggested.

"Shall we?" he said, turning to Guin.

"Sure," she replied.

Craig went over to Betty and gave her a kiss on the cheek. "Just give a holler if you need me."

"I'll be fine," she said, smiling at him.

Guin watched and sighed. If only her marriage could have been that happy. There was something about being with Craig and Betty that made her feel wistful.

Craig gestured toward the lanai.

"You sure we can't help?" Guin asked, glancing back at the kitchen.

"Nah, Betty's fine. I think she secretly likes cleaning up," Craig replied.

They took a seat on the wicker couch.

"So, how was your interview with Billy Simms?" asked Guin.

"Interesting," replied Craig.

"How so?" asked Guin.

"He seemed genuinely upset about Ronnie's death."

Craig paused.

"But he didn't seem altogether surprised."

"Oh?" said Guin, intrigued.

"He said he was always warning Ronnie that she was too much of a flirt, that guys might get the wrong idea."

Guin made a face.

"And what about the two of them? Were they still dating?"

"Billy said it was complicated."

"What does that mean?"

"He didn't elaborate."

If Guin had been there, she would have pressed him.

"Did he have any idea how Ronnie wound up at his grandparents' place?"

"No. And he made a point of telling me he had been away all weekend."

"Can you verify if he was, in fact, away all weekend, or at least Saturday afternoon through Sunday?" asked Guin.

"It's on my list," said Craig.

"So, you learn anything else from Billy?"

"Not a whole lot, I'm afraid. He admitted to being a bit wild his freshman year of college. But he claims he settled down his sophomore year. Said he wanted to set a good example when he became the starting quarterback. He moved back to Sanibel after he graduated to work in the family business. He's the only son, though he has an older sister. He misses football, but he's adjusting."

"Did he know if Ronnie was seeing anyone—anyone else?" asked Guin.

"I asked him, but he said he didn't know," said Craig.

"Do you think he was telling the truth?" asked Guin.

Craig clearly hadn't asked Billy the right questions, in her opinion. Or had let him off easy.

"Hard to say. He didn't seem evasive."

"When was the last time he saw Ronnie?" asked Guin.

"A couple weeks ago."

"Can you be more specific?"

"He said they had had dinner a week before she died."

"Where?" asked Guin.

"Mad Hatter."

"Was it a special occasion?" asked Guin. "Guys, especially twentysomething guys, don't normally take twentysomething women to the Mad Hatter for a casual get together."

"He didn't say," replied Craig. "Just said they had dinner at Mad Hatter."

"Doesn't it seem odd to you that Billy would take Ronnie out for a fancy dinner if they were no longer dating?"

Craig frowned.

"You may have a point. I didn't think about that."

Guin did her best not to roll her eyes. She would have to talk to Billy Simms herself. She didn't blame Craig. He and Betty rarely went out to dinner, and he was clearly not plugged into the Sanibel dating scene. Not that Guin was either.

"So, did he say anything about the dinner?"

"Not really. I asked him if he noticed anything about Ronnie, if she seemed anxious or nervous or worried about anything, and he said she seemed fine."

"So where does that leave us?" asked Guin.

Craig looked thoughtful.

"Not with a whole lot."

They sat on the couch and looked up at the sky, which was filled with thousands of stars. The ones you could see, at any rate.

Guin sighed.

"I never get tired of looking up at the stars. You can see so many on Sanibel."

"I know," said Craig. "It's one of the things I love about it here."

He stood up and offered Guin a hand. She took it and stood up too.

"Well, I should get going," she said. "You okay if I reach out to Billy? I have a few questions I'd like to ask him."

"Go right ahead," said Craig.

"Thanks," said Guin, giving him a smile.

They walked back into the house. Betty was reading a book on the sofa. She put the book down, though, when she heard them come in.

"Guin here is heading out," said Craig.

"You two have a good chat?" she asked.

"Yes," said Guin.

"Well, I hope you two figure out who did that awful thing. So much hate and violence in the world these days," she said, shaking her head.

"Thank you for a lovely dinner," said Guin, smiling at Betty.

"You're welcome. Come on over anytime," she said, returning Guin's smile.

"She misses the kids," said Craig, in an audible whisper.

"They'll all be here over Thanksgiving," Betty said.

"That'll be nice," said Guin.

"It will," Betty replied.

Betty got up and she and Craig walked Guin to the door.

"Goodnight," said Guin. "Thanks again for dinner."

She turned to Craig.

"I'll check in with you tomorrow."

Craig gave her a thumbs up, then closed the door.

CHAPTER 18

Guin sat back in her office chair, staring out the window. Thursday looked to be a busy day.

She had already gone on her morning beach walk, showered, and had breakfast. Now it was time to work.

She was interviewing the owner of a new boutique up on Captiva later that morning and needed to go over her notes. Then she was meeting Ris for lunch near the Shell Museum. After that she planned on transcribing her interview with the boutique owner. Then at five-thirty she was meeting Veronica Swales's two housemates over at Doc Ford's.

"Going to be a busy day, pussycat," she said to Flora, who had plopped herself down on Guin's desk, in front of her monitor. She rubbed Flora's ears and scratched her chin and back. Flora purred more loudly. Guin smiled.

"Okay, time to get to work."

Flora opened her eyes and stared at Guin, who had stopped petting her. Guin could almost hear her saying, "Why did you stop?"

Guin opened her notes on the boutique, a cute shop selling resort wear and jewelry. She had visited the place a couple of times, incognito, to check it out, and had asked the young women working there several questions. She had also done a little research on the owner, a former model turned interior designer from Chicago who had visited

Captiva on vacation and had fallen in love with the place.

She read over what she had typed, including the questions she planned to ask the owner. As she was reviewing the questions, Fauna jumped into her lap and started kneading her. Guin looked down at the cat and stroked her head.

"I have bad news for you, Fauna," she said. "I am about to get up."

Fauna ignored Guin and continued to knead her legs. Then she curled up in Guin's lap and closed her eyes. Guin looked down and sighed.

"Really?"

She looked back up at her monitor. After making a couple of tweaks to the questions, she printed them out. Then she gently removed Fauna from her lap, placing her on the floor. The cat stared up at her.

"Don't give me that look," said Guin. "I told you I had to get up."

Fauna gave her another look, then jumped up on the bed, turned around a couple of times until she found just the right position, then promptly shut her eyes and fell asleep.

Guin smiled.

"Ah, to be a cat."

Flora, still lying atop Guin's desk, tapped Guin with a paw.

"Sorry, girl, I've gotta go. I promise, I'll pet you some more later."

The cat looked up at Guin with her big green eyes.

"Fine, just one more pet, then I have to go."

She scratched Flora's head. Flora closed her eyes and purred.

"Now I *really* have to go," she told the cat.

She grabbed the list of questions she had printed out, along with her microcassette recorder. (She recorded all her interviews, then transcribed them later. It was a bit old fashioned, but it worked for her. And she found it much easier to write after listening to her subject a second time.)

A few minutes later, she was in her purple Mini, heading up San-Cap Road to Captiva.

The interview had gone well. The owner was good at talking about herself and had personally shown Guin around.

"I selected everything myself," she informed Guin. "I went to trade shows, traveled the world, found things no one else had—things perfect for people visiting the islands, as well as locals, too," she quickly added.

"And what have been some of your best sellers?" asked Guin.

"Our charm bracelets," the owner, Maria Farinelli, replied. "Can't keep them in stock. Here, let me show you. We just got a new shipment in yesterday."

She walked Guin over to a display near the cash register, where several bracelets were hung on a display board. Below were boxes of charms, which customers could choose to customize their bracelets.

"I actually had the company design special charms you can only find here on Captiva," she informed Guin.

Guin looked at the display, and suddenly it was as if a light bulb went off. She stopped the microcassette recorder and placed it on the counter.

"Excuse me," said Guin, rummaging around her handbag. "Ah, got it."

She pulled out her phone and opened her photos. She scrolled until she found the photo she had taken of Veronica Swales's wrist, with the charm bracelet on it.

"Do you recognize this bracelet?" asked Guin, holding up the photo.

The boutique owner squinted.

"Sorry, I know it's not a great photo," said Guin.

She enlarged it then handed her phone to the boutique owner.

Mrs. Farinelli examined the photo, then handed the phone back to Guin.

"It does look like one of ours. Why do you ask?"

"The girl wearing the bracelet was found dead the other day."

"Was she murdered? Don't tell me it was here on Captiva."

"No, on Sanibel," Guin replied. Not that that really made a difference. "She had no ID on her, though we believe her to be a young woman who worked and lived on Sanibel named Veronica Swales."

Guin regarded the boutique owner, to see if she had any kind of reaction to the name. But either she was a very good actress or the name didn't ring a bell.

"That's horrible. Well, I hope they catch her killer."

Guin looked down at the photo of Ronnie's wrist, at the charm bracelet, then over at the display and the boxes of charms. Guin hadn't paid much attention to Ronnie's bracelet before. Now she eyed it carefully. Among the visible charms were a sand dollar, a heart, a palm tree, a cookie, and a dolphin, all charms the boutique carried.

"If I show you a picture of the girl, do you think you could tell me if she happened to buy her bracelet here?" asked Guin.

"It's possible we may have sold it to her," said the boutique owner.

"Here," said Guin, opening up the Instagram app. "Tell me if she looks familiar."

Guin pulled up Ronnie's Instagram feed and showed it to the boutique owner.

The woman eyed the photos, then shook her head.

"Pretty girl, but she doesn't look familiar. You should ask Ava if she recognizes her. She's around here somewhere."

The boutique owner looked around the shop until she spied a young woman across the way, straightening a pile of t-shirts.

"Ava," she called. "Can you come here a minute?"

Ava came over and stopped in front of the boutique owner.

"Yes, Mrs. Farinelli?"

"Ava, does this girl look familiar to you?"

Guin handed Ava her phone.

"That's Ronnie Swales," said Ava, matter-of-factly. "Why?"

"So you know her?" asked Guin.

"Sort of," said Ava, handing Guin back her phone.

"Sort of?" asked Guin.

"I mean, she's not, like, my BFF, but we've hung out. Why?"

Ava looked from Guin to the boutique owner, then back at Guin.

"She's dead," replied Guin.

Ava's eyes went wide.

"Ronnie's dead? I don't understand. Was she in some kind of accident?"

Again she looked from Guin to the boutique owner, then back at Guin.

"No, she wasn't involved in an accident. Someone murdered her. And anything you could tell me about Ronnie could help me catch her killer."

"You with the police?" asked Ava.

"No, I'm a reporter with the *San-Cap Sun-Times*, but I'm working with the police."

Ava was still in shock.

"Who would do such a thing to Ronnie?" she asked.

"Ava, do you happen to know anything about this bracelet Ronnie was wearing?"

Guin pulled up the photo of Ronnie's wrist with the charm bracelet and handed her phone to Ava. Ava looked at the photo, then up at the boutique owner, then at Guin.

"It sure looks like one of ours," said Ava.

"Do you recall selling a bracelet to that young woman?" asked the boutique owner.

Ava glanced over at the display.

"I'm pretty sure I didn't sell one to Ronnie," she replied.

"You're sure?" asked Mrs. Farinelli.

"Yeah, I'm sure," said Ava, more confidently. "I would have remembered. Maybe Paloma sold it to her?"

"Paloma?" asked Guin.

"She manages the store," explained the boutique owner.

Guin suddenly had another thought.

"The bracelet, do men buy it for their girlfriends or wives?"

"Oh sure," said Ava.

The boutique was located right across the street from the South Seas Resort and lots of guests of the resort no doubt stopped in to buy something, a little souvenir of their trip, or a gift.

"Would it be possible to find out if that particular bracelet was sold here?" asked Guin.

The boutique had been open barely a month, so there wouldn't be too many receipts to go through.

"It's possible, but we're not the only store on the islands selling these particular charm bracelets," explained the boutique owner. "They're very popular right now."

"What about the charms?" asked Guin.

"The selection varies from store to store," replied the boutique owner.

"But you carry all the charms she was wearing?"

"Oh yeah, and a bunch of other really cute beach-themed ones, too," said Ava.

"So the bracelet could have been purchased here?" asked Guin.

"Yes," said Mrs. Farinelli, though from the look on her face, she didn't think it likely.

"May I email you the photo of the bracelet and the girl, so you can ask your manager and anyone else who works here if they sold that particular bracelet to someone or recognize the girl?" asked Guin.

"If you think it would help," said the boutique owner.

"It's worth a shot," said Guin. Though she knew it was a long shot.

The door to the boutique opened and a middle-aged woman entered. The boutique owner's attention was immediately drawn to the potential customer.

"Did you have any other questions for me?" she asked, turning back to face Guin.

"No, not right now," Guin replied. "I'm going to transcribe our interview a bit later. Can I email or call you if I have any follow-up questions?"

"Email is fine, or text me," said the boutique owner, keeping an eye on the customer, who was looking around.

"And you'll let me know if Paloma or one of your other salespeople sold that bracelet to someone?"

"I will," said Mrs. Farinelli, not looking at Guin. "Just send me those photos."

"I'll do it right now," said Guin.

She quickly sent the boutique owner a photo of Ronnie and the one of the bracelet.

"Done!"

"I'll check my phone later," said the boutique owner. "Now, if you'll excuse me?"

She hurried toward the customer, a big smile on her face, while Ava remained standing next to Guin, not sure what she should do.

"I can ask Paloma and Katya about the bracelet," offered Ava.

Guin looked at the young woman, who seemed to be about Veronica's age.

"So Ava, you said you knew Ronnie…"

"Just a little," she replied.

"And you knew some of the people she hung out with," prodded Guin.

"Ye-es," said Ava, not sure what Guin was after.

"Any of them jealous of Ronnie, not like her?"

"Not that I know of," said Ava. "Though I guess some of the girls might have been a bit jealous."

"How come?" asked Guin.

"Well, she was dating Billy Simms."

She said it as though everyone in the world knew about Ronnie and Billy Simms.

"Billy Simms, the former football player?" asked Guin, just to be sure.

"Yeah," said Ava. "Though rumor had it that they had broken up and Ronnie was seeing some older guy. That's probably why I hadn't seen her at happy hour in a while."

"Would this be the Thursday happy hour over at Doc Ford's?"

"Yeah," said Ava. "You been?"

Guin ignored the question.

"So any idea who this older guy was? Did she ever bring him to happy hour?"

Ava gave Guin a look.

"No way. That would have been weird."

"How come?" asked Guin.

"It just would be. It would be like someone bringing their dad," explained Ava.

Guin suddenly felt very old.

"So your happy hour group, everyone is pretty much in their twenties?"

"Yeah. We all went to high school or college together or work together on the island. That's how I met Ronnie. She started coming with Billy and Jake over the summer. Jake's Billy's best friend. They go way back. We all went to high school together."

"I heard that Jake used to date Ronnie."

"Yeah," said Ava.

"Was Jake jealous of Billy?"

"Jake, jealous of Billy?"

She said it in a way that made Guin feel like an idiot for even asking. Guin waited for her to say something more.

"They were, like, best friends. Besides," said Ava, whispering, "I think Jake might be gay."

"So was there anyone in the group who didn't like Ronnie, maybe resented her?" Guin asked.

Ava looked thoughtful.

"Some of the girls may have been a bit jealous, you know, because of Billy. But it seemed like everyone got along."

"Well, if you think of something, anything you might have heard about Ronnie or anything about this older man Ronnie was supposedly seeing, would you let me know?"

Guin reached into her bag and pulled out her card case.

"Here," she said, giving Ava her card.

Ava took it and stuck it in her pocket.

"You going to be at Doc Ford's tonight?" Guin asked.

"Nah, I can't make it," said Ava. "Gotta have dinner with the folks."

"Well, thanks for your help," said Guin.

She glanced around the boutique, looking for Mrs. Farinelli. She spotted her behind the cash register, ringing up a customer. She caught her eye and waved goodbye. Then she left the store and walked down the stairs, to the parking lot. She knew it was a long shot that the bracelet had come from the boutique, but on the off chance it had....

She looked at the clock on the dashboard. She needed to get going if she didn't want to be late for her lunch date with Ris.

CHAPTER 19

Ris had asked Guin if they could eat at the Sanibel Sprout, the local vegetarian restaurant, and Guin had suggested they call ahead as the place could get crazy busy at lunchtime, even though it was still shoulder season.

They still had to wait a little while for their food, but they used the time to catch each other up on their weeks.

"So, have you reconsidered coming with me to Panama City?" Ris asked.

"I'm sorry, Ris," replied Guin, though she was not at all sorry. "But with this case…" She trailed off.

Ris gave her a look. They both knew she had no desire to spend all day in the car and hang out alone at the hotel while he competed in the Ironman.

"So, you still feeling good about the race?"

"Pretty good. Though I should have done this ten years ago."

"I bet you're in better shape now than you were back then," she said, smiling at him.

He smiled back at her, the smile that revealed his dimples, that made Guin melt a little bit.

"You may be right. When the kids were little, I barely had time to run or bike more than a few miles. Though I ran after them plenty."

"You'll do great. Speaking of your kids, why don't you

get John to go with you? He could meet you there."

John was Ris's son, who was in college at UT-Austin.

"He's busy," Ris replied.

"Fiona?"

Fiona was Ris's daughter, who was a sophomore at University of Florida. She and John were twins.

Ris gave her a look.

Guin chuckled.

"Yeah, I probably wouldn't have wanted to spend the weekend watching my dad run some race either," she said.

Just then the server came over with their food.

"One classic burger," she said, holding up the plate.

"Here!" said Guin.

"And one happy belly salad," she said, placing the salad in front of Ris, who smiled up at her. "I'll be right back with your kombucha and your juice."

"So after the race, can we go back to eating pizza?" asked Guin.

"We've gone out for pizza," replied Ris.

"You know what I mean."

They ate in silence for several minutes, during which time the server deposited their drinks.

"So, did you find out who the dead girl was?" asked Ris.

Guin looked around the restaurant. It was full of people.

"I did, but let's not discuss it here."

Ris looked around. No one seemed to be paying any attention to them.

"I don't think anyone's listening."

Guin eyed the people at the two tables next to theirs. Both parties seemed to be involved in their own conversations.

"Still…"

"Fine," said Ris. "You can tell me on the ride back to the museum."

They finished their meal, making small talk in between bites.

"You guys want anything else?" asked the young woman who had brought over their food.

Guin glanced over at the dessert case.

"No, I'm good."

"Just the check please," said Ris.

The young woman reached into her pocket and pulled out her pad.

"Here you go," she said, ripping off their bill. "Pay at the cashier."

They got up and headed over to the cashier, an older woman who smiled up at Ris.

"I know you!" said the woman. "You're that nice man who talks about shells and things!"

"Guilty," said Ris, giving her a warm smile.

"I went to that lecture you gave all about the different shells you can find on Sanibel," she continued. "Is this your wife?" she asked, looking at Guin.

Guin felt her face getting warm.

"Not yet," replied Ris, taking Guin's hand and gazing down at her. (Guin was at least a head shorter than Ris, even in heels.)

Guin felt a bit queasy, but she forced herself to smile back at the woman.

"You're a very lucky lady!" said the older woman.

"Yes, I am," replied Guin, squeezing Ris's hand, and wishing they had just left some money on the table.

"Well, here's your change!" said the woman, continuing to smile at the two of them. "You have a real nice day."

"Thank you," said Ris. "You too."

He gave her another big smile, then left the cafe, still clutching Guin's hand.

"You okay?" Ris asked Guin, after they had exited the cafe.

Guin's cheeks were still a bit flushed and she had a hand on her middle.

"I'll be fine," she said. "Must be a little indigestion."

Ris offered to drive them back to the museum, but Guin insisted she was fine.

They got in the car and he turned to Guin.

"So, the dead girl…"

"Right!" said Guin, thrilled not to have to talk about why she had freaked out at the cafe. While she cared for Ris, for some reason the idea of marrying him, really marrying anyone right now, made her anxious.

"The dead woman was one Veronica Swales, known to her friends as Ronnie."

"Was she from around here?" asked Ris.

"I don't think so. She seems to have shown up on Sanibel this summer, after she graduated from UCF. She was dating Billy Simms, the—"

"The Knights star quarterback," interrupted Ris.

"I thought you weren't into football?" said Guin, glancing over at him.

"I follow college ball a bit," he replied. "So she was Billy Simms's girlfriend?"

"Or was. It seems they may have broken up or were taking a break."

"Was she living here on the island?"

"She was," replied Guin. "I'm meeting her two housemates over at Doc Ford's later, after they get off work."

"You going to speak to Billy?"

"Craig spoke with him, but I'm going to follow up."

"Anything else?" asked Ris.

"Oh yeah. Polly asked if we could go see some more places Saturday. I said I'd check with you."

"Can I get back to you?"

Guin knew Ris was not excited about her house hunt.

"Fine."

Ris sighed and was about to say something when Guin cut him off.

"I know you think it's silly of me to get my own place when you have your cottage, which, by the way, I love, but…"

They pulled into the employee lot and Guin parked the Mini.

Ris turned to look at her.

"I know this is really important to you, Guin."

"It is," she replied, looking into Ris's gray-green eyes.

Ris sighed again.

"Fine."

"So you'll go with me?"

"Yes," he replied. "But no dead bodies this time, okay?"

"Promise!" said Guin.

She reached over to give him a kiss on the cheek, but he moved his head so that their lips touched instead. Several minutes later, as the car started to fog up, Guin pulled away.

"Go! I know you need to get back to work, and I have to go home and transcribe an interview and make some calls."

Ris grinned at her.

"Go!" she repeated, pointing out the passenger door.

He got out of the car, then walked around to the driver's side and tapped on the window.

"What?" she asked, rolling it down.

"I love you."

Guin blushed.

"I love you too."

"I'll check in with you later."

"Okay. Have fun at work!"

Ris smiled at her then turned and headed toward the museum. Guin watched as he opened the door to the employee entrance, then disappeared inside.

Suddenly, she heard her phone. She grabbed her bag from the back seat and rummaged around inside until she found it. By the time she pulled it out, however, the call had already gone into voicemail.

CHAPTER 20

Of course, it was the detective. Guin immediately called him back at the police department, but she was informed by the operator that the detective was on another call.

"Just put me through to his voicemail," Guin sighed.

She left him a message then sent him a text. Then she wondered if she should just drive over there. As she sat there, still in the Shell Museum employee parking lot, her phone started buzzing. She checked to see who was texting her. Shelly.

"How's it going? Need any help with the case?" read the text.

Guin smiled.

"Slowly," Guin wrote back. "Thanks for the offer. Will let you know."

"OK," replied Shelly. "Steve and I are having a BBQ Sunday. You free?"

Guin cast her mind to her calendar. She didn't think she had plans Sunday. But she'd need to check her calendar at home and with Ris.

"Let me get back to you," Guin typed. "Gotta go. Later."

"OK," replied Shelly. "Don't be a stranger!"

Guin smiled and put her phone down.

She stared at the dashboard, then made her decision. She would go back to the condo and transcribe her interview with the boutique owner. If she was fast, she could get it typed up before she left to meet Ronnie's housemates over at Doc Ford's.

Guin arrived at Doc Ford's promptly at 5:30 and went over to the bar, where a group of twentysomethings were laughing and drinking beer.

"Excuse me," she said to one of the young women. "I'm looking for Pam and Gillian. Are they here?"

"Gill went to the ladies' room, but Pam's just over there," said the young woman, pointing to an attractive brunette a little way down the bar.

"Thanks," said Guin.

She made her way down the bar and lightly tapped Pam on the shoulder.

"Excuse me," said Guin. "Are you Pamela Miller?"

"That would be me!" said the young woman.

"I'm Guin Jones, with the *San-Cap Sun-Times*. We had an appointment to talk about your housemate, Veronica Swales."

"Poor Ronnie," said Pam, looking downcast. "Who would want to do that to her?" she said, taking a swig of her beer.

"Is there someplace a little quieter we could talk?" asked Guin, looking around. "Maybe we could step outside for a few minutes, when your friend comes back?"

Just then Gillian, a tall, model-thin blonde, returned.

"What's up, Pam?" she asked, looking from Pam to Guin.

"This is that reporter," explained Pam. "The one who wants to talk to us about Ronnie."

"Poor Ronnie. I still can't believe it," said Gillian.

"Shall we go outside?" suggested Guin.

"Let's go," said Pam, hopping off her barstool. "Hey, Dave," she said, tapping the young man in the next seat, who was talking to a friend.

"Yeah?"

"Watch my seat for me? I'll be right back."

"Sure," said Dave. Though he immediately turned back to continue his conversation with his friend.

Pam sighed.

"Let's go."

They made their way onto the deck, which wasn't too crowded. Guin suggested they go to a quiet corner and the girls followed her.

"So how long had the three of you been living together?" Guin asked.

"Gill and I have been sharing a place for just over a year now," replied Pam, who, Guin observed, was around her height, while Gillian towered over them both. "Then Ronnie moved in this past May. She had just graduated."

Guin was momentarily confused.

"We graduated last year," Pam clarified.

"Ah," said Guin. "And how did you two know Ronnie?"

"We were sorority sisters," said Gillian.

"And did the three of you get along?" asked Guin.

"Oh yeah," said Pam.

Guin looked at Gillian, who didn't seem to share Pam's enthusiasm.

"She was cool," replied Gillian.

"And she was dating Billy Simms, the football player?" asked Guin.

Pam grinned.

"Oh yeah. She and Billy had been together for years."

Guin looked over at Gillian, who was stony-faced.

"I heard a rumor that they were taking a break," Guin continued, "that Ronnie was seeing someone else."

Pam and Gillian exchanged a quick look.

"What?" Guin asked, looking from one to the other.

Again, Pam and Gillian exchanged a look.

"Ronnie said not to tell anyone," said Pam.

"You mean she didn't want Billy to find out," interjected Gillian.

"But she told you two?" Guin asked.

"We saw them," replied Pam.

"So do you know who the guy was?" asked Guin.

Pam and Gillian shook their heads.

"We didn't get a good look," said Gillian. "He dropped her off late at the house one night. We knew it wasn't Billy's car and we asked her what was up. She had this look on her face, you know, when you have a secret."

"She told us she was seeing this man—she emphasized *man*. Said he wasn't like the immature boys she had dated," said Pam.

"So she considered Billy a boy?" asked Guin.

"Maybe," said Pam. "I don't know. Anyway, we asked who this mystery man was, but she wouldn't say. Then she showed us this bracelet he had gotten her, with all her favorite things on it."

The bracelet! thought Guin. So there was a good chance it was bought on the island or somewhere nearby.

"And how long ago was this?" asked Guin.

"Maybe a month?" said Pam, looking at Gillian.

Gillian nodded.

"And do you know of anyone who would want to hurt Ronnie?"

Again, Pam and Gill exchanged looks.

"No," said Pam. "Ronnie got along with everyone."

Guin glanced at Gillian and saw a sour look cross her face. She filed it away and continued.

"I heard that Ronnie had a tattoo, just above her heart.

Do you know what it was or what it said?"

"It was a heart," said Gillian.

"With Ronnie and Billy's initials," added Pam.

"Do you know if she covered up the tattoo with a permanent marker?" asked Guin.

Pam and Gillian looked at Guin as though she had just swallowed a goldfish.

"Why would she do that?" asked Pam.

"That's what I'd like to know," said Guin. "Maybe she and Billy had broken things off, and she did it in a fit of pique?"

"Why would she do that?" asked Gillian.

Guin did not have an answer.

"Well, thanks for your help, ladies," said Guin, not knowing what else to ask them right then. "If you think of anything, anything having to do with Ronnie, or with this mystery man she was seeing, please call or text or email me."

She reached into her bag and pulled out her card case.

"Here," she said, handing each of them one of her business cards.

"Thanks," said Pam. "I hope you find out who did it."

"Yeah," said Gillian.

"Me too," said Guin.

They moved toward the entrance to the restaurant when Guin stopped.

"Any of your friends in there worth talking to, about Ronnie?"

The girls stopped and thought for a minute. Then Gillian leaned down and whispered something into Pam's ear.

"Have you talked to Jake Longley?" asked Pam.

"A bit. Why?"

"Apparently they had a big row just before she died. One of Gill's friends heard about it and told her."

Gillian nodded.

Interesting, thought Guin. She would have to talk to Jake again.

"Anything else?"

Pam and Gillian exchanged another look. Gillian shook her head.

"Nope," said Pam.

"What about Billy?" asked Guin.

"What about him?" asked Pam.

"Is he the jealous type?"

Pam and Gillian exchanged yet another look. It was like they couldn't speak without telepathically communicating with the other.

"He would never harm Ronnie," said Pam.

Guin turned to Gillian, who was looking off into the distance.

"Well, thanks again for your help," said Guin. "You have my card if you think of anything."

The girls headed back inside and Guin headed back to her car. She made a mental note to contact Billy and arrange an interview.

CHAPTER 21

Guin got into the Mini and checked her phone. No reply from the detective. She sighed. It always felt like they were playing phone tag. She would follow up with him first thing the next morning if he didn't get back to her tonight. Or first thing after her beach walk. Some things were sacred.

She realized she hadn't gotten back to Polly, so she sent her a text, letting her know she and Ris were available to check out more houses that Saturday afternoon. "Just no dead bodies, please," she had typed, followed by a winky face.

She started the car and made her way out of the parking lot, down Tarpon to San-Cap Road. Her phone started buzzing as she was driving, but she ignored it, knowing better than to answer her phone while driving. When she arrived back at the condo fifteen minutes later, she checked her messages. There was a text from Polly.

"Let's chat," she had written. "I'll be up til 10. Or call me tomorrow."

Guin got out of the car and jogged up the stairs. She turned on the hall lights to find Flora and Fauna a few feet from the front door, giving her accusatory looks.

"What did I do now?" she asked.

She looked from one cat to the other.

"Meow!" said Fauna, as if saying, "You know what you did!"

"How many times have I told you two, I don't speak cat," Guin said with a sigh.

She headed into the kitchen to get herself a glass of water. The cats trotted after her.

"Meow!" repeated Fauna as Flora sat down in the middle of the kitchen floor and looked up at Guin.

"Are you guys hungry? Is that it?" she asked, looking down at them.

She walked over to their bowls. There was still some food in them, but not a lot. She opened the door to the pantry and removed the bag of cat food. Then she poured a little kibble into each bowl.

"There," she said.

The cats continued to look up at her.

She sighed and put the bag of cat food away, making sure to clip it shut.

"I give up," she said.

She walked down the hall to her office/bedroom. The cats followed her.

"Oops, forgot my phone," she said, looking over at the cats. "Be right back."

When she got back, both cats were curled up on her bed. She made a face, then turned to her phone. She entered Polly's number and waited for her to pick up.

"Hey!" said Polly.

"Hey," said Guin. "What did you want to chat about?"

"I just wanted to run some houses by you."

"Can't you just send me the listings?"

"Not all of them are officially on the market or have pictures posted online," said Polly.

"Fine," said Guin. "Describe away."

Polly spent the next ten minutes describing the three places she wanted to show Guin. All of them seemed fine.

"So you and Ris want to meet me at the first place at two?" asked Polly.

"Fine," said Guin. "See you then."

They ended the call and Guin put down the phone and stretched. Then she headed back into the kitchen to fix herself some dinner.

She looked in the fridge. She had once again forgotten to stock up at Bailey's. So she wound up fixing herself a peanut butter and jelly sandwich on multigrain bread and put some baby carrots on the plate.

She refilled her water glass, then brought it and her plate to the dining table.

As she ate, she read through the news on her phone. Ugh, she thought, as she scrolled past one depressing story after another. She put down her phone and stared out past the lanai. It was dark outside, but the area just outside the condo was lit up, and she could see palm trees in the moonlight.

She finished her sandwich and put her plate in the dishwasher. Then she went into the living room, flopped on the couch, and turned on the TV. She wound up flipping back and forth between Food Network and HGTV.

Finally, around nine-thirty, as she found herself nodding off, she went into the bathroom to brush her teeth. When she came back into the bedroom, she saw her message light flashing. It was a text from her brother, Lance.

"Long time, no text. What's up?" he had written.

Guin smiled. She'd been so busy the past week, she hadn't spoken to or texted Lance.

"Just busy," Guin wrote back.

Lance was pretty busy himself, what with owning a successful boutique ad agency in Brooklyn and living the good life in New York City with his husband, Owen, who ran a gallery in Chelsea.

"You have time to chat? I miss that melodic voice of yours. :-)"

Guin made a face.

"Liar. Sure, call me," she texted him back.

A second later her phone rang. She smiled.

She spent the next half an hour on the phone with her brother, listening to him complain about a particularly picky client (though they all were, if Lance was to be believed) and then talk about this new fabulous restaurant he and Owen had found. Guin smiled and let him talk. Then when he asked her what was up with her, she told him about her latest assignment.

"Billy Simms, Billy Simms," muttered Lance. "Why do I know that name?"

"Unless you've been following college football, you wouldn't."

There was a pause on the other end of the line.

"Oooh, *that's* why I know him."

Guin raised her eyebrows and waited.

"He's totally gay."

"He is not," said Guin. "He has a serious girlfriend, or had until recently."

"Means nothing," said Lance.

Guin rolled her eyes. Lance thought all good-looking guys were secretly gay.

"So how do you know him?" asked Guin.

"His picture was everywhere last year. Where were you?"

Clearly not paying attention, thought Guin.

"He played for some college football team. Anyway, you think he killed that girl? What was her name again?"

"Veronica Swales. Ronnie."

"Just proves it," said Lance.

"Proves what?" asked Guin, confused.

"That he was gay!" said Lance.

"I don't follow," said Guin.

"He was dating someone named Ronnie! Isn't it obvious?"

"Lance, not every good-looking guy is gay."

Lance made a noise that sounded like 'phft.'

"I need to get some sleep. Is there anything else you wanted to discuss?" asked Guin.

"You coming home for Thanksgiving?"

"I hadn't thought about it," said Guin.

"Mom hasn't guilted you yet? I'm shocked."

Uh-oh, thought Guin.

"What do you know, Lancelot?"

"Nothing!" said Lance.

Guin yawned.

"Well, if there's nothing else, I'm going to bed."

"Fine," said Lance.

"Good night, Lance. Love you. Send my love to Owen. And tell mom I'll phone her this weekend."

"Tell her yourself," said Lance.

Guin sighed. She tried to be a good daughter, but she often forgot to call her mother, who expected both children to check in regularly with her.

"Bye," she said and ended the call.

CHAPTER 22

Guin got up at 6:30 and thought for a minute about not going to the beach. Then she reminded herself that no one would be up or answering their phone until at least 8:30. So she got out of bed, went to the bathroom, and threw on a pair of shorts and a t-shirt. Then she gave the cats some food and water, grabbed her keys, fanny pack, and shelling bag, and headed out the door.

She parked over by Blind Pass and saw her friend Lenny's car parked nearby. Lenny was a retired middle school science teacher and Shell Ambassador, and they often looked for shells together, though she hadn't seen him lately.

She walked down to the beach and spied Lenny wading into the water with his shell catcher.

"Lenny!" she called, waving an arm.

He turned around and smiled when he saw her.

She walked down to the water, happy to see him.

"Hey! Where have you been? I was starting to get worried."

"If you were so worried, you could have just called," he said, in his New York accent. (Like Guin, Lenny was originally from New York and was a big fan of the New York Mets.)

"I know. I should have. I've just been busy."

"No doubt with that marine biologist of yours," said Lenny. "Ah, to be young."

"I actually haven't seen much of him lately either," said Guin.

"Oh?" said Lenny. "Trouble in paradise?"

"No, things are fine. He's just been really busy. He's training for the Ironman up in Panama City."

"Ah," said Lenny.

"And I've been busy with work."

"Oh? Anything interesting?" asked Lenny.

Guin then told him about finding Ronnie Swales.

"I heard about that," said Lenny.

Guin raised her eyebrows.

"Annie was all bent out of shape about it."

"Annie?" asked Guin. Lenny was a widower, and as far as she knew, he was single.

"It was her listing. Now she's worried no one will buy the place."

"Wait. You know Ann Campbell?"

"Of course I do," said Lenny. "We play bridge together every week."

"Huh," said Guin. "You think 'Annie' would help me out?"

"Maybe. What is it you need help with? You want to switch real estate agents?"

Lenny knew about Guin's quest to find the perfect beach cottage. Funny he hadn't mentioned Annie. Then again, Guin had told him she was working with Polly, and he had probably not wanted to rock the boat.

"No, I'm hoping Ann could tell me who had access to the Simms place, or was there last weekend."

"Why don't you just ask her?" asked Lenny.

"I don't think she likes me very much."

"What makes you think that?"

"I don't know, maybe finding a dead body in her house?" Lenny chuckled.

"Well, I can't promise you anything, but I'll talk to Annie, see if she'll help you out."

"Thanks Lenny. You're a prince."

"And here I thought I was just an ambassador," he said, grinning.

"Ouch," said Guin.

They spent the next hour or so combing the beach, making small talk—and trading puns—and looking for shells.

Guin headed home a little before nine, leaving Lenny on the beach. He had been stopped by a family with some questions about shells, and once Lenny got going, there was no stopping him. So Guin had politely excused herself. (Lenny loved chatting with people he saw looking for shells and would happily help them identify their finds and tell them how to clean them.)

Upon returning to the condo, she immediately checked her phone. Still no word from the detective. Though the cats had plenty to say.

"What?" said Guin, looking down at the two felines, who had met her at the door and were now following her around, meowing. "I gave you food!"

Fauna gave her an accusing look.

"Fine," said Guin, squatting down and petting the black cat. Immediately Flora came over and started rubbing herself against Guin's legs. Guin sighed and petted her.

"What am I going to do with you two?" she asked them, as she stroked one and then the other.

They purred happily in response.

Guin got up, much to the annoyance of her pets.

"Sorry team. I've got to make some calls and do some work."

She took her phone and called the Sanibel Police Department. After going through the usual pleasantries, she was transferred to Detective O'Loughlin, who amazingly picked up.

"O'Loughlin."

"Good morning, detective."

"We'll see about that," replied the detective. "What do you want, Ms. Jones?"

The detective was in a particularly grumpy mood. I wonder what's up? thought Guin.

"You get back the toxicology report?"

"She was clean, no drugs."

"What about Billy Simms?" asked Guin.

"What about him?" asked the detective.

"Have you spoken with him?"

"We have."

"And?" asked Guin, her annoyance with the detective increasing. Getting information out of him was like trying to coax a pearl out of an oyster.

"And I'm not at liberty to discuss it."

"You know Craig spoke with Billy?"

"Then why are you asking me?"

"Because I want to know if you found out anything!" she practically yelled.

She took a deep breath, then slowly exhaled.

"What about the house?"

"What about it?"

"Did you find out who had access to it over the weekend?"

"You mean your agent hasn't told you? I'm shocked."

Guin could feel the steam starting to come out of her ears. The detective was enjoying this. She could just picture him leaning back in his chair, smirking.

"Look detective, I have a story to write, and you have information I need. Are you going to help me or what?"

"What fun would that be? You want to play detective, Nancy Drew, go for it. I have work to do and a murder to solve."

"Fine!" said Guin, clenching her teeth.

"Is there anything else I can help you with?" asked the detective, sweetly.

He was definitely enjoying this.

"What's the point? You probably won't tell me," she said, a bit sulkily.

"Now, now, Ms. Jones. It's not personal. I'm just doing my job."

"I have a job, too, you know, and you are not helping me do it," Guin retorted.

"Thanks again for the pastries," said the detective. "Quite a place that Jean-Luc has. I can see why he's so popular."

"You're welcome," said Guin, a bit confused by the change of topic. "Glad you liked them."

She paused. There was something about the way the detective said the last two sentences that pricked up her ears. Was it a clue? She wanted to ask him, but she knew he wouldn't admit anything.

"Well, I must be getting back to work. Have a good day, Ms. Jones."

"Thanks for your help," Guin replied, her tone laced with sarcasm.

She ended the call and paced around the condo. Why had the detective mentioned Jean-Luc's? Of course, it could have been innocent. She had brought him pastries from there. But she had a feeling he was trying to tell her something. After all, it was where the dead girl had worked.

Just then Guin's stomach gurgled quite loudly. Right. Food. She had yet to eat something. And she could use some coffee. If only Jean-Luc's was closer.

She headed into the kitchen and made herself some toast and eggs, along with some coffee. When everything was ready, she brought her plate and her mug over to the dining table. As she ate, she stared out past the lanai, which overlooked the golf course, her mind going over what she knew about Ronnie Swales.

From everything she had heard, Ronnie had been an outgoing, friendly young woman about whom no one had anything bad to say, except for Madame Fournier. Though that could have just been an older woman jealous of a younger one.

Guin finished off the last of her eggs and toast and sighed. Fauna was sitting by her feet, looking up at her.

"Here you go, Fauna," she said, placing the plate on the floor.

Fauna sniffed it, then turned up her nose.

"Sorry, that's all there is."

She leaned down and retrieved the plate, taking it into the kitchen and putting it into the dishwasher.

Something was nagging at her, but she didn't know what it was.

"Well, may as well get some actual work done," she said to Fauna, who had followed her into the kitchen.

She walked back to her office/bedroom and sat down at her computer to write up the profile of the boutique on Captiva.

CHAPTER 23

Guin had lost track of time. That often happened when she was working on a story. She had turned off the ringer on her phone and placed it in the drawer of her nightstand, so she wouldn't be distracted. Now that she was done with the first draft of her article, she would take it out. But first she needed a good stretch. She got up and took a deep breath, reaching her arms up over her head. Then she slowly bent over, touching the floor with her hands. She did a few more stretches, then retrieved her phone.

There were several text messages, most of them from Shelly.

"You coming to the BBQ Sunday?" read the first one.

"Yo, you get my message?" read the second one, sent an hour later.

"You OK?!" read the third, sent a little while ago.

Guin sighed. She had forgotten to ask Ris about the barbeque that Sunday, probably because she figured he would not be interested.

"I'm fine, just WORKING," Guin texted back. "Can I get back to you re the BBQ later?"

"Let me know by TONIGHT," came the immediate reply.

"Will do," wrote Guin.

"How's the case?" asked Shelly. "You find the killer?"

"Not yet," typed Guin. "Working on it. Gotta go."

"Yeah, yeah, yeah," wrote Shelly. "Bye."

Guin shook her head. She knew Shelly meant well, and was grateful for her friendship, but sometimes….

She checked the rest of her messages. She would need to send a few emails, but there was nothing urgent. Her stomach gurgled. She walked into the kitchen and opened the refrigerator. Nothing looked appealing. She glanced up at the clock on the microwave. It was nearly two o'clock. Should she run into town and get some food? Probably not a bad idea.

Her stomach growled, as if in response.

"Fine," she said, looking down at it. "I'll go get us some food."

She grabbed her bag and her keys and told the cats she'd be back in a little while.

She parked her car and entered Jean-Luc's. May as well kill two birds with one stone, she had thought, wincing slightly at the analogy. She walked in to find Jake behind the counter.

"Hi, Jake," Guin said pleasantly.

"Good afternoon, Ms. Jones," he replied. "Can I help you?"

"As a matter of fact, you can. First, I need something to eat. And as I recall, you guys did sandwiches," she said, looking at the case, but not seeing anything. "Or are you all out?"

"We're out of the ready-made ones, but I can make you something in back. What would you like? We do this killer brie sandwich with granny smith apples and turkey, and we also—"

"Stop," said Guin, interrupting him. "I'll have that brie sandwich."

"Would you like it on our signature baguette?"

"Sure," said Guin.

"Coming right up," said Jake. "I'll be back in a minute."

He disappeared into the back, and Guin eyed the pastry case. Everything looked so good.

Jake reappeared a few minutes later with her sandwich on a piece of butcher paper and held it up for her to see.

"Anything else?"

"Just a bottle of water," she said. She waited a few seconds while he retrieved one. "So what were you and Ronnie arguing about right before she died? I heard you two had a major blowout."

Jake look confused, then angry.

"Who told you that?"

"Is it true?" asked Guin.

"It's not what you think," he replied.

"You don't know what I think," said Guin. "Did it have to do with her and a certain older man?"

Jake's eyes darted around the shop, then he looked back at Guin.

"I can't talk about it. Not here."

There was a noise from the kitchen. He quickly glanced back. Then he turned to Guin again.

"Will that be all, Ms. Jones?" he asked, his voice raised.

"Yes, thank you," Guin replied, a bit confused.

Just then Jean-Luc emerged from the back.

"Ah, Ms. Jones, so nice to see you again," he said, a smile on his face.

He noticed the sandwich and the bottle of water sitting on the counter.

"Is this for Ms. Jones?"

Jake nodded.

"Well then, why don't you give it to her?" asked Jean-Luc.

He picked up the sandwich and placed it into a bag.

"May I get you something else, a pastry perhaps?" asked Jean-Luc.

"No, thank you. Though I am very tempted," she said, smiling. Jean-Luc slipped a macaron into the bag. "Is it okay if I eat outside, at one of your tables? It's such a lovely afternoon."

"*Bien sûr!*" said Jean-Luc.

Jean-Luc rang her up then handed her the bag and the bottle of water.

"*Merci*," said Guin, smiling at the proprietor.

"It is I who should be saying thank you to you," he replied, smiling back at her. "Now, if you will excuse me, I have much work to do. A pastry chef's work is never done! Jake, your assistance please."

Jean-Luc departed to the back of the bakery. Jake made to follow him but Guin stopped him.

"Please, Jake. I just have a few more questions. Is there someplace we can talk?"

"Jacob!" came Jean-Luc's voice from the back.

"Coming chef!" Jake called back.

"I've really got to go," he said, keeping his voice low. "I'll text you later."

He then disappeared into the back.

Guin took a seat at one of the tables outside. She unwrapped the sandwich and took a bite. She closed her eyes. Oh my God that was good. She took another bite, savoring the different flavors and textures.

"Good sandwich?"

Guin opened her eyes to see the detective looking down at her. He was smiling, or what passed for a smile on him. She swallowed and started coughing.

"You okay? Didn't mean to startle you."

Guin nodded her head and took a sip of water.

"What are you doing here?" she asked.

"A man needs to eat."

"Isn't it past your lunchtime?"

"I've been busy," he replied.

Guin eyed him suspiciously.

"Jean-Luc's doesn't seem like your kind of place."

He put a hand over his heart.

"You wound me, Ms. Jones."

Guin made a face. She doubted that.

"Well, don't let me stop you."

"What are you having?"

"Turkey and brie with some granny smith apple on one of their baguettes."

"Sounds good," said the detective.

"It is," replied Guin.

"I'll be back," said the detective.

Guin watched as he entered the bakery. Did he mean for her to wait for him? She did have over half of her sandwich left. Maybe he'd be more amenable to answering some questions with some food in him.

She took another bite of her sandwich and stared at the little garden. She was almost done eating when the detective finally emerged.

"What took you so long?" she asked.

"Here, I got you something," said the detective, placing a small box in front of her.

She looked down at the box and then back up at the detective.

"Aren't you going to open it?" he asked.

"Aren't you going to eat?" she replied.

He sighed, sat down opposite her, and took out his sandwich. She watched as he unwrapped it.

"You get the turkey and brie with granny smith apples?"

He raised it up.

"I did."

He took a bite and chewed thoughtfully as Guin watched.

"Not bad."

Guin smiled.

"So, you going to open the box?" he asked her.

She looked down at the box and then opened it. Inside were a piece of opera cake and a mocha eclair, two of Guin's favorites. How did he know?

"Thank you," she said. "They're my favorites."

He grinned and took another bite of his sandwich, followed by a sip of fruit-flavored sparkling water.

"They don't have Coke?"

"No," said the detective, frowning. "Though this stuff isn't bad."

"And it's a lot better for you," said Guin. "So, what's the real reason you're here, detective," she said, eyeing him.

"Can't a man enjoy a sandwich without being given the third degree?"

He took a large bite of his sandwich, showing how much he was enjoying it. Guin looked on skeptically. Something was up.

"You were asking them some questions, weren't you?" said Guin.

The detective continued to eat his sandwich. Guin sighed.

"Aren't you going to have your pastries?" asked the detective.

"I'm kind of full from lunch."

She still had a couple bites left of her sandwich. The detective continued to look at her.

"Fine," she said, lifting the mocha eclair out of the box and taking a bite.

"Oh my God," she moaned, her eyes closing briefly.

The detective let out a bark of laughter.

Guin quickly opened her eyes. She felt her cheeks turning red.

"Glad you're enjoying it. Go on, take another bite," he said, clearly amused.

"I think I should save it," she said, hastily returning the eclair to the box.

"Suit yourself," he said, taking another bite of his sandwich.

Guin wrapped the remains of her sandwich and placed it back in the bag.

"So, are you going to tell me why you're really here?" she asked.

"I told you, to get lunch," said the detective, continuing to eat his sandwich. "This isn't bad."

Guin felt her annoyance increasing, but she held it in check.

"Come on. Give."

"I just did," said the detective, looking over at the box.

Guin sighed.

"You know what I mean."

"Why can't you just leave the detective work to the police?"

"Because," said Guin. "I'm just trying to do my job."

"And so am I," said the detective.

This was starting to be a familiar refrain.

They sat there staring at each other for several seconds.

"Fine," said Guin, standing up. "Thanks for the pastries."

She picked up the box, along with her bag and her water bottle.

"My pleasure," said the detective.

Guin wanted to get right in his face and demand he tell her what he knew, but she knew that was useless. Instead she smiled and bid him good day.

She walked as casually as she could to her car, which was parked a little way away, feeling like the detective was watching her. She unlocked the door and got in, placing the bag and the box on the passenger seat, along with the bottle of water. She desperately wanted to check her phone, but she felt odd about it with the detective watching her. At least she assumed the detective was watching her. She had purposely not turned around to check.

She started the car and quickly turned her head to where the tables were. The detective waved. Guin clenched her teeth and put the car in reverse.

Fine, she thought. You don't want to help me? I'll just find out the truth myself.

Her phone started ringing as she walked through her door. It was Ann Campbell. Guin couldn't believe it. Lenny must have spoken to her.

"Ann, thank you so much for giving me a call."

"Lenny said it was urgent," said Ann. Though from the way she said it Guin knew she didn't believe it.

"Can you tell me who had access to the Simms house over the weekend?"

"I gave that information to the police."

Guin gritted her teeth.

"Could you also send it to me? Please?" she added.

"Why do you need it?"

"I'm covering the story for the paper," Guin explained.

"So why don't you just ask the police?"

Guin dug her nails into the palm of her hand.

"I have. But they're a bit busy."

"And I'm not?" replied Ann.

Guin got the distinct impression Ann Campbell did not like her.

"Did Billy Simms have a set of keys?" Guin asked.

"Yes, but don't you go thinking he had anything to do with that girl's death."

So Billy could have been at the house.

"Well, if I knew who else had access to the house over the weekend, it could help put Billy in the clear," Guin replied.

It wasn't a lie.

There was silence on the other end of the line. Clearly Ann was thinking it over.

"Fine, I'll send you the list."

"Thank you," said Guin. "Do you have my email address?"

"Go ahead and give it to me."

Guin told her the address.

"Just do me a favor," said Ann.

"If I can," said Guin.

"Say something nice about the house when you write about it."

Guin smiled. This whole thing must be very hard on Ann.

"Of course," said Guin. "It's a lovely little place."

"You want to buy it?" Ann asked.

Guin was momentarily taken aback. She hadn't really thought about the Simms place, other than as a murder scene, the last few days.

"I could get you a good deal," Ann said.

"I'll think about it," said Guin. "Thank you."

"Well, if you want to make an offer, just let Polly know."

"I will," said Guin.

She said goodbye, then ended the call. Hopefully, Ann would be as good as her word and would send her the list of people who had accessed the house that weekend.

CHAPTER 24

Guin called Craig right after she got off the phone with Ann.

"Hey, I just spoke with Ann Campbell, the listing agent for the house."

"And?"

"She said she would send me a list of the people who were there over the weekend."

"Good."

"Both Billy and his folks had a set of keys."

"Not surprising."

"Have you been able to find out if Billy was in town Saturday?"

"I'm working on it," said Craig.

"Can you also check to see where his folks were?" asked Guin.

"I'll try."

"Thanks Craig. So, you have plans this weekend, other than helping me solve this case?"

"Just the usual," he replied. "Going to go fishing with some of the guys tomorrow. And I've got my poker game later. You?"

"I'm going to look at a few more houses with Polly tomorrow. Then Ris and I are having dinner."

"Give him my regards," said Craig.

"I will," said Guin.

She wished him a good evening and they agreed to check in with each other Sunday.

Guin had been unable to fall asleep and wound up not waking up until seven the next morning, which was late for her. Instead of springing out of bed, she petted the cats for several minutes. Eventually, she got up and opened the shades. It was raining outside.

"Well, I wasn't really in the mood to go to the beach anyway," she told the cats, who gazed lazily at her from the bed.

She took her phone out of the drawer in her nightstand and turned it on. She entered her password, and a few seconds later the phone began to buzz and continued to do so for several seconds, indicating she had several messages.

That's odd, she thought. Who could have called or messaged her in the middle of the night? It was very un-Sanibel like. Oh no, could something have happened to her mother?

She felt a momentary sense of panic. She really should have called her mom. She took a deep breath and slowly exhaled. Calm down, she told herself.

There was a text message from Ris, left at six that morning, saying he had to skip the house hunt but could meet her for dinner. Guin made a face. She wasn't surprised, but she was disappointed. At least they'd still have dinner together.

"Do you want to come over here for dinner?" she texted him back.

There was also a text from Craig, left just a few minutes before.

"Jake Longley's car was found abandoned just over the Causeway early this morning. No sign of him. Doesn't look good."

Guin stared at her phone, then immediately called the detective's mobile, not caring that it was seven-thirty on a Saturday.

"Yes?" came the curt reply.

"Craig said the police found Jake Longley's car in Fort Myers Beach, by the Causeway, but he wasn't in it."

There was a short silence on the other end of the line.

"Hello?" said Guin. "You there?"

The detective sighed.

"Is it true?" asked Guin.

"Yes," replied the detective.

"Is Jake okay? Were the police able to find him."

"I don't know," said the detective. "The Lee County police have been unable to locate him."

"Any clue as to what happened?"

"Not yet," replied the detective.

"Did they try calling his phone?"

"Wouldn't have done much good," said the detective.

"Why not?"

"They found it in the car, between the seats. Must have fallen down there without him realizing it."

"Oh," said Guin.

"And here's the interesting thing," said the detective.

Guin waited.

"He tried calling you a little after ten last night."

"What?" said Guin. She wanted to check her phone for missed calls, but she was worried about dropping the detective. If only she hadn't turned off her phone!

"Any idea why he'd be calling you?" asked the detective.

Guin thought for a second. Suddenly she remembered the scene at the bakery. She had told Jake to call or text her.

"Maybe," she finally replied.

"What aren't you telling me, Ms. Jones?"

Guin sighed. She hadn't had her morning coffee yet, or

food, and she hadn't had a great night's sleep and wasn't prepared to spar with the detective.

"Veronica Swales was supposedly seeing an older man. I thought Jake might know who this man was. He wouldn't tell me at the bakery, but he said he'd be in touch. Maybe he was calling to tell me?"

Again Guin waited for the detective to say something. When he didn't, she spoke again.

"Had you spoken to Jake?"

"I did," he replied.

"And?" asked Guin.

"And this is an ongoing police investigation."

"What does that mean?" said Guin. She had gotten off her bed and was making her way to the kitchen, to fix herself some coffee. "Did he say anything about Billy Simms?"

"Only that he would never hurt Ms. Swales."

"Did you believe him?" asked Guin.

There was a pause.

"So you didn't believe him," said Guin.

"I didn't say that, Ms. Jones. It doesn't matter what I believe. It's about finding out the truth."

Guin rolled her eyes.

"Do me a favor," began the detective.

"Me, do you a favor?" said Guin, stopping what she was doing.

"Call me if you hear from Jake Longley."

"Of course," Guin replied. "Will you do the same?"

"I'll be in touch," replied the detective.

Yeah, right, thought Guin.

"Well, it was lovely chatting with you, detective. But I really must go. I'll let you know if I hear anything from Jake."

"Thanks," he replied.

She ended the call and immediately checked her call history. There was a call from a 239 number she didn't recognize, no doubt Jake's, a little after ten, but the person hadn't left a message. Why had he called? thought Guin. And why hadn't he left a message? She assumed he had called to tell her who the older man was, if there was, in fact, an older man, or to arrange a meeting. What had happened to him?

She finished preparing her coffee, then phoned Craig.

"How did you hear about Jake's car?" she asked when Craig picked up.

"My buddy in the Lee County Sheriff's Office. He phoned me to say he couldn't go fishing with us this morning."

Maybe I should take up fishing, Guin thought.

"And? Any idea what happened to Jake or his car?"

"No. They're having the car towed. No sign of the kid. They found his phone between the seats."

"So I heard," said Guin.

"Oh?" said Craig.

"I just got off the phone with O'Loughlin. Apparently Jake tried to call me last night, but I had turned my phone off. You think Jake is in trouble?"

"Could be. They found some blood inside the car, on the driver's side."

"Jake's?"

"Most likely. They're checking it out."

"Any theories?"

"Not at this point," said Craig. "Could be he was involved with drugs, a deal gone down bad."

"Though he doesn't seem the type," said Guin.

"You'd be surprised," Craig replied.

Guin thought about that. Jake seemed like a clean-cut, all-American young man, but what did she know? There were probably lots of baby-faced, nice-seeming guys out there selling and doing drugs.

She sighed.

"Well, thanks for texting me."

"No problem," he replied.

"Oh, and Craig?"

"Yes?"

"Hope this didn't interfere with your fishing trip."

"The fish will be there tomorrow," he replied. "Gotta go. Catch you later."

"Bye."

They ended the call and Guin put the phone down and drank some coffee. What had happened to Jake? she wondered. And did it have anything to do with Veronica's death? She tried not to let her imagination run away with her, but she had a bad feeling. Hopefully, the police would find Jake, alive.

She took another sip of coffee then opened the refrigerator and took out the container of milk. Next, she opened a cabinet and pulled out a box of Cheerios and a container of raisins. She poured the cereal into a bowl, added a few raisins and some milk, then ate it while she leaned against the counter.

Suddenly she felt something furry rubbing against her leg. Fauna.

"What?" asked Guin, looking down at the cat.

"Meow," said Fauna, who then jumped up onto the counter and rubbed up against the container of milk Guin had left there.

"Ah," said Guin.

She opened a cabinet and took out a small Pyrex bowl, into which she poured a little milk.

"Here you go," she said, placing the bowl of milk on the floor.

Fauna immediately jumped down and began lapping it up. So much for cats not liking milk (though she knew too much wasn't good for them).

Guin smiled and took another sip of her coffee.

CHAPTER 25

Guin paced around the condo. It had been raining all morning, and she was feeling restless. She had so many questions and no answers. If only the detective would share a little information, it would make her job, and her life, so much easier.

She sat at her computer and ran a Google search for Billy Simms. There were thousands of hits, most of them having to do with his football career. She scrolled through, hoping to find something, though she wasn't exactly sure what. She found the story from his freshman year, when a freshman woman had accused him of groping her, but other than that she could find no negative stories. No accusations of assault, no shoplifting, not even breaking curfew.

She sat back in her chair. No one's that perfect, she thought. What about Ronnie Swales?

She typed *Veronica Swales* into her browser, hoping to find out a little more about the young woman. She had already done a search, when she had found out the young woman's name, but maybe she had missed something. She scrolled through the search results. Who knew there were that many people named Veronica Swales?

She typed *Veronica Swales UCF*. That narrowed it down.

She clicked on "Images" and saw several of Ronnie in a cheerleading outfit. In the pictures she was jumping and smiling. So alive. Guin sighed and kept scrolling and saw photos of Ronnie with Billy, Ronnie in her cheerleading outfit, Billy in his football uniform. They made a handsome couple.

She went back to the main page and clicked on a couple of the links. Veronica was from the Atlanta area and had been a cheerleader in high school.

Guin also found her Facebook page, but she was only able to see a few photos. She grabbed her phone and went to Ronnie's Instagram page. She scrolled through the photos again, more slowly this time, and found a few that had been taken at the bakery, including one of Ronnie with Jake and Jean-Luc. There were also a few older photos of her with Billy and Jake. Something about the way Jake looked at her…

Had Jake been telling her the truth about them being just friends? Maybe he wasn't entirely over her. And what had he and Ronnie argued about just before she was killed?

Guin sighed.

"Where are you Jake?" she said aloud.

She glanced back down at Ronnie's Instagram feed. Just then her stomach let out a loud gurgle. She looked at the time. How did it get to be one o'clock already? She needed to meet Polly at two. But if she didn't eat something, she wouldn't be able to focus.

She went into the kitchen and opened the refrigerator. Why hadn't she gotten more food at Bailey's when she was in town? She checked the freezer. Well, there was always ice cream and Trader Joe's chocolate-covered almonds! She thought about having ice cream for lunch for a few seconds, then she shook her head. What she needed was protein, not sugar. She sighed again and made a mental note to make up some meals to keep in the freezer.

She opened the door to the refrigerator again and stared

inside. It was either a cheese sandwich or peanut butter and jelly. She compromised and toasted two pieces of whole grain bread and put PB&J on one and some cheese on the other. Then she poured herself some water from the pitcher she kept in the fridge and went to sit at the dining table.

As she ate, she went over everything she knew, which wasn't much. Which reminded her, Ann Campbell hadn't sent her the list. She made a face. She'd have to text or email her later. Why couldn't people just do what they said they would do?

She stared out past the lanai at the golf course. Soon it would be filled with golfers again, as the snowbirds returned. She looked around the living area. It was a nice condo. Just the right size for her and the cats. If only it was closer to the beach.

She got up and brought her plate and glass back into the kitchen. She glanced at the clock. Time to go meet Polly.

Guin grabbed her keys and her purse.

"Goodbye!" she called to the cats, who were no doubt napping someplace.

She paused by the door, as if expecting them to reply, then left.

Guin arrived at the first house a little before two. Polly had yet to arrive. She waited a couple of minutes in the driveway, then decided to walk around the place.

The grounds were well maintained. And there was a pool in the back. Guin had no need for a pool, but it wasn't a deal breaker, and she knew that if she ever sold, a pool would be good.

She finished her circuit, taking in the view—the place was situated on a small lake, like the Simms house. A minute later, Polly pulled in.

"Sorry I'm late!" Polly called as she stepped out of her car, a silver Audi convertible.

"No worries," said Guin. "I showed myself around."

"Is the door open?" asked Polly.

"I don't know. I just walked around the outside," Guin replied.

"Oh, okay," said Polly, clearly relieved.

She walked over to the front door. There was a lock box on it. She typed something into her phone, and a few seconds later the lock box beeped and opened. Polly pulled out the key.

"Shall we?" she said, putting the key into the lock.

Guin stepped inside.

"Hey, Polly. That lock box on the front door, is it the same type of lock box as the one over at the Simms place?"

"I think so," she said. "Why?"

"So you unlock it with your phone?"

"Yes. There's an app you get at the app store, just for real estate agents."

"And can you tell who accessed the lock box?"

"Oh yeah," said Polly. "It keeps a record of who used the app and can generate a report."

That's probably what Ann sent the detective, thought Guin. If only she'd send me the report. Of course, it was possible people could have gotten into the house without accessing the lock box. Billy's folks and Billy both supposedly had a set of keys. And it was possible a neighbor had a set too.

"You want to take a look around?" Polly asked, breaking Guin out of her reverie.

"Sure," said Guin.

They entered the cottage and glanced around. The place seemed okay. A little dated and in need of a fresh coat of paint, but it had good natural light.

"It has two bedrooms and there's another little room off the kitchen I thought you could use as your study," said Polly, walking over to show her.

Guin peeped in, a small part of her worried there would be another dead body inside. But the room was empty.

"Where are the owners?" asked Guin.

"They moved back to Canada. The husband apparently missed having four seasons."

"Not me!" said Guin.

Polly showed Guin around the rest of the place. There was barely any furniture and both bathrooms and the kitchen would need to be updated. But it had good bones, as they liked to say.

They walked out onto the lanai and took a look at the pool, which was enclosed by screens, and the lake beyond.

"Isn't this a lovely spot?"

Guin looked out at the lake. It was a nice spot.

They went back inside.

"Well?" asked Polly, standing in the living area.

"It's nice," said Guin.

"But," said Polly, sensing Guin's hesitation.

"But I don't think it's right for me. It just lacks…"

She looked around the living area and back at the kitchen.

"That beach house feel."

"You can give it that beach house feel with the right decor, Guin! And did I mention you are only a ten-minute walk to the beach?"

Guin sighed.

"Let me walk through the place one more time."

"Take your time," said Polly.

Guin made her way back through the two bedrooms, the two bathrooms, the living area, the study, and the kitchen. You put a hundred thousand dollars into the place, it could be something special. But she didn't have a spare hundred thousand dollars, and this place was already at the top of her budget.

"Well?" asked Polly.

"Sorry, Polly. It's got a lot going for it, but…"

Polly sighed.

They went back outside and Polly put the key back in the lock box. Guin was tempted to take out her phone and email Ann Campbell right there, but she refrained.

"The next place is just a little way away from here. You want to follow me?"

"Sure," said Guin.

She followed Polly to the next place and to the one after that. Neither of them was what Guin was looking for. As Polly replaced the last set of keys, she turned to Guin.

"If you want to find a place near the beach, Guin, you're going to have to compromise."

"I know," said Guin. Though part of her kept hoping she could find the perfect place without having to do so or go way over her budget. She didn't mind spending some money on renovation. Pretty much every place would need some paint and repairs. But she didn't want to have to do a major remodel. And she had to be able to walk to the beach in under 20 minutes.

She sighed.

"Any chance we could go by the Simms place? Did the police say it was okay to show it?"

Even though she had seen the place twice, she had a sudden urge to see it again. Hopefully the police were allowing people back in.

"Let me give Ann a call," said Polly. "One sec."

She reached into her bag and pulled out her phone.

"Just do me a favor, don't tell her it's me."

Polly gave her a quizzical look, then shrugged.

"Okay."

She dialed Ann's number.

"Hi Ann? it's Polly," she said, putting on her real estate agent smile. "I have a client who'd like to see the Simms place. Okay if I take her over there now?"

She waited. A few seconds later she gave Guin a thumbs up.

"Excellent. Thanks Ann."

She hung up and put her phone in her purse.

"You sure it's okay?" asked Guin, surprised they would be able to get in.

"Ann said it was fine by her."

Guin wondered if it would be okay with Detective O'Loughlin, then brushed the thought aside.

They got in their respective cars and headed over.

There was a car parked in the driveway.

"Do you think someone's in there, showing the place?" Guin asked.

"Ann didn't mention anything, though maybe she forgot?"

Guin looked at the car. It wasn't the detective's. She'd know his car anywhere.

"Well, shall we?"

Polly hesitated.

"I doubt it's a burglar. Come on."

She headed up the stairs, Polly behind her. The front door was ajar. Polly and Guin exchanged looks.

Guin opened the door slowly and took a step inside.

"Hello? Anybody home?" she called out.

Polly followed her inside.

"Hello?" Polly called.

They heard the sound of a toilet flushing and exchanged looks. A minute later a man walked out of the guest bathroom.

"Oh my God, you nearly scared me to death!" said Polly, placing a hand over her heart.

It was Billy Simms. And he looked as surprised to see them as they were to see him.

"Sorry, Ms. Fahnestock. I didn't mean to scare you."

"What on earth are you doing here? Ann didn't say anything."

Billy looked bashful.

"I was just checking up on the place. I always check up on the place Saturday afternoons."

"Were you here last Saturday afternoon?" asked Guin.

Billy looked over at Guin.

"This is Guin Jones, she's…" Polly began.

"I'm the one who found Veronica's body," Guin said, finishing her sentence.

"I can't imagine what a shock that must have been," said Billy.

It had been a shock.

"So were you here last Saturday?" Guin asked again.

"Like I told the police, I stopped by here on my way out of town, but I didn't see Ronnie. I was heading out of town on a business trip, to Orlando. I was meeting some buddies of mine for dinner up there."

Guin eyed Billy. He looked like a quarterback, in the Tom Brady mold: tall, good looking, with a TV-ready smile. She wondered if he had wanted to pursue a career in the NFL. From what she had read, he could have. But he had decided to return to Sanibel and the family business instead. Curious.

"Any idea how her body wound up here?"

Billy ran a hand through his hair.

"No, none."

"You ever take her here?"

Billy's lips twitched, and he had balled one of his hands into a fist.

"We had dinner here a couple of times with my grandparents," he finally said.

Guin had a feeling, looking at him, that he wasn't telling her the whole truth, but she didn't press him.

"Any idea who'd want to strangle her?"

"Well, she could be annoying," he said, smiling, as if recalling something. Then his face clouded over. "But I can't believe anyone would literally strangle her. Everyone loved Ronnie. If anything, that was the problem. She was always attracting strays."

"Strays?" asked Guin, confused. "As in dogs?"

"Them, too," he said, smiling again. "She loved animals. But I meant men. She had a soft spot for guys who were down on their luck. Wanted to cheer them up. Probably why she was such a good cheerleader."

"I heard that the two of you had broken up and she was seeing someone, an older man," continued Guin.

"Where'd you hear that?" asked Billy.

"Around," said Guin, not wanting to give away her sources.

He sighed.

"We were kind of taking a break," Billy answered. "But I didn't know she was seeing someone else."

"So no idea who the older man was?"

"Ask her housemates," he replied.

Clearly she was not going to get any information about Ronnie's love life out of Billy Simms.

"Well then, if you two are done, is it okay if I show Guin around the place, Billy?" asked Polly.

"You interested in buying it, Ms. Jones?"

Guin glanced around. It was a rather sweet place. Except for the dead body.

"Maybe," replied Guin, surprising herself.

"Well, I need to be on my way," said Billy. "Just put the

keys back in the lock box when you leave. I left them on the counter."

Guin and Polly both looked over at the counter. There was indeed a set of keys there.

"What happened to your set?" asked Guin.

"I lost them," Billy replied.

Guin looked skeptical.

"Well, thanks for letting us have a look around, Billy," said Polly. "Tell your mom I said hi."

"Will do, Ms. Fahnestock. Nice to see you," he said, smiling at her.

They watched him leave, then Guin made her way around the cottage, stopping for several minutes in each room. Her bed would definitely fit in the master bedroom, and she liked the big walk-in closet. And the master bath looked like it didn't need too much work.

She walked to the other side of the house. The guest room, like the rest of the house, could use a coat of paint and new carpeting or flooring. She paused before the door to the office. She put her hand on the knob and breathed in. She opened the door and peered inside. If you hadn't known there had been a dead body there six days before, you would never have guessed. Guin slowly exhaled.

She walked around the room, inspecting the desk and the book shelves, then opening the closet. It would make a nice office. It just needed some freshening up.

"Well?" asked Polly, when Guin had returned to the kitchen.

"I like it," said Guin.

Polly beamed.

"I bet you could get a really good price on it, too," she said, conspiratorially.

"Polly!"

Though Ann Campbell had basically said the same thing.

"Well, you could," said Polly, defensively.

Guin laughed. She had no doubt Polly could get her a good price, but it was a bit macabre.

"Well, I should get going. I need to stop back at home then head over to Ris's place."

After several texts back and forth, they had decided it made the most sense for Guin to go there instead of for Ris to go to her place.

"Send him my love," said Polly, a big smile on her face. "Sorry he couldn't join us this afternoon."

"Me too," said Guin.

They headed out the front door, which Polly locked behind them. She then placed the keys in the lock box.

"Well, let me know if you want to make an offer on the place," said Polly.

"You will be the first to know," said Guin.

They hugged then got into their cars.

As Guin drove home, she kept thinking about Billy. She had a feeling he knew something, but what?

She still had too many questions and no answers.

CHAPTER 26

Guin headed over to Ris's place a little after five. As the season had not officially begun, she didn't encounter much traffic and made it there in under an hour.

She stood by the front door and was about to ring the doorbell when she remembered she had the key. She felt around in her purse for her keys, then rang the doorbell before letting herself in.

"You know you don't have to do that," said Ris, walking to the front door, looking handsome and relaxed in drawstring pants and a polo shirt.

"I know," said Guin, "but it still feels strange to just let myself in, no warning."

"You don't have to warn me, Guin. You said you'd be here around six."

"Still," said Guin, feeling awkward. "What if you were in the middle of something?"

"Even more reason for you to have the key and just let yourself in," he replied, smiling. "Now, are you just going to stand there or…"

Guin walked over to him, stood on her tiptoes, and gave him a kiss. When they finally broke off, Ris gently ran a hand through her reddish blonde hair and looked down at her.

"You know, you wouldn't have to feel awkward if you actually lived here."

Guin looked up at him. If only it was that simple. But she just wasn't ready. Why? She wasn't sure. She mentally kicked herself. Here was this handsome, caring, intelligent man, who could have any woman, but he seemed to want her, so much so that he had given her a key to his home and invited her to live with him, after dating her only a few months. Maybe that was the problem. It had happened so fast. She had been divorced over a year now, but she still didn't feel ready to live with someone again, or to live with someone beyond a few days.

She sighed inwardly.

"So, what are we having for dinner?" she said, looking over toward the kitchen.

Ris smiled at her, still holding her close.

"I know what you're doing," he said.

"Yes, asking what's for dinner."

She smiled up at him sweetly and gently pushed herself away from him.

"I'm making poke," he said, heading to the kitchen. "I found this great recipe in the Ironman group and got a nice piece of tuna and some cucumbers, tomatoes, avocado, and mango to go with it."

"Sounds delicious. And very healthy."

"That's the idea," said Ris. "Could I interest you in a cranberry cooler?"

"A cranberry cooler?" asked Guin.

"It's iced mint tea with a splash of cranberry. Very refreshing."

"Sure," said Guin. "Why not?"

Guin kept Ris company in the kitchen while he went about fixing the poke. She loved it when he cooked. As he moved around, chopping and mixing the ingredients, they caught each other up on their weeks.

"So the police still don't know who killed that girl?"

"Nope," said Guin. "Or they haven't shared it with me or anyone else at the paper."

"Any ideas?"

"Well, Billy Simms is the obvious suspect. He and Ronnie had been going out, but word has it they had broken up and she had been seeing someone else. Maybe he was jealous? After all, the body was found at his grandparents' place, and he had a set of keys."

"Any other suspects?"

"Several. That's the problem. But I'm working on it."

"Isn't that the police's job?" asked Ris.

"It is, but I found the body. I feel a responsibility to find out who killed her, and Craig and I are covering the story for the paper."

"Just be careful."

"Yes, *dad*."

Why was it that all the men in her life were always telling her to 'be careful'?

Ris put the bowl of poke in the refrigerator.

"We should let that sit for an hour," he said.

"What do you want to do to pass the time?" asked Guin.

"Oh, I have a couple of ideas," he replied, grinning at her.

Dinner had been delicious: simple but tasty. Which was fine by Guin. Then they had watched a movie, a documentary about someplace in Australia Guin had never heard of. Guin had been prepared to head home, but Ris insisted she stay over. She agreed on the condition he wake her when he went running the next morning, no matter how early, so she could get to the Sanibel Farmers Market right when it opened. He dutifully did so, at 6 a.m., though they wound up staying in bed until after six-thirty.

By seven they were both dressed, Ris for running, and Guin in a pair of shorts and a t-shirt she kept there. They headed out the door together. Guin gave him a kiss goodbye by the Mini, then watched as he ran down the driveway. They both had busy weeks coming up, but they made a date to see each other that Tuesday.

Guin smiled as she drove back across the bridge linking Fort Myers Beach to the mainland. It had been a good evening. And she would miss Ris the following weekend, when he was off to Panama City to compete in the Ironman race. He had asked her again if she would go with him, but she had begged off, citing work and the fact that she would barely see him even if she went. She felt a slight twinge of guilt, but she knew it would be better if she didn't go, even though he didn't see it that way.

She headed over the Causeway, glancing to her left, toward the lighthouse. It was still early, and the sun hadn't fully risen yet, but she could just make it out. She smiled. That view never got old.

Guin parked her car in the lot by Big Arts, just next door to the police department, and walked over to the farmers market. It was a little before eight, but the vendors were already there, setting up. She entered and made a beeline for Jean-Luc's booth. While clean living may be fine for Ris, Guin needed her carbs, and her mouth watered at the thought of a freshly baked almond croissant or raisin danish.

She arrived at the stall to find both Fourniers laying out trays of baked goods.

"*Bonjour!*" said Guin.

"*Bonjour*, Guinivere," replied Jean-Luc, a smile on his Gallic face. "You are here bright and early. What can I get for you?"

Guin looked over the pastries on display. Everything looked so good. Screw it, she said to herself.

"I'll have a *pain au chocolat* and one of those raisin pastries," she said, pointing. "What do you call them in French?"

"*Pain aux raisins*," said Jean-Luc.

"I should have known," said Guin, feeling slightly embarrassed. She had studied French in high school and college.

"*Bon*. Anything else?"

Guin was sorely tempted to get a couple more things, but she controlled herself.

"No, that's it for today."

She looked around.

"Where's Jake? Is he back at the shop?" She had hoped that by some miracle Jake had reappeared.

"No," said Madame Fournier. "I just hope the poor boy is all right."

Clearly the police had spoken with them.

"So you haven't heard from him?" asked Guin.

"Not a word since Friday," Madame Fournier replied.

"Any idea what happened to him?"

"No, none at all," said Jean-Luc. "The police said they found his car just over the Causeway. Maybe he ran out of gas or was having car trouble?"

"But where did he go?" asked Guin.

Jean-Luc shrugged.

"Perhaps he has a friend…"

"I just hope the lad's okay," said Madame Fournier. "We miss him at the shop. He was a dab hand with the pastry."

Jean-Luc nodded.

"If he hasn't shown up by tomorrow, we're going to have to hire someone new," said Madame Fournier. "Jean-Luc and I are already stretched as it is."

"Well, please let me know if you hear anything," said

Guin, handing her card to Madame Fournier. "And how much do I owe you for the two pastries?"

Jean-Luc told her and Guin handed over some money. He gave her the box containing the two pastries along with her change, then they said their goodbyes.

Next Guin got herself some coffee, which she drank as she finished her rounds. She bought some cheese from her favorite cheese vendor. Then she bought some crab cakes from the seafood vendor she liked and some meat from the organic ranch. Finally, she picked out some fruit and vegetables. Her purchases made, she headed back to her car. She put everything in the back seat, except for the box containing her pastries, which she placed next to her. She was tempted to eat one now but decided to wait until she had gotten back to the condo and put away her groceries. But a few seconds later she gave in and quickly took a bite of the *pain aux raisins*.

Guin was sitting at her dining table, eating her pastries—she had cut the *pain au chocolat* and the rest of the *pain aux raisins* in two and was eating half of each, saving the rest for later—when her phone started ringing. It was Craig.

"Hope I'm not calling you too early," he said.

"Are you kidding?" said Guin. "I've been up for hours. What's up?"

"I have news."

"Did they find Jake?"

"No, or at least not as far as I know."

Guin was disappointed.

"What's your news?"

"You remember my friend, Jimbo?"

"The one with the same name as the college football coach?"

"That's the one," replied Craig.

"What about him?" asked Guin.

"Well, he says he saw Billy Simms out with some leggy blonde last night."

"Is that a crime now?" asked Guin.

"No, but Jimbo said they looked awfully cozy, if you catch my drift."

"Craig, you of all people shouldn't jump to conclusions."

"Here's the thing: Jimbo says he's seen that girl before, over at Doc Ford's, during happy hour."

"So?" asked Guin. "Lots of people go to Doc Ford's for happy hour."

Craig sighed.

"Would you let me finish?"

"Sorry," said Guin.

"He says he saw this girl with Ronnie, not long before she died, and they were arguing."

"What were they arguing about?"

"Jimbo can't remember exactly. He was trying not to listen. But he said the tall skinny one was in Ronnie's face and called her a little bitch."

"What did Ronnie say?"

"He doesn't remember, but he said Ronnie seemed pretty calm, just smiled back at her."

Odd, thought Guin.

"Does Jimbo know who the tall, skinny girl was?"

"He thought he heard Ronnie say, 'Chill Jill' to her, but he can't be certain."

Guin paused. One of Ronnie's housemates, the tall, skinny one, who had blonde hair, was named Gillian, Gill for short. When Guin had asked her about Ronnie, she hadn't mentioned an argument. Was Gillian hiding something?

"Hello? You still there?" asked Craig.

"Sorry, I was just thinking," Guin replied.

"About?"

"One of Ronnie's housemates is named Gillian, Gill for short, and she happens to be a tall, leggy blonde."

"Hmm…" said Craig.

"And she didn't say anything to me about getting into a fight with Ronnie or about seeing Billy Simms."

Guin paused. There had been a guy named Jimbo at the bar over at Doc Ford's when she had been there the other day. Could it be the same Jimbo? Then again, how many Jimbos could there be on Sanibel?

"So how does Jimbo know all of this anyway? Isn't he a bit old to be hanging out with a bunch of twentysomethings?"

Craig cleared his throat.

"Jimbo lost a daughter when she was around Ronnie's age a few years back," replied Craig.

"Oh, I'm sorry to hear that," said Guin.

"Apparently Ronnie was the spitting image of her."

"Oh wow."

"Yeah. Jimbo saw her at happy hour one day and nearly fell off his chair. He thought he was seeing a ghost. Even went up to her and asked her her name."

"How did Ronnie react?"

"He said she was very sweet. Ever since then, she'd say hi to him if she saw him over at Doc Ford's and would ask how he was doing. I think he felt kind of protective about her."

I wonder how protective, thought Guin.

"And how did you find all this out?"

"We were playing poker Friday night, and I may have brought up the case. Jimbo seemed real interested. Then he called me this morning, to let me know he had seen Billy Simms with this girl, the one who got into that fight with Ronnie."

Hmmm… thought Guin. Something about Jimbo's story just didn't sit right with her, but she didn't say anything to Craig.

"I'll text Gillian later, see if she'll speak with me."

"Sounds good," said Craig.

"What are you up to?"

"I'm on my way to go fishing with some of the guys, off Blind Pass."

"Well, have fun," said Guin. "Let me know if you catch anything—or hear anything else."

"Will do," said Craig.

They ended the call and Guin walked back over to the dining table. She had been pacing around the living room while she and Craig were talking. She took another bite of the *pain au chocolat* and closed her eyes, savoring the bittersweet chocolate.

She had been hoping to narrow down her list of suspects, but instead the list kept getting longer.

CHAPTER 27

Guin looked at her notes, which now spanned several pages. She had read them over several times, but she felt no closer to figuring out who killed Veronica Swales or how she had wound up at the Simms place.

She rested her head in her hands, pulling her hair away from her head. Think, Guin, think, she told herself. There must be some clue she was missing

She reread what Craig had told her about Ronnie getting in a fight with a tall blonde. It had to be her housemate, Gillian.

Guin picked up her phone and sent a text to her, asking if she had a minute to chat. A few minutes later she received a response. Gillian was working that afternoon, but she could meet Guin for a quick coffee on her way there. They agreed to meet over at the Sanibel Bean at noon.

Next Guin sent a text to the detective, asking if he had any news about Jake. She hit "send" and stared at her phone, willing the detective to text her back or call her.

She nearly jumped when her phone started ringing, but it was not the detective.

Guin sighed.

"Hi Mom."

"You don't sound very excited to hear from me."

"Sorry. I was just hoping it was someone else."

As soon as Guin said it, she regretted it.

"Sorry I'm not who you wanted," sniffed her mother.

Guin rolled her eyes.

"Can we start this conversation over? Hi Mom! Thanks for calling! What's up?"

"Really Guinivere," began her mother.

Guin waited for her mother to continue.

"I was calling to see if you would be coming home for Thanksgiving. It's less than a month away, you know."

"I hadn't planned on it," Guin replied.

"What if I paid for your plane ticket?"

"That isn't the issue."

"Then what is?"

"I was thinking I'd spend Thanksgiving here, with Ris," said Guin. Though, in fact, the two of them had only touched on the topic. Ris normally spent Thanksgiving at his ex's house, with their children, but he had said Victoria would be happy to have Guin join them. Guin just wasn't sure how happy she would be.

"He's welcome to join us," announced her mother.

"That's very nice of you, mother, but he usually spends Thanksgiving with his children."

"As he should. Parents and children should spend Thanksgiving together. It is, after all, a family holiday."

Guin rolled her eyes. She was in a no-win situation. Instead of arguing with her mother, she changed the subject.

"How are you and Philip? Did you two have a good time with his family in Bath?"

Guin's stepfather was British and he and her mother would visit his relatives in the UK at least once a year. For Guin's mother, an Anglophile, Philip had been a dream come true. Not that she hadn't loved Guin's father. She had. But Philip, whose family was very distantly related to the royal family, or so they claimed, was the epitome of the Proper British Gentleman.

"We had a marvelous time," her mother replied. "Philip's sister and her family are the loveliest people—and their new place is divine. You should really go and visit. They would be happy to have you. In fact, Lavinia specifically asked after you."

"Oh?" said Guin, surprised.

She had met Philip's sister Lavinia and several members of Philip's family a few times over the years, but she never felt particularly warm and fuzzy about them.

"She was wondering if you and Dr. Hartwick were serious. It seems her dear friend Harriet's son, who is also recently divorced, lives in Naples of all places, and she thought the two of you might hit it off. Alfred is in finance, I forgot what exactly, but apparently he's quite well off, despite the divorce, and has a little place just steps from the beach."

Guin closed her eyes and silently counted to ten. She knew her mother meant well, but she had no desire to be fixed up, now or ever, with the son of some friend or friend of a friend of her mother's.

"Hello?" queried her mother. "You still there?"

"I'm here," replied Guin. "That's very kind of Philip's sister, but I'm good. Ris and I are very happy."

"Well, if you change your mind…"

"I'll let you know. So, any other news?"

"Have you spoken with your brother lately?"

"Not in the last few days, why?"

"Did he tell you he's thinking about opening an office in San Francisco."

"Good for him. No, he hadn't mentioned it."

"I'm just worried he and Owen will move out there and leave me here all by myself."

Guin rolled her eyes. Her mother was far from being alone. She had Philip and at least a dozen friends, and every time Guin communicated with her she seemed to have just gotten back from or was about to go to some new exhibit or show or restaurant or trip.

"You could always go visit him."

Her mother sniffed.

"Hey mom, I have to go."

"Oh?" asked her mother. "You and the marine biologist having brunch?"

"No. He's in training for the Florida Ironman. I need to go meet with someone regarding a story I'm working on."

"On a Sunday?"

Her mother sounded appalled.

"Yes, on a Sunday."

"What's the story?"

Guin hesitated. She didn't think her mother was all that interested in her work, and she would probably be appalled that Guin was involved in another murder.

"Really Guinivere. I thought I taught you not to be rude."

"Sorry. I found a dead girl in a house I was looking at, and I'm trying to find out what happened to her."

"Another dead body? I hope this isn't becoming a habit."

"I hope so too," Guin replied.

"Shouldn't the police be investigating?"

"They are. I'm covering the story for the paper."

Her mother made a little noise, the one she made when she disapproved of something.

"I'll be fine, mom. Really."

"This is the second dead body you've found in a matter of months. One would think you worked in a cemetery."

Was that her mother's attempt at humor?

Guin sighed.

"I love you, mom. Gotta go."

"Just be careful. And think about my offer regarding Thanksgiving!" she added.

"Bye," said Guin.

She ended the call and looked at the time. She still had a little while before she needed to head over to the Sanibel Bean to meet Gillian.

Her phone started buzzing. It was a text from Shelly.

"ARE YOU COMING TONIGHT?!" it read.

Oh no, I forgot to get back to her, Guin realized. She stood and stared out the lanai. She didn't really want to go, but she didn't have other plans and didn't want to offend Shelly.

"Sorry. Been busy. I'll be there," she wrote back.

"Ris coming?" Shelly typed.

"No," Guin replied. "Just me."

"OK," Shelly texted back. "See you at 6."

"See you then," Guin wrote.

She sighed and looked down. Flora was rubbing against her legs. Guin knelt and stroked the cat.

"Hi Flora. You need some loving?"

Flora purred and continued to rub herself against Guin's legs. Guin smiled.

A minute later she got up.

"Sorry, girl. I need to do some work then head out."

Flora looked up at her with big green eyes.

Guin sighed and gave Flora's ears another rub.

"Now I really have to go," she said, standing up again.

She went back to her computer and stared at the screen. "Screw it," she said aloud. She closed the file she had opened and opened the *New York Times* instead, clicking on the Sunday crossword. Before she knew it, it was time for her to go meet Gillian. She grabbed her bag and her keys and hurried out the door.

CHAPTER 28

Guin arrived at the Sanibel Bean at noon. She looked around but didn't see Gillian. As the day was warm, she ordered herself an iced decaf, then took it out to the shaded porch to wait for Ronnie's former housemate.

Gillian arrived a few minutes later, looking like an ad for Ralph Lauren. She was wearing a long, striped sundress and wedge sandals, and had her hair tied back in a neat ponytail.

Ah, to be tall and thin, thought Guin. She waved to the young woman.

"I only have a few minutes," Gillian announced as she climbed the stairs. "What did you want to ask me?"

Guin ignored her rude tone.

"Would you like to get yourself a coffee? My treat."

Gillian thought about it for a few seconds.

"Sure," she said. "Why not?"

"What'll you have?"

"A cappuccino. A small one is fine."

"Coming right up."

Guin went inside, followed by Gillian, and ordered a small cappuccino. When it was ready they headed to a table on the enclosed porch, near the back.

"Thanks," said Gillian, taking a sip of the cappuccino. "So…?"

"So," said Guin, not sure how to phrase her question. "I

heard that you've been seeing Billy Simms. Is that true?"

"What if it is?" snapped Gillian. "Is there some kind of law against it?"

Someone woke up on the wrong side of the bed this morning, thought Guin.

"Is it true?" Guin repeated.

Gillian took another sip of her cappuccino.

"Billy and I are… friends."

"Did Ronnie know you and Billy were 'friends'?" Guin asked.

Guin assumed that by "friends" she meant friends with benefits.

"I don't know," Gillian retorted. "But she was seeing her mystery man, so it really wasn't any of her business."

"By mystery man, you mean the one Pam mentioned?"

"Unless there was some other one we didn't know about. I wouldn't put it past Ronnie to be seeing more than one guy."

Clearly there was no love lost between Gillian and her former housemate.

"Do you happen to know the mystery man's name?"

"No. She only referred to him by his initials, J.L."

J.L., thought Guin. Immediately her brain started thinking of all the people she knew on the island with the initials J.L. Of course, the mystery man might not even live on Sanibel, and those might not even be his initials, but it was something. She would have to tell Craig and the detective. That is, if they didn't know already.

"Any idea what J.L. stood for, or whom?" asked Guin.

"Nope," said Gillian.

Guin decided to ask her again about Billy.

"So how long have you and Billy been 'friends'?"

Gillian looked annoyed but answered.

"Since we were at UCF."

Guin tried a different tack.

"Shortly before Ronnie died, a number of people saw you two arguing about something over at Doc Ford's." Though what Guin had heard was that Gillian was yelling at Ronnie, and Ronnie pretty much ignored her. "Was it about Billy?"

Gillian made another face. For someone so attractive, she had mastered the ugly expression.

"It was private, okay?"

"Gillian, Veronica is dead. Someone strangled her and dumped her body at a beach house. Don't you want to help find her killer?"

Guin regarded Gillian, but it seemed like bitch face was pretty much Gillian's default look.

"It may have had something to do with Billy," she begrudgingly replied. "I don't remember."

Guin didn't believe that for a minute.

Gillian stood up.

"Look, I need to get to work. If you have any more questions, text me."

Guin stood up and followed Gillian out to the parking lot.

"Thanks for the cappuccino," Gillian said, as they walked down the stairs.

"You're welcome," said Guin. "If you think of anything, anything at all that could help find Ronnie's killer, please contact me."

"You working with that detective?" Gillian asked.

"As a matter of fact, I am," said Guin.

"Well, if I hear anything, I'll let the police know," she said.

She then walked to her car.

Well, that was unhelpful, thought Guin, as she watched Gillian depart. Though she would bet even money that

Gillian was sleeping with Billy or wanted to. She walked to her car and quickly checked her phone. No messages, or none from anyone she was waiting to hear from. She looked at the time and wondered if Craig was back from his fishing trip. Well, only one way to find out, she thought.

Guin called Craig's mobile and was preparing to leave him a message when he picked up.

"Hey Guin, what's up?"

"You still fishing?"

"No, I just got off the boat."

"You catch anything?"

"Nothing to write home about," he replied. "You got some news?"

"I do. I just had coffee with Veronica Swales's housemate, Gillian. She says Ronnie referred to the mystery man by the initials J.L."

"Jake Longley?"

"Could be, but the mystery man was supposedly much older than Ronnie and she and Jake were the same age, or nearly."

"Hmm…" said Craig. "Unless her housemates were lying about the other guy being older. They could have been covering for Jake."

Guin hadn't thought about that.

"What about your friend, Jimbo?"

"What about him?" asked Craig.

"Does his last name by any chance start with the letter L?"

There was a momentary silence on the other end of the line.

"Jimbo's last name is Leidecker, but I can't believe he would have done something like that, especially after losing his own daughter."

"I know he's a friend, Craig, but we can't rule him out."

"You're right. I just hate to think he was somehow involved."

"I know, but we need to check him out."

"Let me do it," said Craig. "I promise not to go easy on him."

"Fine," said Guin. "Just don't let your friendship cloud your judgment."

She knew as soon as she said it that she sounded like the detective. Speaking of whom…

"By any chance you hear from the detective or your buddy over in the police department?"

"As a matter of fact, guess who I saw out fishing this morning?"

"The detective?"

"On the nose."

"Did you get a chance to speak with him?" asked Guin.

"He was on another boat. We just waved."

Darn, thought Guin.

"Do you know if he's back on shore?"

"Probably, but I don't know for sure. Why?"

"I want to ask him about J. L. and if he knows about Billy and Gillian."

"You can always leave him a message."

"I know. I just figured I'd ask."

"Hey, I've got to go," said Craig. "Catch up with you later?"

"Sure," said Guin. "Thanks for taking my call."

"Always," said Craig.

Guin smiled. At least someone was happy to hear from her.

They ended the call, and Guin thought about calling the detective. She decided to send him a text instead.

"Please call me when you have a minute," she wrote. "I have news."

She hit "send" and waited a few seconds, but her phone

remained quiet. She sighed and got into the Mini. Shelly's barbeque was later that day, and she didn't want to arrive empty handed. She thought about making chocolate chip cookies, her go-to, but she was feeling lazy. I should go to Bailey's, she said to herself. After all, she was already in town.

She sat in the car, staring out the windshield, debating what to do. Then her phone started buzzing. She looked down. Wonder of wonders, miracle of miracles, it was the detective, returning her text.

"What's up?" he had written. "Can't talk."

"When can you talk?" Guin wrote back.

"I'm busy until 5," he texted her.

Guin suddenly had an idea.

"You free for dinner?" she impulsively wrote.

"Why?" asked the detective.

"I need to talk to you + you need to eat."

She waited for a reply.

"Shelly + Steve are having another BBQ. Free food + beer! They'd love to see you. Please?" she hurriedly typed and hit "send."

Guin stared down at her phone, feeling a bit nervous and embarrassed. Should she write him back and say never mind? She was about to do just that when he wrote back.

"Fine."

Guin stared at her phone in disbelief.

"Great," she wrote back. "Let's meet there at 5:45. That way we can talk beforehand."

"How bout I pick you up at 5:30?" he replied.

Huh. She didn't know where the detective lived, but chances were it was closer to Shelly and Steve's than she was.

"You sure?" Guin typed back. "Aren't I out of the way?"

"See you at 5:30," he responded.

Guin could tell that was the end of that. There was no

use arguing. She didn't even bother to reply.

She put her phone in her bag and started the car. She couldn't believe she had just asked the detective to dinner, again! And that he had accepted. She smiled to herself then headed to Bailey's.

CHAPTER 29

The doorbell rang at exactly 5:30.

"Coming!" Guin called, though she knew the detective probably couldn't hear her.

She hurried down the hall and opened the door to let him in.

"Good evening, detective. You're right on time," she said, smiling.

She quickly gave him the once over, taking in his neat, button-down shirt and chinos. His standard uniform. His face had a ruddy, healthy glow, as if he had spent time out in the sun, which he had. And his short, curly, chestnut hair, which was turning gray, looked like it had been tamed with some product, either a bit of gel or mousse.

"Please, come in. I'll just be a second."

She walked him into the living area and indicated for him to have a seat.

"I just need to go grab a necklace. Then I'm all set."

Guin had gone back and forth about what to wear to the barbeque. She knew it was informal, but she wanted to look nice. (She dismissed the idea that it was because the detective was joining her.) She had stood in her walk-in closet for several minutes going through her wardrobe, casting aside outfits, until she finally settled on a pair of white skinny jeans and a pretty blue top that brought out the blue in her eyes.

She had applied a little mascara and lip gloss and was about to put on some jewelry when the doorbell had rung.

Guin scooted back to her bedroom, leaving the detective with the cats, who had immediately trotted over to check him out. She put on her rings and grabbed the necklace she had picked out and went back out to the living area, to find the detective squatting down, petting both felines. She grinned.

"Hope you don't mind," she said, looking down at him. "I have a lint roller if you need it."

The detective stood up and looked down at his pants and shirt, which were covered with cat hair.

"Hmm… I think I'll take you up on that offer."

Guin reached into a drawer and handed him the lint roller.

"Thanks."

She watched as he quickly brushed away the fur.

"They like you."

The detective handed her back the lint roller.

"You ready?"

"Sorry, just need to put this on," she said, holding her necklace, a simple gold chain with a heart-shaped pendant.

"Here, let me," he said, taking it from her hand and placing it around her neck.

Guin lifted her hair and could feel herself go goose-pimply as he affixed the slender chain around her neck.

"There," he said, gently resting his hands on her shoulders.

Guin shivered slightly and released her hair.

"Thank you," she said, turning to face him.

They stood there for a few seconds, looking at each other. She felt her cheeks go warm and broke off the gaze.

"Well, we should probably get going," she said, turning and heading back toward the front door.

The cats followed them down the hall.

"I just need to give them a little food and get the fruit plate. Be right back," she said, turning into the kitchen.

She grabbed the bag of cat food, emptied a little into the cat bowls, put the bag back, then grabbed the fruit plate she had made up from the fridge.

"Okay, all set," she said, smiling as the detective opened the front door for her.

"Thanks for picking me up," Guin said to the detective as they drove to Steve and Shelly's. "You really didn't have to."

"Seemed silly to take two cars," he said, not looking at her.

Guin stared out the window, then looked back at the detective.

"I heard you were out fishing this morning."

"Yup," said the detective.

"You catch anything?"

"A couple of fish."

"Anything good?"

The detective looked over at Guin.

"Do you really care or are you just being polite?"

Guin felt her cheeks turning pink. She didn't really care about fishing, but she wanted to engage the detective.

"Fine. We can talk about baseball."

"I'd rather not."

Guin had forgotten, the Boston Red Sox had just lost the American League Division series to the Houston Astros.

"Oops, sorry about that. Though your Red Sox did a lot better than my Mets."

"Still hurts."

They remained silent the rest of the way. A few minutes later the detective parked down the block from Steve and Shelly's place.

"I need to ask you something," said Guin, looking at the detective.

"Is it about the Swales case?"

"No, though I have questions about that, too," she replied.

The detective waited.

"What happened to you this summer? One minute we were going to ball games and getting coffee and then you disappeared on me. I didn't hear from you for a month, longer, and you didn't return any of my messages. Was it something I said? Because I've been racking my brain and I can't figure out what."

The detective sighed and looked at Guin.

"You didn't do anything."

"Then why didn't you return my calls and messages?"

"It's complicated," said the detective.

Now it was Guin's turn to sigh.

"I thought maybe you had gone into the witness protection program or something."

The detective chuckled.

"Nothing so dramatic, Nancy Drew."

"Then what?"

The detective sighed.

"I got divorced."

"WHAT?!" Guin practically shrieked.

The detective placed his hands over his ears.

"You got a divorce? I thought you weren't married," said Guin, more quietly.

"I wasn't, not in any real sense of the word."

"I don't understand," said Guin.

"Molly, my wife, and I got married young, too young. Typical Irish Catholics, or typical back in those days in South Boston. Next thing you know, we had a kid. It was rough on both of us. We both loved Joey, Joseph, to bits, but the marriage didn't last. I was working crazy hours, trying to make enough money to support the family, and Molly resented me not being around. And she didn't like having guns in the house. She actually moved out, to her sister's, when Joey was around ten, took Joey with her, but she refused to get a divorce, being a good Catholic and all."

The detective made a face. Guin waited for him to continue.

"We pretty much led separate lives, which was fine, though I made sure to be there for Joey. Even managed his little league team. Then, after he graduated college and Molly started seeing another man, I moved down here, to Fort Myers."

"But why get divorced now? What changed?"

"Molly wants to get remarried. She had convinced the church to annul our marriage, but she had to get a divorce if she wanted her second marriage to be legal."

"Wow," said Guin, totally stunned. "And you're okay with that?"

"Okay? I was thrilled. I'd been begging Molly to see reason for years, but she had refused. I wanted to kiss Frank, her new husband, I was so relieved. Even sent them a wedding gift."

"So is that where you were, Boston?"

"Yup. Went up to personally sign the divorce papers and see Joey. He was there for the wedding."

"Did you go, to the wedding?"

"I wasn't invited, but Joey says Frank's a good guy."

"But why didn't you just tell me? Why didn't you return my calls, I—"

Guin was unable to finish because the detective had leaned over and was kissing her, and she was kissing him back.

A few minutes later, though it seemed like far longer, the

detective sat back, leaving Guin sitting there, stunned.

"That's why."

"Oh," said Guin, very quietly.

The detective opened the door.

"Shall we?" he said.

Without waiting for an answer, he got out of the car and opened the trunk, taking out a small cooler.

Guin opened her door and retrieved her fruit plate from the back seat, still a bit dazed.

"You okay?" asked the detective, taking note of Guin's confused state.

Guin snapped herself out of her trance. She had so many questions, but they would have to wait.

"I'm fine," she said, acting as though nothing had happened. She began walking down the block. "Let's go," she said, turning to make sure he was following her.

"Detective! How nice to see you again!" said Shelly, grinning at the two of them.

She looked over at Guin. Guin willed her not to wink or say anything.

"I brought you some beer," said the detective, holding up the cooler.

"Thank you," said Shelly. "You can take it out to the lanai. We have a big ice bucket there."

"And I got you this," said Guin, holding up the fruit plate.

"Give it to me. I'll put it in the fridge, if I can find room."

The detective had already headed back toward the lanai with the cooler. Guin watched as Steve chatted with him.

"Come into the kitchen," Shelly directed Guin.

She followed her into the kitchen.

"So?!" asked Shelly.

"So what?" asked Guin.

"So, you and the detective," Shelly said, still grinning. "Is there something I should know?"

Guin tried to stop her cheeks from turning pink. Easier said than done. She could still feel the detective's lips on hers.

"No," she replied, resolutely.

"Oh, come on. You can tell me," Shelly said, dropping her voice, so no one could hear them.

"There's nothing to tell, Shell," Guin replied, mentally crossing her fingers. "I needed some information from the detective, and I thought this was a good way to butter him up."

"Uh-huh," said Shelly.

"Honestly, Shell."

"Fine, you tell yourself that, but you can't fool me. There's something going on between the two of you."

Guin stubbornly refused to admit there was, to Shelly or to herself, but she couldn't get the kiss out of her brain.

She looked around the kitchen.

"You need help with anything?"

"Here, bring this platter of shrimp out to the lanai," said Shelly, handing her a platter of shrimp with cocktail sauce. "I'll be right there."

"Anyone I know out here?"

"I think so. Go take a look. It's a pretty small crowd tonight."

Guin placed the platter of shrimp on the table, then grabbed a bottle of beer and went over to Steve, who was chatting with two other men. The detective was a little way away, chatting with a couple of women.

"Ah, Guin," said Steve, giving her a quick kiss on the cheek. "Do you know Jeff Keegan and Jimbo Leidecker? Gentlemen, may I present Ms. Guinivere Jones, star reporter for the *Sanibel-Captiva Sun-Times* and one of our dearest friends."

He smiled as he said it and Guin resisted giving him a playful thwack. She didn't like being made a fuss over.

Jimbo Leidecker. She looked him over as she said hello. He was a nice-looking man, not handsome, but friendly looking, of average height, probably around sixty, in reasonably good shape. Could he have killed Veronica Swales? He didn't seem the type, but then again, many killers didn't seem the type.

"I saw you the other day at Doc Ford's," said Guin, smiling and extending a hand to Jimbo. "You're a friend of Craig Jeffers's."

"And you are the infamous Guinivere Jones Craig keeps talking about," said Jimbo, taking her hand and smiling.

"I don't know about infamous…" said Guin.

"You helped nail the guy who killed Captain Ben and that other guy," said Jimbo.

Guin blushed slightly.

"That was you?" asked Jeff Keegan.

Guin looked over at the detective, who had joined them. He was clearly amused.

"I, uh," she began.

"You're embarrassing her, fellas," said Steve.

"So what were you all discussing?" asked Guin, looking around the group.

"Fishing," said Jeff. "You fish, Guin?"

"No, can't say that I do," she replied.

"You don't know what you're missing," said Jeff.

"Jeff here was just telling us about the snapper and snook he caught this morning," said Jimbo.

"Though you should have seen the fish Bill here caught," said Jeff.

Guin was momentarily confused.

"Were you two out fishing together?" Guin asked, looking from Jeff to the detective.

"Sure were. You didn't tell her about your big catch, Bill?"

Guin wasn't used to hearing the detective being called 'Bill,' or anything other than Detective O'Loughlin.

The detective looked momentarily embarrassed. Well, this was a change of pace.

"No, he did not," said Guin, eyeing the detective—Bill. She smiled as she said his name to herself.

"We had a good morning," said the detective. "Some days you get lucky."

"I'll say," said Jeff.

The group continued to make small talk for several minutes. Then Steve excused himself to check on the grill. A few minutes later, dinner, which consisted of steak, chicken, and sausages, a holdover from Steve's Wisconsin days, along with a variety of sides, was served. There were a dozen people total, and the evening passed pleasantly, with Guin barely having a chance to speak with the detective.

Finally, after dessert had been served, Guin took the detective aside.

"You okay if we go?"

"Fine by me," said the detective.

"Let me just say goodbye to Shelly and Steve."

Guin found them chatting with a couple of the guests.

"We have to head out," said Guin.

"So soon?" asked Steve.

Guin stifled a yawn.

"I've got an early start tomorrow."

The detective had walked over with Guin.

"Nice seeing you again, Bill," said Steve.

"Likewise," said the detective.

Shelly leaned over and whispered in Guin's ear.

"I think he likes you."

Guin poked her with her elbow.

"Ow," said Shelly.

"Thanks for having us over," Guin said to Steve, trying to ignore her friend.

"You two are welcome any time," said Shelly, grinning.

A couple of minutes later, Guin and the detective were back outside. It was dark out, with only the stars and a bit of light from the houses to guide their way.

They headed down the block, neither saying anything. The detective unlocked his car and held the door open for Guin. She got in.

"Thank you for coming with me," she said to the detective when he was seated beside her.

"No problem," he replied.

"I think you may have known more people there than I did."

"When you work on Sanibel…"

His voice trailed off, and he started the car.

They didn't talk on the ride back to her place, though Guin wanted to ask him why he had kissed her and about the case. But she didn't know where to start.

They arrived back at Guin's condo a little while later. The detective parked the car in the spot reserved for guests.

"Thanks again for coming with me tonight," said Guin, nervously, leaning slightly toward the detective.

Part of her was hoping he might kiss her again, but he just sat there. She let out a sigh.

"Well, goodnight, detective."

"Goodnight, Ms. Jones."

She slowly got out of the car. The detective remained motionless. She walked around to the driver's side and stood there. The detective rolled down the window.

"I didn't get a chance to discuss the case with you. Do

you want to come up for a minute?"

"I don't think that would be a good idea," said the detective.

Guin was on the verge of saying "please," but she stopped herself.

"Shall I call in the morning to arrange an appointment? We need to talk."

The detective sighed.

"Fine. Give me a call in the morning."

Guin continued to stand there.

"Well, goodnight again," she finally said.

"Goodnight again, Ms. Jones."

She walked towards the stairs and stopped and turned to see if the detective was still there. He was. A part of her wanted to walk back over to his car, lean in, and kiss him. Instead she ran up the stairs, not looking back. She hurriedly unlocked the door and went inside, her heart pounding inside her chest.

CHAPTER 30

That night Guin had a horrible dream. She was in her living room, getting ready to head to the barbeque. The detective was there, just as before, offering to help her with her necklace. However, this time, instead of fastening the necklace, he started to strangle her with it. She felt herself gasping for air and managed to turn around—to find that it was not the detective who was trying to strangle her but Ris.

She sat upright in bed, trying not to hyperventilate. She instinctively reached around her neck, but there was nothing there. She slowed her breathing and placed her right hand over her heart, which was beating rapidly.

"Oh my God," she said aloud, her hand still over her heart.

Fauna, who had been curled up alongside her legs, looked up at her.

"What a nightmare!" she said to the cat.

Fauna blinked, turned around, then curled up and went back to sleep.

"Nice for you," said Guin, looking down at the black cat.

She looked over at the clock. It was 4 a.m. Ugh.

She lay back down and stared up at the ceiling. The dream had been so real. What did it mean? Actually, she knew what it meant. It was her subconscious, or conscience, nagging her. She sighed and closed her eyes, but she was afraid to go back to sleep and didn't know if she could. She did some breathing exercises, slowly breathing in through her nose to the count of eight, then out through her mouth to the count of eight. That helped calm her down, but she didn't feel any sleepier. Finally, at four-thirty, she got out of bed.

She headed to the kitchen to make herself some coffee. The cats, suddenly awake, joined her.

Fauna started to meow.

"I'll give you some Friskies in a minute," she told her. "First, coffee."

She scooped some coffee into her French press and boiled some water. Then she went into the pantry and grabbed a can of cat food. Immediately, Fauna started to meow again.

"Dude, hold on!" she admonished the feisty feline.

She divided the contents of the can equally between the two cat bowls, and both cats dove in. A few minutes later, she was sitting at her dining table, sipping her coffee. It was still dark out, and the sun wouldn't be up for several hours. She thought about going to the beach (serious beachcombers often went before dawn), but she blew off the idea. With her luck, she would trip over a piece of a driftwood in the dark and sprain her ankle.

She stared out into the darkness, the dream continuing to haunt her. She placed a hand around her neck and shuddered. She thought of the dead girl. Had she known her attacker, trusted him?

She got up and went into her bedroom/office and grabbed a yellow legal pad and a pen, then went back to the dining table and sat.

"Who killed Ronnie Swales and why?" she wrote at the top of the page. She then made a list of the suspects to date.

Next she wrote: "Who had access to the Simms place?"

and made another list. She knew Ann and Polly and members of the Simms family all had access to the cottage. Who else did? She made a face and wrote: "Follow up with Ann!"

She looked around for her phone and realized it was still in her nightstand. She got up and retrieved it, turning it on on her way back to the living room. Was it too early to email Ann? If she was sensible, she kept her phone off while she slept, as Guin did. And Ann seemed like the sensible type.

Guin sent a text to the listing agent, asking her, again, to please forward the list of people who had access to the house that weekend.

What else? thought Guin, her mind going over the events of the past week. Jake. What had happened to him and why? She made a note to follow up with the detective and Craig, to see if they had learned anything. Maybe there was some clue in his car.

She stared down at the yellow pad and sighed. There were so many loose ends, and it was too early to call anyone. But she could send emails and texts. That at least would kill some time.

She sent Ris a text, just saying hi.

She sent Shelly a text, thanking her for the barbeque.

She sent Craig a text, asking him to message her with any updates—about Jake, or Ronnie, or anything.

She started to compose a message to the detective and stopped. Her mental camcorder was replaying the scene where he kissed her. She could feel herself growing warm and chided herself.

"Focus, Guin," she said aloud.

"I want to make an appointment," she typed. "Let me know when I can swing by the PD. I need some information about the Veronica Swales case."

She hit "send" and stared at her phone.

That was totally professional, right? Totally neutral. If only she could get that stupid kiss out of her head. It probably meant nothing. Just the detective being enigmatic, as usual.

As she was staring into space, her phone started buzzing. Guin jumped. She looked down at the phone. It was the detective. What was he doing up at 5 a.m.?

"Meet me at the PD at 8."

Guin thought about suggesting another time. An 8 a.m. meeting meant she couldn't go for a morning beach walk.

Impulsively she wrote, "You want to just come over here now? I'll make a fresh pot of coffee. :-)"

Immediately after sending it, she chastised herself. What the heck was she doing? She could feel her cheeks burning.

She stared at her phone, dreading the detective's reply. She waited several minutes. No response. She was in the kitchen when her phone buzzed. She raced back to see who had messaged her. It was the detective.

"I'll see you at the PD at 8."

Fine, she would see him at eight. And this time she would bring a list of questions with her, and she wouldn't leave until she had answers.

She congratulated herself for keeping her emotions in check and being professional, even if it was a lie. Then she headed back into her office/bedroom to do some work. She had that other article Ginny had asked her to do, and she could probably knock it out today if she focused—and there was no new information regarding Veronica Swales or Jake Longley.

As soon as she had seated herself at her desk, Flora jumped up in front of her and began rolling around the desktop, clearly seeking attention. At the same time, Fauna climbed into her lap. Guin sighed. Did other writers with cats have the same problem?

She pulled up her notes and the first draft she had started and began to type. Before she knew it, two hours had flown by, and it was nearly seven-thirty.

"Gotta go!" she announced to the cats, gently placing Fauna on the floor.

Guin went into the bathroom and examined her face and hair. As usual, her hair, which was curly, and tended to frizz, was acting up. Instead of trying to tame it, she grabbed a ponytail holder from her drawer and put her hair back.

"That'll have to do," she said, eyeing herself in the mirror.

She slapped some cold water on her face, then quickly brushed her teeth. She had thought about taking a quick shower, but there was no time. Instead she applied some antiperspirant, flapped her arms to dry it, then headed into her closet.

She glanced at her clothes and pulled on a blue t-shirt and a chino skort. Casual yet professional, or what passed for professional for a reporter on Sanibel. She put on her rings and watch, picked up her phone, grabbed her legal pad and microcassette recorder, went into the living area and grabbed her bag and car keys, then headed out. If there was no traffic, she should still be able to make it to the Sanibel Police Department on time, or else just a few minutes late.

She drove down Sanibel-Captiva Road as fast as she dared (which was just under 40 mph, the speed limit being 35 mph), keeping an eye out for hidden police cars, and continued straight onto Palm Ridge Road. She made a left onto Wooster Lane and followed it until it became Dunlop, where the police department was located.

She parked the car in the lot and glanced at the clock. It was 8:05. She had thought about stopping someplace to pick up some breakfast, but she didn't want to be late. Suddenly her stomach let out a loud growl. Maybe she should have stopped along the way. Well, too late now.

She got out of the car, locked it, and ran up the steps to the police department. The door was open, but there was no one behind the plate glass partition where visitors checked in. She knocked on the glass.

"Hello? Anyone there?"

She waited a few seconds, but no one appeared. She peered through the glass, but she couldn't see very far. She reached into her purse and took out her phone. She was about to text the detective when the front door opened. Guin turned. It was the detective, carrying a white pastry box and one of those insulated to-go cups, no doubt filled with coffee.

"Ms. Jones," he said.

Guin eyed the box and her stomach let out a low growl. She felt her cheeks start to turn pink.

The detective smiled.

"Let's go back to my office."

"There doesn't seem to be anyone here," Guin informed him.

The detective sighed.

"Here, hold this," he said, handing her the box.

Guin noticed it was from the Sanibel Bean. Her stomach growled again.

"Shh!" she scolded it.

The detective pounded on the glass.

"Anyone here? Open up!"

He pounded on the glass again.

A few seconds later a young officer came over and slid open the window.

"Sorry, detective, I was in the back."

"Buzz me back, will you?"

"Yes, sir!" said the young officer.

The young man looked over at Guin.

"She's with me," said the detective.

The door buzzed, and the detective opened it for Guin, who was still holding the box.

"I believe you know the way," he said.

Guin walked down the short hallway to the detective's office, stopping in front of it.

"Just a sec," he said, pulling out his keys and opening the door.

He entered and turned on the lights.

"You can put the box on my desk and help yourself."

Guin dutifully placed the box on his desk, then hesitated.

"Go ahead and open it," urged the detective.

Guin opened the box. It was filled with a variety of breakfast pastries. Her stomach immediately started to make gurgling noises.

"Shh!" she ordered it.

"I wasn't sure what you were in the mood for, so I got a bunch of stuff," said the detective, busying himself around his office. "Whatever you don't want, the vultures will grab."

Guin stared at the muffins and doughnuts.

"Go on, eat," said the detective, turning to face her. "You could stand to put on a few pounds."

Guin looked up at him and made a face.

"Fine," she said. She picked out a cranberry nut muffin. "Thank you."

"Take as much as you want," said the detective, seating himself behind his desk.

"Don't you want something?" asked Guin.

"Ladies first," he said.

"Got a napkin?" Guin asked, looking around.

The detective bent over and opened a drawer.

"Here," he said, placing a small pile of those little deli napkins on his desk.

"Thanks," said Guin, taking a few.

She seated herself in the chair opposite the desk, the muffin in her lap.

"Go on," he said, looking from her to the muffin she was holding.

Guin pulled off a bite of muffin and popped it into her mouth.

"Happy now?" she asked him.

"Thrilled. So, questions…"

He grabbed the baseball he kept on his desk.

"Yes," said Guin, swallowing the bite of muffin. "Let me just get out my notes."

She placed the muffin on the edge of the desk and grabbed her legal pad and a pen from her bag.

"Any idea who gave Ronnie that bracelet she was wearing? I've been checking out jewelry stores and no one recalls selling it to Ronnie. I'm pretty sure it was a gift from a male admirer."

She looked over at the detective.

"Any other questions?"

"You didn't answer that one."

"Because I don't have an answer.

Guin gave him a look.

"We're still working on it," he said.

"Fine," said Guin. "I guess I'll keep looking. So I asked the listing agent for a list of everyone who had access to the house that weekend. She said she'd send it to me, but she hasn't. But I know she sent you a copy."

Again, the detective didn't respond.

"Oh, come on!" said Guin. "The least you can do is show me the list."

She crossed her arms over her chest and stared at the detective.

"You going to have some more of that muffin?"

"Argh!" Guin replied, uncrossing her arms and leaning

forward. "Has anyone ever told you you're infuriating?"

From the look on the detective's face, it was clear he was enjoying this.

She grabbed the muffin off his desk, ripped off a piece, and crammed it into her mouth.

"Happy now?" she asked him, her mouth full.

The detective grinned at her.

She finished chewing the bite of muffin, then swallowed.

"Fine," said Guin, "I'll keep after Ann."

"Good luck," said the detective.

Guin clenched her hands.

"What about the young man who disappeared, Jake Longley? Any sign of him?"

The detective frowned.

"No," he replied. "But…"

"Yes?" said Guin, leaning forward.

"Looks like someone poured sugar in his gas tank. That's why the car stalled out."

"Who would pour sugar into his gas tank?" asked Guin.

The detective raised an eyebrow. Clearly he was trying to tell her something. Think Guin, think. Of course, sugar! The bakery!

"So you think someone at the bakery poured sugar into his gas tank?"

The detective continued to regard her, moving the baseball from one hand to the other.

"But why?" asked Guin.

"Why don't you tell me, Nancy Drew?"

Distractedly, Guin pinched off another bite of muffin and popped it into her mouth. The detective smiled at her.

"You want some coffee to go with that?" he asked.

Guin nodded her head, not wanting to speak with her mouth full.

"Be right back."

He got up and headed down the hall.

Think, Guin, think, she told herself, as she grabbed another bite of muffin. It wasn't that good, but she was hungry. Why would someone at the bakery, assuming the sugar came from the bakery, want to harm Jake? Because he knew something, her brain immediately replied. But what?

Jake had tried to reach her just before he disappeared. Had he found out something? That must be it. He said he and Ronnie were close. Maybe he knew who the older man was.

Guin stared at the box of breakfast pastries.

"Oh my God!" she said aloud.

J. L. It had to be Jean-Luc! How stupid had she been not to realize that. True, there was a possibility J. L. could be someone else—she still hadn't ruled out Jimbo Leidecker— but Jean-Luc was the obvious choice.

"Idiot!" she said aloud, cursing herself for being so obtuse.

Just then the detective came in carrying a cup of coffee.

"I hope you were not referring to me," he said, placing the cup of coffee on the desk in front of her. "I added a little milk and sugar as I didn't think our coffee was quite up to your standards. Hope you don't mind."

Guin preferred her coffee black, as the detective knew.

"Thank you."

She took a sip. It was pretty vile. She tried not to grimace.

The detective grinned.

"That's why I bring my own," he said, as if reading her mind.

"Smart," said Guin. "And no, I was not referring to you. I was calling myself an idiot for not realizing J. L. probably stood for Jean-Luc."

The detective looked at her.

"Veronica's housemates said she was seeing an older

man who she referred to as 'J. L.,'" she explained. "It had to be Jean-Luc."

The detective continued to regard her.

"I bet he was the one who put sugar in Jake's gas tank," she continued. "Jake must have known or found out that he was seeing Ronnie and Jean-Luc was worried Jake would say something, so he wanted to send him a warning!"

"Take it easy, Nancy Drew," the detective said.

"Come on, that has to be it. Jake was working late. It would have been easy for Jean-Luc to have snuck out and poured some sugar in his gas tank."

The detective sighed.

"Have you at least questioned Jean-Luc?" Guin asked.

"We have."

"And?" asked Guin.

"He says he didn't do it. In fact, he was insulted we could even think such a thing. He actually said to me, 'Do you know how expensive the sugar we use is? I would never pour it in someone's car!'"

Guin smiled. "I can just picture him saying that."

The detective reached into the box and grabbed a doughnut and took a bite.

"What is it with cops and doughnuts?" asked Guin.

"They're good," replied the detective.

"Getting back to Jean-Luc… What about him and the victim?"

"What about them?"

"Did he admit to, you know?" asked Guin.

"You know what?" asked the detective, taking another bite of his doughnut.

The detective was clearly enjoying himself.

"You know," said Guin, wiggling her eyebrows.

"I don't know what you are referring to," said the detective, taking another bite of his doughnut. Though Guin would bet a dozen doughnuts he did.

"Were they having sex?" Guin practically shouted.

She could feel her cheeks immediately start to flush and watched as the detective tried not to laugh.

"Happy now, detective?"

He was about to reply when the phone on his desk rang. He picked up the handset.

"O'Loughlin."

He listened for several seconds, concentrating on whatever the caller was saying.

"I need to put you on hold for a sec."

He pressed a button and placed a hand over the receiver.

"I need to take this," he said, looking at Guin.

"But…" Guin began.

"I trust you can see yourself out, Ms. Jones?"

"But…" she began again. However, one look at the detective's face told her arguing was futile. "Fine, but we're not done here. You haven't answered any of my questions."

"Come back this afternoon."

"Fine," Guin grumbled. "When?"

He held up five fingers.

She gathered her things and headed toward the door.

"Aren't you forgetting something?" called the detective.

She looked into her bag. She had her phone and her pad and pen. Everything looked to be there. She looked at the detective.

"You forgot your muffin," he said, smiling up at her.

She made a face, took two steps forward, and grabbed the muffin.

"Thanks. I'll see you at five."

The detective pressed a button on the phone and began to speak as Guin opened the door. She stood in the doorway and glanced back at the detective, who signaled for her to close the door behind her. She sighed and did as he instructed. Then she made her way out of the police department, back down the stairs, and to her Mini, feeling incredibly frustrated—and hungry.

CHAPTER 31

Guin decided to head over to Jean-Luc's as she was desperate for a decent cup of coffee—and she had a few more questions for the proprietor.

She arrived there to find a pleasant-looking older woman behind the counter.

"May I help you, dear?" asked the woman.

"Is Jean-Luc here?" asked Guin.

"He's in the back. Is there something I can help you with?" she asked, sweetly.

"I'll have a cappuccino and…" She looked over the pastry case. "And an almond croissant." (She had thrown out the half-eaten muffin the detective had given her.)

"Will that be for here or to go?"

Guin thought for a moment. "To go."

"Very good. And would you like a small cappuccino or a large?"

"A large, please," said Guin.

The woman went over to the espresso machine and attempted to make Guin's cappuccino, but she was having some difficulty.

"Oh dear," she said.

"Is everything okay?" asked Guin, watching her.

"These machines are just so complicated," said the woman.

A man came into the shop.

"Would you excuse me for just a second?" she asked Guin.

"Sure," said Guin.

The man and Guin exchanged glances.

A minute later Jean-Luc appeared, along with the woman.

"It is really very easy," he explained to the woman, sounding a bit frustrated. He prepared Guin's cappuccino, showing the woman how it was done. "*Et voilà!*"

He smiled and handed Guin her cappuccino.

"*Merci*," said Guin.

"Now I must get back to work!" said Jean-Luc.

"If you have a minute, Jean-Luc!" called Guin, as he was about to disappear into the back.

"Yes?" he said, stopping.

"Sorry," Guin said to the man behind her. She stepped to the side. "I just have a couple of questions to ask you," she lowered her voice, "about Veronica Swales."

Jean-Luc scowled.

"Now is not a good time, Ms. Jones."

"It will just take a minute," she said, giving him her puppy dog look that always seemed to work on men.

"Fine. Come to the back."

The woman behind the counter cleared her throat, getting Guin's attention.

"Oh, sorry," said Guin, turning toward her. "How much do I owe you?"

The woman told her. Guin paid and grabbed her almond croissant, which the woman had placed in a bag. Then she headed to the kitchen at the back of the store.

"Where is Madame Fournier?" asked Guin, looking around.

"Out," said Jean-Luc, scowling again. "She had some sort of *emergency*."

"I hope everything is okay," said Guin.

Jean-Luc waved a hand. He was rolling out some pastry dough, not paying attention to Guin.

"Have you heard at all from Jake?" asked Guin.

"*Non*, and I am starting to worry," said Jean-Luc, still working on the dough. "It is very unlike him."

"I don't think he's absent on purpose," Guin said. "The police found sugar in his gas tank and suspect foul play."

Jean-Luc looked up at Guin.

"As I told that detective, I had absolutely nothing to do with that. I would never waste ingredients. And why would I want to harm Jake? I need him here, at the bakery. You see how things are without him."

He gestured around the kitchen. The place did look a bit disorganized.

"Have you hired someone to replace him?"

Jean-Luc stopped again and looked up at Guin.

"I do not want to, but what choice do I have? I cannot do everything myself."

"What about Veronica Swales? Did you replace her?" asked Guin.

"Veronica?" he said, looking off into the distance. "*Non*. She was irreplaceable."

He went back to his dough.

"Were you sweet on her?" asked Guin.

Jean-Luc sighed.

"She was a very sweet girl."

"You didn't answer my question," Guin replied.

Jean-Luc stopped what he was doing and looked up at Guin.

"What is it, exactly, you wish to know, Ms. Jones?"

"Were you…" Guin wasn't sure how to phrase her question. "Were you seeing her, outside of work?"

Jean-Luc had gone back to working on his dough. Guin

waited. Finally, when he had formed the dough into a ball and had placed it into a bowl, he turned to look at her.

"As I told Monsieur O'Loughlin, the detective, I was fond of Veronica. She was a very sweet girl. Very interested in pastry. She asked me to help her, teach her what I knew. So, I helped her. Is that a crime?"

He started mixing ingredients.

Guin waited, hoping he would say more. She watched him work. There was something mesmerizing about it. As he worked, he hummed a little tune. Guin smiled. She could see how Veronica could have been attracted to him.

"So what did you and Veronica talk about, when you were, uh, helping her?" Guin asked, hoping Jean-Luc would reveal something.

Jean-Luc stopped again.

"France. Pastry. Veronica said she wanted to go to France and work in a real bakery, a *patisserie*. She wanted to learn the business, one day open her own place. She studied French in college. Her accent was most charming," he said, with a smile.

Suddenly Guin had a vision of Jean-Luc and Veronica working together in the kitchen, of him showing the young woman how to roll out dough and putting his arms around her, moving behind her….

She felt herself blushing.

Guin was about to ask Jean-Luc who he thought might have wished to harm the young woman when the woman from the front poked her head in.

"I'm sorry to disturb you again, Jean-Luc, but I need your help again."

Jean-Luc sighed, wiped his hand on the cotton cloth he had hanging from his waist, and headed to the front of the shop.

"If you will excuse me, Ms. Jones?"

"Of course," said Guin, who was staring at the cloth hanging from Jean-Luc's waist. The detective had said the medical examiner had found cotton fibers on the dead girl's neck. Could she have been strangled with a baker's cloth?

She followed Jean-Luc to the front of the shop. She held up her cappuccino, which was now cold, and said goodbye to the woman and Jean-Luc, who were busy helping customers and didn't notice her leave.

She placed the cappuccino and the bag with the almond croissant atop her purple Mini and unlocked the car. She got in and put her key in the ignition, then remembered she had left her cappuccino and croissant on the roof. She got out and grabbed them.

She sat for a minute, staring out the windshield. Had Jean-Luc been having an affair with Veronica Swales? Even though he hadn't admitted to anything, Guin had a feeling something had been going on between them. Maybe he had fallen in love with her and had gotten angry when he discovered that she was still seeing Billy? Or maybe Veronica had fallen for Jean-Luc, but he had refused to leave his wife, and she had threatened him?

She envisioned several different scenarios. But if Jean-Luc had killed her, how did her body get to the Simms place? Unless they had used it as their love nest. But that seemed unlikely. Though Billy had said he had lost his keys. Could Ronnie have lifted them and then carried on at Billy's grandparents' place as a way to get back at him for breaking up with her?

Guin sighed and took a sip of her cappuccino, nearly spitting it out. All the heat had gone out of it and it tasted like muddy milk. Maybe if she put it in the microwave it would taste better. Or else she'd need to make herself a fresh cup.

She started the engine and put the car into reverse.

Guin checked her phone as soon as she walked in the door. There were messages from Ris and Shelly, as well as from Ginny. She heated the cappuccino in the microwave and took a sip. She made a face, then poured it down the drain. Oh well. She took out her little French press and made herself a fresh cup. While it was brewing she ate some of her almond croissant. God, that was good.

When it was ready, she poured the coffee into a mug and took it and what was left of her croissant to the dining table. Then she spent the next several minutes savoring both. When she was done she retrieved her phone from the kitchen.

She told Ris she missed him and looked forward to seeing him the next day, though she felt somewhat insincere as she wrote it. She had barely given him a thought over the last 24 hours. Shelly had wanted to know what was up with her and the detective, and if there was any news in the Veronica Swales case.

Ginny, as usual, wanted to know how Guin was doing with those articles she had assigned her, and Guin assured her she would have an update on the Swales case as well as the piece on local boat charters for her by the end of day Tuesday, i.e., tomorrow.

Still no word from Ann Campbell. She was tempted to call Lenny and see if he could work on her but decided not to.

She was surprised there wasn't a message from Craig. But it was still relatively early. The heck with it, she thought, and dialed his number.

He picked up after four rings.

"Jeffers."

Clearly he was busy, otherwise he would have known it was Guin calling.

"Hey, Craig. It's Guin."

"Oh, hey Guin. What's up?"

"You busy?"

"Kind of. I'm out running errands with Betty."

Guin smiled. She could just picture them together at Publix or Costco, loading up on stuff for the week.

"It can keep," she said. "You have some time later to chat?"

"We should be home in a little while. Can I phone you later?"

"Sure, just give me a call on my cell. You know how to reach me."

"I do. Okay, speak with you later."

Guin ended the call. She wished her marriage had been as happy and as loving as Craig and Betty's. Those two truly seemed to enjoy spending time together, even after being together for nearly forty years and raising three kids.

She had wanted to tell Craig about Jean-Luc and Veronica and ask him some more questions about Billy and Jimbo. But it could wait.

She popped the last bite of almond croissant into her mouth, then went back to her office/bedroom to finish up the article on boat charters.

CHAPTER 32

Craig called Guin back a little after two.

"Sorry for the delay. Betty and I stopped for lunch."

"No worries," said Guin, though she had wondered what had happened to Craig. No one had been getting back to her, and she was frustrated.

"So, what's up?"

Guin told Craig about her visit to Jean-Luc's.

"You think the baker and the girl were having an affair?"

"I think it's possible," said Guin. "But I just can't picture him killing her."

"What about a crime of passion?" asked Craig. "The French are known for that."

"It's possible, but I just don't see Jean-Luc strangling her in a jealous rage. He always seems so calm."

"You can't judge a book by its cover," Craig replied.

"True. Also, Jean-Luc swore he had no idea how sugar got into Jake's gas tank and was appalled that anyone would think he would waste something as precious as sugar in anything other than pastries."

"Though he could be lying," said Craig.

"I guess," said Guin, "but the way he said it made me think he was telling the truth."

Craig made a noise. It did not seem he felt the same way.

"Which brings me to the other J. L., your buddy, Jimbo

Leidecker," said Guin. "You speak with him?"

"I did."

"And?"

"Jimbo swore he had nothing to do with Veronica Swales's death."

"And you believed him, of course," said Guin, a note of skepticism in her voice.

Craig sighed.

"I've known Jimbo for years, Guin."

"What about that reporter's objectivity you're always telling me about?"

Craig grumbled.

"Fine. You want to talk with him?" he asked.

Actually, she did, but she could tell from Craig's tone that she needed to tread carefully.

"Let's assume Jimbo is innocent," she said, placatingly. "Can you ask him if he saw Ronnie out with someone other than Billy, say at happy hour or around town?"

"No problem," said Craig.

"Thank you. Also," she continued, "I have a few questions for Billy Simms. It turns out he was seeing Ronnie's housemate, Gillian. Maybe there was some kind of lover's triangle."

Guin pictured Gillian and Billy together. They would make a handsome couple. Both were tall and good looking.

"And I should follow up with Gillian. Find out where she was that Saturday night."

"Anything else?" asked Craig.

"Yes, I want to find out what happened to Jake Longley. Where did he go? Can you ask your buddy in the Lee County Sheriff's Office if they've found out anything?"

"No problem. I have a call in to him already about a different matter."

"Great," said Guin. "I'm going back over to the Sanibel

Police Department later to speak with the detective again. We had to cut short our earlier meeting. Maybe this time I can get some information out of him."

"Good luck with that," said Craig.

"Thanks. So, you'll let me know what you hear back?"

"I will, but it could take some time."

"We talking hours or days?"

"Don't know."

"Well, email or call me as soon as you hear anything."

They said their goodbyes and ended the call.

Guin sighed. She was feeling impatient. She looked at the clock on her computer. She still had a couple of hours before she needed to head over to the police department. She checked her email and messages. Still nothing from Ann Campbell. Why hadn't she sent her the list? Was she hiding something?

Speaking of hiding something....

She picked up her phone and sent Ronnie's housemate Pam a text, asking if they could meet, alone, later or tomorrow. Then she put it down and turned back to her computer. A minute later she picked it up again, holding the smooth black rectangle in her hands, staring at it, willing someone, anyone, to text her back. But the phone remained dark and silent.

"Good afternoon, Officer Pettit."

Guin had arrived at the Sanibel Police Department a few minutes before five and greeted the young officer on duty.

"Afternoon, Ms. Jones," he said, smiling at her.

"Could you please let Detective O'Loughlin know that I'm here?" asked Guin.

"Is he expecting you?"

Officer Pettit knew, as did several of the other officers,

that Guin had a habit of showing up at the police department unannounced.

"As a matter of fact, he is," replied Guin, smiling. "I have an appointment."

"I'll just ring him and let him know you're here then."

He moved away and picked up the phone. A minute later he was back.

"The detective's on a call. He said he might be a while."

"Tell him I'll wait."

"The detective thought you might say that. He says he'll come find you when he's off."

"I'll just be outside."

"Has it cooled off any? I've been on desk duty all afternoon."

"It's not too hot. Though I don't mind the heat."

Guin stepped outside and walked along the decking that ran alongside the police department. She stopped at a bench that overlooked some palm trees and stared out. Suddenly her phone started buzzing. She fished it out of her bag, hoping it was a message from Pam or Ann Campbell. But it was her real estate agent, Polly.

"Hey, Polly."

"Am I catching you at a bad time?" she asked.

"No, I'm just over at the police department, waiting to speak with the detective. What's up?"

"I have another listing I want to show you. It just came on the market, and it's going to go fast."

Guin rolled her eyes. She was not in the mood to look at any more houses, and Polly was always telling her places were "going to go fast," but she figured she should probably go take a look. After all, it could be the one. Though she doubted it.

"Where is it?"

"It's off West Gulf Drive. It's a two-bedroom, two-bath,

with a separate office area. It's a little outdated…"

That probably meant it needed a lot of work.

"But it's got good bones. And you can be on the beach in under fifteen minutes."

"How much?" Guin asked.

Polly told her the price, but quickly added that it was negotiable.

"You know that is the top end of my budget, Polly," Guin replied. "And it doesn't leave me much money for renovations."

"Just take a look."

"Fine," said Guin.

They made a date to meet at the house the next day around two.

They ended the call and as Guin was putting her phone away, she saw Officer Pettit leaning out the door to the police department.

"He's off the phone, Ms. Jones. But he says he has another call in a few."

"I'm coming," Guin called, walking quickly back to the police department.

"Was Jean-Luc Fournier having an affair with Veronica Swales?"

Guin was leaning on the detective's desk, looking down at him as he passed his Red Sox baseball back and forth between his hands.

"And did you know that Billy Simms has been seeing Veronica's housemate, Gillian Metzger?"

She waited for a reaction from the detective.

"I see you've been busy," he finally replied.

"Well?"

"Well what?"

"Are you going to answer my questions?"

"It sounds like you already know the answers," replied the detective.

Why did she even bother?

"Have you spoken with Gillian Metzger?"

"We have."

"And did she happen to say where she was that Saturday, when Ronnie was strangled?"

"Working over at the San Ybel."

"Did you check out her alibi?"

"We did."

"And?"

"And she was working at the San Ybel that Saturday."

"All night?"

"No, but—"

Guin cut him off.

"So she could have done it!"

The detective regarded Guin.

"What about Jimbo Leidecker?"

"What about him?" asked the detective.

"I heard he was sweet on Ronnie, Ms. Swales."

"And?"

"Have you checked him out?"

The detective momentarily stopped passing the baseball between his hands.

"Well?"

"We spoke to him."

"And?"

"And he says he was home Saturday evening."

"Alone?"

"Yes."

"So he could have done it, too," said Guin, leaning over the detective.

"And what was his motive?" asked the detective, calmly looking up at Guin.

"He was clearly sweet on the girl. Maybe he was getting a little overprotective. Or even had a crush on her. Maybe he didn't like what Ronnie was up to. Got mad and strangled her in a moment of insanity."

The detective continued to look up at Guin, who had been walking back and forth.

"Sounds like someone's seen one too many Lifetime movies."

Guin stopped her pacing and made a face. She actually hated those Lifetime movies, though she did occasionally watch the movies and mysteries on the Hallmark Channel.

The detective's phone rang. He picked it up.

"O'Loughlin…. Uh-huh. Okay. Give me a sec."

He covered the mouthpiece with his hand.

"I gotta take this. If there isn't anything else…"

"Can you please send me a copy of the list of people who had access to the Simms place?" Guin practically begged. "I've been unable to get it from Ann Campbell."

The detective didn't reply.

"Pretty please?"

"Hold on a sec, Charlie," said the detective into the phone.

Guin put her hands on the detective's desk.

"I'm not leaving here without getting a copy."

"I'll email it to you."

"You promise?"

The detective gave a slight nod.

"Fine," she said, moving toward the door. "And I still have more questions!"

The detective ignored her and started speaking into the phone.

"Sorry about that, Charlie."

Guin gave him a final look, then exited, loudly closing the door behind her. She knew it was childish, but she didn't care. The man was infuriating.

CHAPTER 33

Guin left the police department fuming. Why did the detective have to make everything so difficult? Why couldn't he just cooperate with her?

She clomped down the stairs to her car. Before she got in she checked her messages. There was a text from Shelly.

"You want to go to another happy hour?" it read. "I could use a drink."

Guin was tempted.

"How about we go for a walk instead?" she wrote back.

"Fine. Where?"

"I'm at the SPD. How 'bout I swing by your place?"

"OK," Shelly texted her back.

Guin could tell Shelly was disappointed, but she thought it better to go for a walk than for a drink.

Shelly and Steve's place was off of Middle Gulf Drive, not that far from the police department. And she arrived there a few minutes later. While driving, she had heard her phone ringing, but she had ignored it (or tried to). She made it a habit not to talk on her phone or even to look at it while she was driving. But upon parking she fished it out of her bag.

There was a voicemail. She played the message. It was from Craig, saying to call him back when she could. She immediately pressed his number into the keypad.

"What's up?" she asked, as soon as he answered.

"I just got off the phone with my buddy in the Lee County Medical Examiner's Office."

"Why were you talking to him?"

"We were arranging a fishing trip."

"Ah," said Guin.

"One thing led to another, and he happened to let slip something about the Swales case."

"Oh?"

"It seems Veronica Swales was pregnant."

"WHAT?!" shrieked Guin. It was a good thing she was in her car and no one could hear her, though she looked around nonetheless. "She was pregnant? How did we not know that?"

"Well, we didn't actually see the full autopsy report."

"True," said Guin, thinking back. "The detective only said she had been strangled and there were no drugs involved. You think he could have at least mentioned something so important."

Guin would have to have another talk with the detective. Why hadn't he told her? And who was the father? Was it Billy or the mystery man—or someone else?"

"Anything else?"

"Yeah, Pete said they also found flour on her body."

"As in baking flour?"

"Yup," said Craig.

"Well, she did work in a bakery, so…"

"Around her neck."

"Oh," said Guin. That did seem a bit unusual. Though there could be a logical explanation. She knew Ronnie had been working at the bakery that Saturday.

"Any news about Jake Longley?"

"Not yet. Still waiting to hear back from my contact in the Lee County Sheriff's Office."

"Okay. Let me know what you find out."

"Will do."

"And did you speak with Jimbo yet?"

"No. We're meeting up over at Doc Ford's for happy hour in a few."

"Well—"

Craig cut her off.

"I'll let you know what I find out."

Guin smiled. She knew Craig well enough not to argue with him, at least about certain things.

"Thanks Craig. I'll let you go now."

They ended the call and Guin got out of the car. Shelly would no doubt be wondering what had happened to her.

"Finally!" said Shelly, ushering her into the house.

"Sorry," said Guin. "I was attending to business."

"Anything you can share?" asked Shelly, hopefully.

"I'm afraid not."

Guin thought about telling Shelly what she had just learned but felt it wouldn't be right.

"Come, check out what I've been working on," said Shelly, walking down the hall to her crafting room.

Guin dutifully followed her.

"Ta da!" said Shelly, gesturing toward a large mirror that was covered in shells.

"Wow!" said Guin. "That's amazing, Shell. How long did it take you to do that?"

"I'm still working on it, but I'd say at least forty hours."

"Very impressive," said Guin, walking over and examining the mirror. "You should enter it in next year's Shell Show."

"You think so?"

"I wouldn't suggest it if I didn't mean it. It's really good,

Shell. You could definitely get a ribbon."

Shelly grinned.

"I'll think about it."

Guin looked around the room. There were shells and jewelry-making tools and supplies scattered across several tables, and she could see some finished necklaces, bracelets, and earrings.

"Looks like you've been busy."

"Gearing up for the holidays," said Shelly. "I want to be prepared this year. Last year was a record year, and I'm hoping I'll do even better this year. I have over twenty-five thousand followers on Instagram and several thousand on Facebook."

"Wow," said Guin. "You're a rock star! Or a shell star! Or would that be a sea star?"

Shelly groaned.

"If only 'likes' equaled sales. But I'm working on it!"

"Well, shall we go for our walk?"

"Sure. But we can't be gone too long. Steve called a few minutes ago and said we've been invited over to some friends at six-thirty, so I don't want to get all sweaty."

"No problem," said Guin.

They left Shelly's crafting room and headed out the front door.

A little while later Guin said goodbye to Shelly and checked her phone as soon as she got to her car.

"Finally!" she said, aloud.

Pam had gotten back to her and suggested they meet at the San Ybel Resort, where she (and Gillian) worked, the next day at ten-thirty, when she had her break. Guin immediately wrote back, telling her that would be fine and asking where she should meet her. Pam said to just come to the front desk. They could go for a short walk, if that was all right with Guin. Guin wrote back saying that was fine and she'd see Pam the next day.

There was also a message from Ris, asking her how her day had gone and if she was free for lunch tomorrow. Guin wrote back to say lunch was good, as long as it was on the early side, say noonish, and that her day was okay. She signed it "xo" and hit "send."

She looked at the time, it was nearly six-thirty. Part of her wanted to go over to Doc Ford's and eavesdrop on Craig and Jimbo, assuming they were still there, which they probably were. But she figured neither man would appreciate it, so she abandoned the idea.

Still no reply from Ann Campbell or the detective. And he had promised to send her that list! Why was no one getting back to her? Though at least Pam had. That was something.

She sat there thinking for another minute then grabbed her phone and said, "screw it." She dialed the detective's mobile and waited for him to pick up.

"I know I'm going to regret this…" came his voice.

Guin was surprised he even answered.

"So when were you going to tell me Veronica Swales was pregnant?"

She could hear the detective sighing on the other end of the line.

"Where did you hear that?"

"Craig's buddy in the medical examiner's office let it slip."

She immediately regretted revealing her source. But too late now. She'd apologize to Craig later.

"I'll have to talk to Mike about that," said the detective.

"Yeah, well, the cat is out of the bag. Give."

"What else is there to say?"

"Well, who's the father, for one."

"I don't know," replied the detective.

"Did you ask Billy?"

The detective did not reply.

"What about Jean-Luc?"

Again, no reply.

"What about Jimbo Leidecker?"

"Jimbo Leidecker?"

"According to Ronnie's housemates, Ronnie was seeing some older guy with the initials J. L."

"In case you hadn't noticed, there are a lot of 'older guys' on Sanibel and Captiva, and no doubt more than a few of them have the initials 'J. L.,'" replied the detective.

"Yeah, well Jimbo was apparently sweet on Ronnie. Craig said Ronnie reminded him of the daughter he lost."

The detective didn't say anything.

"And I still haven't received that list of people who accessed the lock box that weekend. I thought you were going to forward it to me."

"Fine," said the detective. "I'll send it to you tomorrow. I'm not at the office."

"You better, or else…"

"Or else what, Ms. Jones?"

"Or else, or else… I'll come over there and wait until you give it to me."

"You know we can have you arrested."

"For what?" asked Guin.

"Disturbing the peace."

Guin made a noise.

"Can I go now, Ms. Jones?"

"Not yet. Any word on Jake Longley?"

"In the last two hours? No."

Well, at least it was an answer.

"Now, if you don't have any other questions…"

Guin had more questions, but she could tell from the detective's tone he was unlikely to answer them.

"They can wait… I guess."

"Thank you," replied the detective.

"Well, goodnight, I guess."

"Goodnight, Ms. Jones," he replied. "No doubt I will be hearing from you again."

Guin was about to say something but ended the call instead.

CHAPTER 34

Guin arrived at the San Ybel Resort & Spa right at 10:30. She left her car with the valet and headed inside to the front desk. There were pumpkins, some carved, others whole, and cute cutouts of witches and ghosts and monsters in beach attire throughout the lobby. That's right, she remembered. It was Halloween. She had forgotten.

"May I help you?" asked one of the receptionists.

"I'm just waiting for someone," Guin replied.

"Well, let me know if I can assist you. Is the person a guest?"

"No, she works here," said Guin.

"Would you like me to page her?"

"Oh, I don't think that's necessary."

Guin decided to walk around a bit. She strolled over to the large plate-glass windows that looked out onto gardens and was staring out into the distance, toward the beach, when she heard her name.

"Ms. Jones?"

Guin turned around. It was Pam.

"Sorry to be late. Had a minor crisis I had to deal with."

Guin gave her a sympathetic look.

"Another guest wanting a refund because the water was the wrong color."

"The wrong color? What color were they expecting?"

"Per the guest, on our website the water was distinctly turquoise. However, when she got here it was brownish-green."

Guin looked incredulous.

"Did you explain to her that the color of the water constantly changes—and the hotel has no control over it?"

Pam shrugged.

"It wouldn't have made a difference."

"Wow," said Guin.

"You'd be surprised at the things people complain about," Pam replied.

"Shall we go for a walk?" Guin suggested, noticing all the people passing through the lobby.

"Sure," said Pam.

They headed outside to the path that led down to the pool and the Gulf.

"So what did you want to ask me? I assume it's about Ronnie."

"Yes. Did you know she was pregnant?"

"What?!" said Pam, stopping and grabbing Guin's arm. "Oh my God, does Billy know?"

Guin regarded the young woman. She looked truly surprised.

"I don't know," replied Guin. "Why do you think Billy is—was—the father?"

"Who else could it be?" asked Pam.

"What about this J. L. Veronica was seeing, the older man?"

Pam scrunched up her face.

"I don't think she was seeing him for that long, and I don't know if they were actually sleeping together. How far along was she?"

"I don't know," said Guin.

"Wow, Billy must have freaked out—assuming he knew," she added.

"Why do you say that?"

"His folks were not too keen on Ronnie. They didn't hassle him too much about her while he was in college, figuring he'd dump her as soon as they'd graduated. But they were not pleased when Ronnie showed up on Sanibel. They had big plans for Billy, and Ronnie plus a baby would have upset them, big time."

Interesting, thought Guin. Assuming Billy was the father, and Ronnie had told him, and he had told his parents—unlikely, but possible—would they try to get Ronnie out of the way?

"What do you know about Billy's parents?" asked Guin.

"Not a whole lot. They own Island Trust and a lot of property on the island. Been here for generations. Billy's dad is a big-time Republican donor. He went fishing with the VP when he was down here."

Interesting, Guin thought.

"What about Gillian?"

"What about her?" asked Pam.

"Do you think she knew that Ronnie was pregnant?"

"Doubtful. Ronnie didn't confide in Gillian."

"So they weren't close?"

"Hardly," said Pam.

"And did you know Gillian and Billy were seeing each other?"

Pam sighed.

"Yeah, though I told Gillian it was a really bad idea. Billy and Ronnie were still kind of seeing each other, even if word on the street was that they had broken up."

"But she didn't listen to you."

"No. Gillian thought she and Billy were soulmates." She made a face. "And that Ronnie would probably be happy to have him off her hands now that she was seeing someone else."

Hmm, thought Guin.

"What are you thinking?" asked Pam, looking over at Guin.

"I'm thinking I need to have a chat with Billy Simms and talk to his parents. See what they know."

"Good luck with that. Knowing the Simmses, they're going to do everything in their power to keep this hush-hush."

They had reached the end of the path.

"Well, I have to get back to work," said Pam.

"Thanks for your help," said Guin.

"No problem. Ronnie and I weren't the best of friends, but she didn't deserve to die. I hope they catch whoever did it and put him in jail."

Pam turned to head back to the hotel. She took a few steps then stopped.

"Aren't you coming?"

"I can find my way back," said Guin. "I'd like to stay here a minute and just look at the ocean."

Pam smiled.

"I understand. It's very soothing, isn't it? I often come out here during my break."

Guin smiled at the young woman.

"Well, goodbye," Pam said.

Guin watched her depart, then turned back to look out over the water.

Guin sat in the parking lot of the Shell Museum, watching a family make their way up the stairs. She had arrived at the museum early, not wanting to drive all the way back to the condo, only to turn around and go to the museum to meet Ris for lunch. She looked down at her phone, to check her email. Nothing urgent. She had meant to stop by the office that morning, to meet with Ginny, but had texted her to see if she could come by that afternoon instead, which Ginny had said worked out better.

She got out of the car and headed toward the museum. She could always walk around the museum if Ris wasn't ready. She stopped before climbing the stairs and decided to give Craig a call.

"I was just about to send you an email," he said.

"Oh?"

"I got some interesting information out of Jimbo."

"Oh?" said Guin again.

"He says he saw Ronnie's car parked over at the bakery Saturday evening."

"Oh?" said Guin, for the third time.

"Don't you know any other letters?" asked Craig.

Guin chuckled.

"Go on."

"Like I said, he saw Ronnie's car parked outside the bakery Saturday evening—"

"But doesn't the bakery close at four on Saturdays?" Guin interrupted.

"Will you let me finish?"

"Sorry," said Guin.

"So anyway, he sees Ronnie's car around six and figures maybe the bakery is open late. So he pulls in and goes to the front door. But the place is locked, and he can't really see in."

"Maybe she was working in the back? They had a lot of stuff to get ready for the farmers market the next morning, and I think they were catering some event."

"That's what Jimbo figured. He said he knocked on the door, but no one answered. So he just drove away."

"And this was around six that Saturday?"

"Yeah, according to Jimbo."

"And when was the last time Jimbo saw Ronnie?"

"A couple days before, at Thursday happy hour. That's when he saw Ronnie and the other girl arguing."

"Huh," said Guin. The pieces were starting to come together, but she still didn't know what the finished puzzle looked like.

"You still there?" asked Craig.

"Sorry. I have a feeling the other girl was Gillian, and that Billy was involved."

"You think Gillian knew about the baby?"

"Maybe," said Guin. "Pam, Ronnie's other housemate, didn't know, and said she doubted Gillian did either. But you never know. The question is, did Billy know that Ronnie was pregnant?"

"Good point. And do we know for sure if it was Billy's baby?" mused Craig.

"You want to ask him?"

"Billy?"

"Yes."

There was a pause on the other end of the line.

"We need to find out if Billy knew about the baby, Craig."

"Why don't you ask your friend, the detective?"

Guin made a face.

"I did. He's not talking."

Craig sighed.

"Fine. I'll go speak to him."

"Tell you what, I'll speak with him."

"You sure?" asked Craig.

"Yes," said Guin. She had been wanting to speak with Billy. "I'm also curious to know what Billy's parents knew."

"Why?" asked Craig.

"According to Pam, the Simmses didn't think Ronnie was wife material and would not have been pleased to learn their son had gotten her in the family way."

"Hmm…" said Craig.

"I'd ask them about it, but I'm not sure they'd talk to me. You on the other hand…"

"Fine. I'll go speak to them, but I wouldn't get your hopes up."

Guin glanced at the time. She needed to go meet Ris.

"Hey Craig, I've gotta go. Talk to you later?"

"Sure," he said.

Guin ended the call and tossed her phone into her bag. She then walked quickly up the steps and into the museum.

Upon entering the lobby, Guin immediately spied George straightening some items in the gift shop. George was in charge of merchandising and also the museum's displays.

"Hi George!" Guin called. "Long time, no see."

"Hey Guin," George replied, turning around and smiling at Guin.

"The gift shop looks great. Getting ready for the season?"

"Yup," he replied. "Got lots of new things at the trade show I went to end of August. Just figuring out what to put out."

"Well, knowing you, you'll figure it out. How've you been?"

"Pretty good," he replied.

George was an introvert and a man of few words. He was also a skilled craftsman and shell artist who had won ribbons at various shell shows for his shell sculptures.

"Well, take care of yourself, George. I'll be back soon to pick up a few things for the condo."

George smiled at her and returned to his shelving.

Guin went over to the front desk. Bonnie was there,

greeting visitors. She had retired and moved to Sanibel a while back, but she volunteered at the Shell Museum several days a week. Said it was her way of giving back. And she loved meeting fellow shell lovers.

"Hi Bonnie."

"Hi Guin. Let me guess," she said, grinning. "You're here to see Dr. Hartwick."

"With your mind-reading abilities you should take up fortune telling," said Guin, teasingly.

"Yeah, well, doesn't take a mind reader to know why you're here," she said, winking.

Guin could feel herself starting to blush.

"Is he around?"

"I'll ring him and let you know."

Bonnie picked up the phone and dialed Ris's extension.

"I have a Ms. Jones here to see you," she said, winking at Guin again. "Okay, I'll send her up."

Bonnie started to open her mouth but Guin stopped her.

"I know the way. Thanks Bonnie."

Guin headed to the stairs and went up.

"Hey there," said Ris, getting up and going to the door to intercept her. He leaned down and gave Guin a kiss.

"Hey there, yourself," said Guin, a minute later, looking up at him.

Ris still had his arms around her.

"So, lunch…?"

"About that…" Ris began.

"Let me guess," she said, looking around his disheveled office. "You need to reschedule."

Ris looked a bit sheepish.

"It's just that with me taking off Friday…"

"Say no more," said Guin. "I get it. Can I get you something?"

"Oh no, I'm fine," he replied.

"You need to eat," Guin retorted.

Ris grinned.

"I'm glad you're concerned for my welfare, but I'll be fine. I still haven't eaten the breakfast and snacks I brought to work with me."

Guin made a face.

"But if you're so concerned about my well being, have dinner with me Thursday."

"Aren't you leaving for Panama City early Friday?"

"I am," Ris replied. "But I still need to eat. And I'll be carbo loading. And I know how you love your carbs," he said, grinning.

When he looked at her like that, she was unable to refuse him anything. Also, she did love carbs.

"Fine. I'll come over for dinner. Or would you rather go out? But I'm telling you now, I'm not staying over. You need a good night's rest."

Ris, still holding her, laughed, then kissed her forehead.

"I do love you, Guinivere. Always looking out for me."

Guin smiled up at him. She felt she should say "I love you, too," but she couldn't get the words out for some reason.

She untangled herself from Ris's embrace.

"You sure I can't get you something from Bailey's or the Sanibel Sprout?"

"No, really, I'm good. But thank you."

"Okay. Then I'll see you Thursday. Just text me the time and place."

"Will do."

Ris went back to his desk and was going through a pile of papers. Guin smiled and let herself out.

Bonnie was on the phone when Guin walked past the reception desk. Guin waved to her and she waved back. She looked to see if George was around, but he had disappeared. He was probably doing something in the back or was outside having lunch.

She jogged down the steps and into the parking lot. Before getting into her car, she checked her phone. Craig had texted her Billy's number, in case she didn't have it. She thought about calling him, but just then her stomach let out a loud rumbling sound.

"Okay, okay," she said aloud. "First food."

CHAPTER 35

Guin thought about heading home to eat, but she was supposed to meet Polly at two and didn't really have time to drive there and back and eat lunch. So she decided to check out Traders 2, a new branch of Traders Restaurant that had just opened on the west end of Periwinkle. Ginny would probably want her to check it out anyway, she reasoned, though she would need to visit it a few times before actually writing a review. Maybe she would take Shelly. Shelly loved going on restaurant review trips with Guin as she could order whatever she liked and didn't have to pay.

As it was early in the season and the place had just opened, there were only a few people there when Guin arrived and she was promptly seated. Cute place, she thought, looking around. It had a very tropical feel.

She looked over the menu and ordered the pulled pork tacos and an Arnold Palmer from a friendly young man who introduced himself as Noah. A few minutes later her drink arrived, followed a few minutes after that by her pulled pork tacos.

Guin thanked the young man and dug in. The tacos were good. She took another bite then got out her little notebook and a pen and made some notes. A few minutes later she asked Noah for the check.

"No dessert or coffee?"

"Sorry, maybe next time."

She paid with her credit card and made a note on the back of the receipt. She would submit it to Ginny when she submitted her monthly expense report.

"Any way you could meet me at the first place a few minutes early?" Guin had texted Polly while she was waiting for her check.

"How early we talking about?" Polly had replied.

"1:30? 1:45?"

It was 1:15 now, and Guin could be at the address Polly had sent her by 1:30.

"Let me check with the listing agent and get back to you," Polly had written back.

A couple of minutes later, Polly texted her again.

"1:45. See you there."

"C u soon!" Guin wrote back.

She thought about calling or texting Billy but decided she'd wait until after she was done house hunting.

She arrived at the house a few minutes later, figuring she could walk around if no one was there. There was a car in the driveway. Probably the listing agent's, thought Guin, or maybe the owner's. May as well go ring the doorbell.

She jogged up the steps and rang the doorbell. A minute later it was opened, by Christina Fournier.

"Madame Fournier," Guin stuttered.

Christina Fournier smiled.

"I get that a lot from people who are used to only seeing me at the bakery," she replied.

Guin didn't know what to say.

"Come in, come in," said Madame Fournier. "I assume you're Polly's client."

Guin nodded.

"You probably want to know what I'm doing here, yes?"

Guin nodded again.

Madame Fournier continued to smile.

"Well, someone in the family had to make some money."

"The bakery's not doing well?" asked Guin, surprised.

"Oh, the bakery's doing well enough. That daft husband of mine," she said, her Irish accent becoming stronger, "opening here in May." She shook her head. "I don't know what he was thinking."

"It is a bit of an odd time to open a new place here," said Guin, recovering. "But the bakery always seems busy. I see cars parked there all the time."

Madame Fournier crossed herself.

"Saints be praised for that. But it hasn't been easy. Just in case, I decided to get my real estate license a while back. Seemed like a good way to make some extra money."

"So who do you work for?" Guin asked.

"Do you know Ann Campbell?"

It took all Guin's willpower to keep from saying something rude.

"So is this her listing?"

Madame Fournier smiled.

"No, it's mine. My first. The seller is one of our best customers over at the bakery. The man's an addict. Comes in every morning to get a croissant and a cappuccino—and comes in again in the afternoon to get himself a pastry. He's partial to our opera cake. He heard me mention to Jean-Luc that I had to run off and do a showing and asked if I was in real estate. I told him I was, and he said he was thinking of selling his place and buying a condo, and would give me a shot at selling it if I would give him free pastry."

She laughed at the memory.

"I'm assuming you agreed," said Guin, smiling.

"I did."

When Madame Fournier smiled, especially with her hair down and wearing a dress instead of her starched white baking attire, she looked years younger and more relaxed.

"Well, congratulations," said Guin. "I hope you sell lots of houses, but I hope this won't affect the bakery. I'm also addicted to your pastries."

Madame Fournier laughed.

"I'm hoping it will help the bakery. If I can sell a few houses, maybe we can hire more people. I can't remember the last time Jean-Luc and I had a vacation."

Guin gave her a sympathetic look. With many places on Sanibel and Captiva selling for over a million dollars, there was a lot of money to be made in real estate.

"It must be hard with Veronica and Jake not there to help you," she said.

As soon as she said Veronica's name it was as if a dark cloud had settled over Madame Fournier's face.

"If that little tramp had stuck to making bread instead of making eyes at my husband—"

She was cut off by the sound of Polly entering.

"Hello-o," she called from the front door. "Sorry I'm late!"

She glanced over at Guin and Madame Fournier, who had forced a smile on her face.

"Guin and I were just having a nice chat."

"Did you have a chance to look around?" Polly asked Guin.

"Not yet. You want to give me the tour?" Guin asked Madame Fournier.

"I'd be happy to."

"I'll just tag along," said Polly.

Madame Fournier showed Guin around the house. It wasn't terribly big, but it was cozy and well laid out, and it had a nice view out the back. It just needed some updating, as did all the houses Guin had seen, especially the bathrooms and kitchen.

As if reading Guin's mind, Polly piped up.

"Of course, it needs a little freshening up, but it has good bones—and it's a less than fifteen-minute walk to the beach."

That seemed to be Polly's stock answer.

"Is the owner negotiable?" Guin asked Madame Fournier.

"He has his eye on a condo down on the East End, so…"

"*Everything* is negotiable," Polly cut in.

Guin walked around the place again, taking in the kitchen, which opened onto the living area, and the two bedrooms, each of which had an en suite bathroom and were located on either side of the house.

"Oh, and I nearly forgot!" said Madame Fournier. "Come with me!"

She headed out to the lanai. Guin and Polly followed. There was a flight of stairs that led down to a patio. Guin followed Madame Fournier to a door just underneath the stairs, which she flung open. Guin peeped in, but it was dark.

"Oh, sorry," said Madame Fournier, flipping on the lights.

Guin stepped in, followed by Polly.

It was a finished basement, of sorts, probably not permitted. But it was very nice. There was an open space with a ping pong table and a little room to one side with some workout equipment.

"And over here," announced Madame Fournier, walking to the other side of the space and opening another door, "is a little office with a half bath."

Guin poked her head in. The office was small, though certainly big enough for a desk and chair and a couple of filing cabinets. And there was a window, so it would get some natural light.

"This would be perfect for you!" said Polly.

Guin wasn't so sure. It was nice, but…

"And the only way to get down here is by going outside the house?"

"Yes," answered both real estate agents in unison.

Guin smiled.

"And there's a garage on the other side—and a door connecting the two," said Madame Fournier.

They left the downstairs area and walked around the building to the driveway.

"Did you want one more look around?" asked Polly.

"No, I'm good," said Guin.

"Well then, I'll just go lock up and put the keys back in the lock box," said Madame Fournier.

"Thanks for showing me the place," said Guin.

"My pleasure," Madame Fournier replied.

She then excused herself and headed back up the stairs.

"So?" asked Polly.

But Guin wasn't paying attention. She was too busy staring up at Madame Fournier and the lock box.

Guin said goodbye to Polly then drove over to the *San-Cap Sun-Times* office over on Periwinkle. When she got there, everyone was scurrying around.

"What's up?" Guin asked Mark, the copyeditor, who was going through some papers.

"We can't find a story," he explained. "Ah! Found it!"

He ran down the hall.

"Jasmine! I found it. I sent it over to you last Wednesday. Look for…"

He read the file name.

"I'm checking!" called Jasmine, the paper's head designer, who was in charge of laying out the print and online editions. "Ugh! I forgot to put it in the print file. My bad."

"You find that story?" boomed Ginny.

"Got it!" shouted Mark and Jasmine simultaneously.

"Good," said Ginny.

She came into the main room and spied Guin.

"You see the fun you're missing?"

Guin grinned. She had worked at a newspaper up in New England and knew all about the craziness behind getting each edition out.

"Is this a bad time? I can come back later in the week."

"Nah, you're here," said Ginny. "May as well come back. Everything was all set, except for that one hole."

Guin followed Ginny back to her office.

Ginny flopped into her chair.

"You okay?" asked Guin.

"Nothing that a cosmo wouldn't cure. So, whatcha got for me?"

Guin filled her in on the latest on the Swales story.

Ginny whistled.

"Sounds like you've got your work cut out for you. So O'Loughlin's been no help, as usual?"

Guin sighed.

"He says I'm on a need to know basis, and apparently he doesn't think I need to know that much."

"Well, you and Craig keep working on it. You think this thing will be wrapped up by next edition?"

"I hope so," said Guin.

"So, you got time to tackle a couple of other pieces?" Ginny asked her.

Guin knew better than to say no.

"Sure, what've you got? By the way, I just had lunch at Traders 2. It was good. I was thinking I could review it."

"Sure, why not? And speaking of restaurants, I want you to do a roundup of places in the area to have Thanksgiving."

"Just Sanibel and Captiva or including Fort Myers?"

"Whatever you think," said Ginny. "I just need copy by November 11th at the latest. You know the drill."

"Got it," said Guin.

"Speaking of Thanksgiving, you have plans?"

Guin sighed.

"My mother wants me to go to New York."

"So?" asked Ginny.

"I don't really want to go."

"Why not?"

Guin sighed again.

"I get it. Family. Say no more," said Ginny. "What about that cute beau of yours?"

"Ris?"

"You got some other one I don't know about?"

Guin's mind immediately flashed on the detective, but she quickly scrubbed the image and shook her head no.

"He invite you to his place for Thanksgiving?"

"He did. Except he celebrates it at his ex-wife's."

"Ah," said Ginny. "And you don't want to go."

"No, not really."

Guin suddenly felt sad.

"You can always join us orphans."

"Orphans?" Guin was confused.

Ginny chuckled.

"That's what we call ourselves. People with no family to go home to for Thanksgiving. We have a big pot luck. This year it's at my place. You're more than welcome to attend. You just have to bring something."

"That's very kind of you, Ginny."

"Well, the door's open. Let me know if you want to attend."

"I will," said Guin.

"Hey Ginny!" called a male voice.

"Coming!" called Ginny. "I've got to go."

Guin stood up.

"I'll see myself out."

She followed Ginny down the hall, towards the front door. She was about to call out goodbye, but she doubted anyone would pay attention. So she quietly let herself out.

CHAPTER 36

Guin stood in the parking lot outside the *San-Cap Sun-Times*, her back to her car, debating whether to call, email, or text Billy Simms.

"Just call him, Guin," she prodded herself.

She looked at the text Craig had sent her with Billy's phone number and typed it into her phone.

"William Simms," came a deep male voice.

"William, also known as Billy, Simms?" asked Guin.

For a second Guin thought maybe Craig had given her Billy's father's number.

"Yes. May I help you?"

"Yes, this is Guinivere Jones, with the *Sanibel-Captiva Sun-Times*. We met the other day at your grandparents' place."

There was a brief pause on the other end of the line.

"Is this about Veronica?"

"It is," replied Guin.

"I already spoke with your colleague, Mr. Jeffers, and the police. I have nothing more to say."

"I just have a couple more—"

"Was I not clear, Ms. Jones?" he said, cutting her off.

"Did you know Ms. Swales was pregnant?"

There was silence on the other end of the line.

Guin waited several seconds.

"Mr. Simms? Are you still there?"

"Ronnie was pregnant?" came his voice, so soft Guin could hardly hear it.

"You didn't know?"

Either Billy Simms was a very good actor, or he hadn't known. Though Guin found it surprising that the detective still hadn't told him. And he would no doubt be pissed at her for spilling the beans.

"No," said Billy, very softly.

Guin waited a few seconds, to see if he would say more.

"How far along was she?" he finally asked.

"I don't know," said Guin.

"Are you sure she was pregnant? Absolutely positive?" asked Billy.

Guin felt bad for the young man.

"It was in the autopsy report," she told him. Which wasn't a lie.

"She told me she was on the pill," Billy said, though he spoke it more to himself.

Guin wanted to explain to Billy that women can still get pregnant even on the pill and that it was possible Ronnie had missed a day or stopped taking the pill. But she didn't say any of those things.

"I know this must be very hard for you, Mr. Simms. But if you could spare me just a few minutes in person. I just have a few questions…"

She held her breath.

Billy sighed.

"Fine. Meet me over at the Bailey Tract. I need to get some air."

"What time?"

"Fifteen minutes? Not like I'm going to get any more work done today."

"That's fine," said Guin. "I'll see you there."

She ended the call and put her phone in her bag.

Guin arrived a few minutes later at the Bailey Tract, part of the wildlife refuge. There were a couple of cars parked in the lot. She locked the Mini and walked to the entrance. She immediately spied Billy—he was hard to miss—a few feet away, looking out at some trees in the distance.

"Mr. Simms?" Guin called, though she knew it was him.

He turned toward her.

"Ms. Jones."

Guin smiled and held out her hand, but Billy didn't take it.

"Let's walk," he said.

Billy turned and headed down the path. Guin had to practically jog to keep up with him.

"I can't believe Ronnie was pregnant and didn't tell me," he said, not looking at her.

"She didn't say anything to you, not even hint?"

"No. Though…"

Guin waited several seconds. Billy sighed.

"She did call me that Friday. Said she had something important to tell me. She wanted to get together in person, but I told her I was going away for a few days—I was meeting some clients up in Orlando—and we could talk when I got back."

He paused.

"She got kind of annoyed and said it was really important, so I told her to meet me over at my grandparents' place at three. I had promised them I would make sure everything was okay before I left town."

"And?" asked Guin.

"And she didn't show. I waited until almost three-thirty

and texted her, but she didn't reply. So I left. Figured she had changed her mind. Ronnie could be a bit mercurial."

"And you didn't hear from her again?"

"No," said Billy. "I didn't hear about what happened to her until I got back."

"And when was the last time you actually saw Ronnie?" Guin asked.

"We had had dinner the weekend before she…"

He stopped and ran a hand through his wavy brown hair, not finishing the sentence.

"I thought that you and Ronnie had broken up."

Billy looked down at Guin.

"Who told you that?"

"Her housemate, Gillian."

Billy smiled. It was not a friendly smile.

"Gill would have liked that."

"So, it wasn't true? Some of Ronnie's friends were under the impression you two were taking a break."

Billy sighed.

"That's what we wanted people to believe, so my parents would stop hassling me."

"They didn't like Ronnie."

"They were okay with her, just not for their only son. Ronnie was a bit of a free spirit. They thought I should be with someone more serious, someone more like them."

"Ah," said Guin.

"So I asked Ronnie if we could cool things for a bit, though I said we could still see each other on the QT."

"And how did she react to that?"

Billy made a face.

"She wasn't too thrilled."

I'll bet, thought Guin.

"But you continued to see each other?"

"We did."

"So you and Gillian…?"

"Are just friends," replied Billy.

"Well, she seems to be under the impression the two of you are dating. And you were spotted having dinner together the other night."

Billy let out a bark of a laugh and shook his head.

"Sanibel really is a small town. Amazing what people choose to believe."

He shook his head again.

"Look, I like Gillian. We've known each other since college. But dating? No."

He looked at Guin, who continued to listen.

"I was in love with Ronnie, Ms. Jones. And Gill knew that."

"But you did go out with her, Gillian, a few times."

Billy ran a hand through his hair.

"Sure, we had dinner a couple of times, and, okay, maybe fooled around a bit, but it was nothing serious."

Guin didn't think Gillian saw it that way, but again she didn't say anything.

"And did Ronnie know about you and Gillian?"

Billy shrugged.

"Maybe. But like I said, Gillian and I were just friends."

Guin was skeptical.

"And was Ronnie seeing anyone else?" she asked.

Billy made a face.

"I heard she was seeing an older man," Guin continued.

Guin watched Billy for any signs. He seemed to be struggling with something.

"Do you think she was trying to make you jealous?"

Billy sighed.

"She was really pissed off when I suggested we take a break. But I didn't think she'd go and actually start seeing someone else. I mean, I told her we could still see other, just on the sly. Then Gill told me she was seeing this guy."

"Whose initials were J. L.," Guin said, hoping to get a reaction out of Billy.

"I didn't know his name. For all I knew, Gillian was making it up, to get me to drop Ronnie."

"Did you confront Ronnie?"

"No. What was I going to say, 'Sorry I can't date you, but I don't want you to see anyone else?'"

He had a point, though looking at and listening to him Guin was pretty sure that was exactly what he had wanted, even if he never said it.

"So you have no idea who she was seeing?" Guin asked again.

"No. I didn't want her to think I was jealous."

"Though you were."

Billy ran a hand through his hair again.

"Yes, sort of. But what was I supposed to do?"

"Did you ever take Ronnie to your grandparents' place, the one I saw you at?"

"We had dinner there a few times. My grandparents got a kick out of her."

Unlike your parents, Guin wanted to say.

"Did you give Ronnie a heart-shaped locket?"

Billy stopped and looked at Guin.

"Yes, for graduation. Why?"

"It was found at your grandparents' place, by the bed in the master bedroom."

Billy's cheeks turned a slightly reddish hue.

"I'd appreciate you not mentioning that to anyone."

"No worries," said Guin. "Though the police know."

Billy ran a hand through his hair and started walking again.

"So, any idea who killed her?" asked Guin, trying to keep up with him.

He stopped and stared down at her.

"You don't think I did it, do you? No way. I loved Ronnie! I would never hurt her. Even when she pissed me off. Ask anyone."

"What about Gillian?"

"Gillian?" asked Billy, confused.

"Was she jealous enough to want Ronnie out of the way?"

"I've known some psycho chicks," said Billy. "But I don't think Gill is one of them."

"I heard the two of them had gotten into a big fight the Thursday before Ronnie died."

"Probably just girl stuff," said Billy, dismissing it.

Guin felt her eyes start to roll but stopped them.

"You ever bring Gillian over to your grandparents' place, when they weren't there?"

Billy looked distinctly uncomfortable.

They had stopped walking and Guin realized they were back at the beginning of the trail.

"I should get going," said Billy.

Guin dug into her bag and pulled out her card case.

"Here," she said, handing him a card. "If you think of anything, regarding Ronnie or who she may have been seeing, call, text, or email me."

He silently took her card.

"One more thing," she said. "Any idea what happened to your friend, Jake Longley?"

"No," said Billy. "I just hope he's okay."

"Me too," said Guin. "Well, thank you for your time, Mr. Simms." She didn't even bother to extend her hand. "Call or message me any time. I'm always looking for a good story, particularly about companies giving back. And I hear Island Trust does a lot of good work."

"Sure," he said, distractedly.

She turned and walked back to her car. She could be wrong, but she had a feeling Billy was not the killer.

CHAPTER 37

Guin drove home and raced up the stairs to her condo. She was greeted by the cats, who chided her for not leaving them enough food. Or that was how Guin interpreted their pitiful meows.

"Sorry team, but I'm not feeding you until later," she said.

Fauna immediately protested.

"Too bad," said Guin, placing her bag on the counter and extracting her phone.

Flora rubbed up against Guin's legs. Guin leaned over and stroked her.

"Sorry, got to go make some calls," she announced a minute later, straightening up.

She walked to the lanai, holding her phone, and stared out at the golf course, which had more birds than golfers on it at present. She stood there for several minutes, just admiring the view. Later on she would have a view of the sun setting.

"Back to work," she said aloud.

She entered the number for the Sanibel Police Department, which she had long ago memorized, only to find that Detective O'Loughlin had just left for the day. The woman asked if she wanted to leave a message for the detective, but Guin declined. As soon as she ended the call she tried his cell phone. His voicemail picked up.

"This is Ms. Jones. Please call me when you get this. I just met with Billy Simms."

She ended the call and phoned Craig.

"What's up?" he asked.

"I just met with Billy Simms."

"And?"

"He claims he had no idea Ronnie was pregnant."

"You believe him?" asked Craig.

"I don't know. He seemed pretty surprised when I told him. Either he's a really good actor or he didn't know."

"Hmm…" said Craig.

"He also swears he didn't kill her."

"You asked him?"

"I did."

"That was either very brave or very stupid," said Craig.

"What was he going to do, pull a gun on me in the Bailey Tract?"

"You'd be surprised what people do when cornered."

Guin was about to reply that she could handle herself, but she knew Craig had seen more bad stuff go down in Chicago than she ever had covering business up in Connecticut.

"I also asked him if he had any idea who might want to harm Ronnie."

"And?"

"He said he had no idea."

"What about the housemate, Gillian, the one Jimbo saw arguing with Ronnie right before she died?"

"Billy said they were just friends, though I got the distinct impression from Gillian she didn't feel the same way."

"You think she was jealous of Ronnie?"

"Definitely," said Guin.

"Enough to want to her out of the way?" asked Craig.

"You mean kill her? I can't really imagine it coming to that."

"Jealousy can be a nasty thing. They don't call it the green-eyed monster for no reason."

"Speaking of jealousy, Billy thinks Ronnie was trying to make him jealous."

"With J. L.?"

"Yes."

"He have any idea who J. L. is?"

"No."

"So we're basically not a lot closer to figuring out who killed the girl."

Guin sighed. Her head hurt. Solving mysteries always seemed so much easier in books.

"So, what next?" asked Craig.

"I want you to speak with Billy's parents."

"Already arranged an appointment to meet with them."

"When?"

"Tomorrow morning at eight-thirty."

"Good. Ask them, as diplomatically as possible, if they knew about Ronnie being pregnant."

"Do we even know for sure if the baby was Billy's?" asked Craig.

"Even though they had supposedly broken up at the end of the summer, they were still seeing each other on the sly," Guin told him. So while it's possible the baby could have belonged to the mystery man, chances are the baby was Billy's. Did your buddy in the medical examiner's office say how far gone she was?"

"No, but I got the impression not far."

"Can you follow up with him?"

"It's a bit sensitive."

"Do what you can."

They chatted for a couple more minutes, Craig promising to call Guin after he had interviewed the Simmses, then they ended the call.

Guin glanced at her phone, hoping there was a text or voicemail from the detective. She had heard some kind of message coming in while she was speaking to Craig but didn't want to interrupt their conversation.

It was a text from her brother Lance.

Instead of texting him, she called.

He picked up after just two rings.

"Hey sis. What's up?"

"You texted me."

"I did. I haven't heard from you in days and was getting concerned."

"Sorry. I've been kind of busy."

"Still working on that case you told me about?"

"Yeah."

"You figure out who done it?"

"Not yet," said Guin, sighing.

"Well, I have total confidence you will catch the killer. I bet Colonel Mustard did it in the library with the rope."

"That's Clue, you idiot." Though Guin was smiling as she said it.

"I knew I saw it somewhere. So, you coming home for Thanksgiving?"

"Sanibel is my home now."

"You know what I meant."

Guin sighed.

"So did mom tell you to call me?"

"Puh-lease. Don't give her that much credit. Though it's all she talks about. 'Tell your sister she'll break her mother's heart if she doesn't come home this Thanksgiving,'" he said, imitating his mother's voice.

Guin rolled her eyes.

"So, you coming? You don't have to stay with her, you know. You can bunk with us. Owen would love to have you here."

Guin smiled. It had been ages since she had been to Lance and Owen's place. It could be fun.

"I can hear those wheels spinning…"

"I'll think about it."

"Don't think too long. Mom is driving me nuts—and you know how expensive airfare can be this time of year."

"Mom volunteered to pay."

"Well then, what the heck are you waiting for?! Come on down—or up. You know what I mean."

At that moment, going to New York City for Thanksgiving seemed like not so bad an idea.

"I'll think about it, Lance."

Lance sighed.

"Whatever. So, what else is new with you?"

Guin told him about what she had been working on and her conversation with Billy.

"I bet he did it."

"How come?" asked Guin.

"I just don't trust football players."

"He doesn't play football anymore. He works at his parents' financial services business."

"Even worse!"

"You would make a terrible journalist. No objectivity."

"That is why I am in advertising, darling."

Guin smiled.

"I need to go. Is there anything else big brother can help you with?"

"No. Besides, you're the one who texted me. Any news? Mom said you were opening an office in San Francisco."

"Oh that. Fingers crossed. It's not a done deal yet, but…. Look, I've got to run. Got a big meeting. Talk more this weekend?"

"Sure," said Guin. "Ris is away."

"Oh? And where is that big, hunky dreamboat of yours off

to now? Diving with dolphins? Scuba diving in the Seychelles for seashells?"

Guin laughed.

"No. He's competing in the Florida Ironman this weekend, up in Panama City."

"How fun!" said Lance. "Though you wouldn't catch me running and swimming and biking for, like, a hundred miles."

"Nor me," said Guin.

"Well, I'd love to chat some more, Guinivere, but I really must go."

"Okay," said Guin. "Give my love to Owen."

"Will do."

They ended the call and Guin walked into her bedroom/office. She didn't have plans for the evening, so she figured she might as well get some work done. She sat down at her computer and began to type.

It was nearly eight o'clock when she finally looked at the clock. Wow, she thought. Where did the time go? Her stomach grumbled. Right, food. Frankly, she was surprised the cats had not bothered her, though Fauna had passed out in her lap over an hour before, and Flora was still asleep on the bed. She smiled.

"Sorry, pussycat," she said, placing Fauna on the floor. The cat looked up at Guin accusingly.

Guin took her phone out of the drawer she kept it in when she was working. There were several messages.

Her stomach growled again. Okay, first food, then messages.

She opened the refrigerator and looked inside.

"May as well make myself an omelet," she said aloud, taking in what she had, though she was not excited about the prospect. If only there was a pizza place or a Chinese restaurant or an Indian place close by that delivered or did takeout. She sighed. It was one of the things she missed about New York City (though she hadn't lived there in years). You could order in any kind of food you could think of, and it would be delivered to your door in minutes. Even when she lived in Connecticut you could have pizza or Chinese food delivered. But not on Sanibel. Oh well.

She would just have to make do with an omelet.

She grabbed the carton of eggs and cracked two into a bowl. At the sound, Fauna came running into the kitchen.

"Hold your horses," said Guin. "I'll give you the bowl when I'm done."

Fauna meowed and pawed Guin's leg, but Guin ignored her. She took out some vegetables and chopped them up. Then she grabbed a couple of slices of multigrain bread out of the freezer and put them in the toaster oven. Finally she placed the carrots, pepper, zucchini, and onion in a pan with a little olive oil and butter and sautéed everything, adding the eggs at the last minute. Then she slid the finished omelet onto a plate.

Suddenly she was reminded of the detective. When she had been trying to secure a confession from Anthony Mandelli in the Matenopoulos murder case, and had drunk too much in the process, and the detective rescued her (though, she told herself, she really hadn't needed his help), he had made her an omelet very much like this one. She smiled at the thought, then frowned. She needed to stop thinking about the detective, at least that way.

She poured herself a big glass of water and took her omelet and toast to the dining table, along with her phone, though she forced herself not to look at it until she had had a few bites of omelet. Her omelet and toast half eaten, she picked up her phone and checked for messages. Amazingly, there was a text from the detective. Guin nearly choked.

She quickly opened it. It read, "You rang?"

"That's it?" said Guin, staring at her phone. She sighed. Well, at least he responded. That was something.

Guin hastily ate another bite of omelet and toast. Then she called the detective.

The phone rang several times, and Guin was preparing to leave a voicemail message when he picked up.

"Isn't it a bit late, or is this a social call?"

Guin felt herself starting to blush but forced herself to focus.

"I know you think I'm sticking my nose in where it doesn't belong, but it's my job to cover the news on this island, and that means finding out why a twentysomething young woman with everything to live for was strangled in her ex-boyfriend's grandparents' house. And I could really use your help here and…"

"What makes you think she was strangled at the grandparents' house?" interrupted the detective.

Was he kidding? Did he forget who found the body?

"Hello? I was the one who found her, or had you forgotten?"

"I didn't forget," he calmly replied. "But how do you know she was killed at the house?"

Guin was about to say something but stopped. She did not, in fact, know if Veronica had been killed at the Simms house. She had just assumed she had. But if she hadn't been killed there, where had she been killed, and why dump her body there?

As if reading Guin's mind, the detective continued.

"According to the report from the medical examiner's office, chances are she was already dead when her body was placed at the scene."

Guin cast her mind back to Ronnie lying on the floor. Now that she thought about it, the place did seem awfully tidy for a murder scene.

"So where was she killed?"

Guin waited for the detective to say something, but he did not reply.

"Either you know and are not telling me, or you don't know."

Again, Guin waited. And again the detective did not reply. Guin sighed.

"Did you tell Billy Simms about Ronnie being pregnant?"

"Not yet."

"Why on earth not?" asked Guin, astonished.

"We had our reasons," he replied.

Guin's mind suddenly flashed on Billy's parents. Was it possible they had convinced the detective not to say anything to their son? That is, assuming they knew or had found out. After all, they were very prominent members of Sanibel society and were known for their very generous charitable contributions and support of the local police and fire departments and many local charities. But Guin couldn't imagine the detective agreeing to withhold evidence, no matter where the request came from. But she had to find out.

"Did someone order you not to say anything to Billy?" Guin asked.

"No one tells me how to do my job, Ms. Jones. Except for you."

Guin couldn't see the detective's face, but she would lay odds that he was smirking. She made a face.

"Ha ha. Very funny."

"I thought so," replied the detective.

He seemed to be in a good mood. Why not take advantage? Guin thought.

"So, you have anything else to share with me?"

"You free Saturday morning?"

Huh? Guin wasn't expecting that.

"Hello? You there?"

"Sorry," said Guin, refocusing. "I think so. Why?"

"I'm going out fishing with Captain Al. One of the guys I usually go with just cancelled, and I thought maybe you'd like to join us."

"Why didn't you ask one of your other fishy friends?"

"Because I'm asking you," replied the detective.

Guin was about to say, "but you know I'm not into fishing," but she stopped herself. Here was her opportunity to get into the detective's good graces, and maybe do a little networking. Was she really going to say no?

"Sure. Why not? Though you know I know next to nothing about fishing."

"We'll teach you. It'll be fun."

Guin wasn't so sure about that.

"What time?"

"Seven at Al's boat. Is that a problem? I know how you ladies like your beauty sleep."

Guin rolled her eyes.

"Nope, no problem at all," she said, forcing a smile, even though she knew the detective couldn't see her face.

If the detective made comments like that to his now ex-wife back in the day, no wonder she left him.

"I'm usually up by six-thirty and Al's boat is less than ten minutes from here."

"What about your boyfriend?"

"What about him?"

Guin had picked up on the detective's slight emphasis on the last word. Could it be he was jealous? Guin found herself smiling, then immediately wiped the stupid grin off her face. The detective was not the type to be jealous, and she shouldn't even be thinking that way about him.

"He's heading out of town on Friday, driving up to Panama City to compete in the Ironman."

"Impressive."

"I think so."

There was a pause.

"I'll let you go now," said Guin.

"How very considerate of you," replied the detective.

"Oh, one more thing."

"Yes?"

"Any word about Jake Longley?"

"No," said the detective. "At least I haven't heard anything. You may want to check with the Lee County Sheriff's Office. They're handling the case."

"Well, at least no one's found a body. That means he could still be alive."

"Or someone hid it," said the detective.

Way to be positive, thought Guin.

"Well, goodnight, detective."

"Goodnight, Ms. Jones."

CHAPTER 38

Guin woke up the next morning feeling surprisingly refreshed. She checked the clock next to the bed. It was 6:45. Too early to call anyone, but not too early to go for a beach walk, though the sun wouldn't be up for at least another half hour.

She turned on her phone and headed to the bathroom as it booted up. She checked the weather a few minutes later. Looked like a perfect beach day. She loved that she could go to the beach in November—and didn't have to put on a down jacket.

She threw on a pair of shorts and a t-shirt and headed to the kitchen, the cats trotting after her. She gave them some food and water, then poured herself a glass of water while she was at it. A few minutes later, beach bag and keys in hand, she was out the door.

She drove down Sanibel-Captiva Road to Rabbit Road. Then she turned right and right again, onto West Gulf Drive, and parked at Beach Access #4.

The sun was just beginning to rise and Guin watched as the sky started to lighten and glow pink and mauve. She loved dawn. She looked out at the ocean and said her silent prayer to the god of the sea to send some shells her way. Then she headed off down the beach.

The beach was quiet. Just a couple of people walking

their dogs and a few beachcombers. Guin walked a little way then noticed the man ahead of her, wearing a bright blue Shell Ambassador t-shirt. She squinted. Could it be? It was. Guin smiled and jogged to catch up with him.

"Lenny!" she called.

Lenny stopped and turned around. When he saw Guin, he smiled.

"You didn't have to run. Wasn't like I was moving very fast."

"I just didn't want to miss you."

"Well, you got me. Now what are you going to do with me?"

He grinned.

"Throw you back in the sea!"

"You just try, young lady."

Guin laughed.

"It's good to see you, Lenny. You find anything good?"

"Nah. With all the red tide we've been having, it's been slim pickings."

"I hear you, though I've found a few things."

"Well, maybe you'll bring me some luck."

They walked together, looking down at the sand in search of shells, picking up and discarding ones that didn't meet their high standards. (They both had so many shells they refused to take broken ones or any more Florida fighting conchs or cockles.)

"So, what's new with you, kid? Did Annie ever get back to you?"

"No, but that's okay," Guin lied. "She's probably just real busy."

Lenny made a face.

"I'll have another talk with her. I told her it was important."

"Well, she turned over the list to the police. Maybe the

detective will share it with me," though Guin had pretty much given up hope of that happening. "Has she mentioned anything about the place?"

Guin was curious to know if finding a dead body had turned prospective buyers off.

"We haven't talked about it. Work talk is off limits at bridge."

"Ah," said Guin.

"So, how are you and the marine biologist?"

"Okay."

"Just 'okay'?" Lenny asked, stopping and looking at Guin.

"Isn't 'okay' okay?" Guin replied.

"You two should be madly in love! You're young, good looking… What's wrong?"

"Why do you think something's wrong?" asked Guin, slightly irritated.

"Fine, if you don't want to discuss it with your Uncle Lenny…"

"You're not my uncle," though Guin smiled as she said it. She would love to have had Lenny as her uncle. "And really, Len, everything is fine between me and Ris."

"Then what are you doing out shelling at seven o'clock in the morning with me? You should be in bed!"

Guin felt herself blushing.

"It's not like we spend every minute together. Besides, he's been training for that Ironman up in Panama City this weekend."

"You going?"

"No, I've got work to do, and I'd barely see him."

Lenny made a face.

"Can we change the subject, please?" Guin asked.

"Fine. So have you figured out who killed that girl?"

"Not yet," said Guin.

"But you got your suspicions?"

"I do, but…"

She looked out at the sea. She wished she did know. Just one more piece of the puzzle and she felt for sure she'd be able to figure it out.

"Well, keep me posted, and let me know if there's anything I can do."

"Thanks Len," she said. "Now, can we focus on finding some shells?"

Lenny smiled.

"Sure, kid, sure."

They spent the next several minutes in companionable silence, as they made their way down the beach along West Gulf Drive, heading west, until Lenny happened upon a father and daughter looking for shells. Even though Shell Ambassadors were not supposed to speak until spoken to, Lenny couldn't help striking up a conversation with the pair, but they didn't seem to mind. Guin smiled. It was moments like this Lenny lived for. And the little girl seemed very excited when Lenny gave her a shiny lettered olive shell he had found, along with a pretty pink tellin.

Guin arrived back at the condo a little after nine-thirty.

"Coffee!" she announced, walking quickly toward the kitchen. "I need coffee!" She also needed food.

A few minutes later she was seated at her dining table, drinking her mug of java and spooning granola mixed with yogurt and fresh fruit into her mouth as she checked her messages on her phone.

Her mother had forwarded her an email for a special on airfare to New York City from Fort Myers that was good for two days only. Would Guin please let her know if she should buy her a ticket? Guin sighed.

"Fine mom. You win," she said aloud.

She emailed her mother a one-word reply: "Sure."

A few minutes later, her phone rang. It was her mother.

"Oh Guinivere! I'm so happy you'll be coming home! Everyone will be so excited to see you!"

"Everyone? Who's everyone?" asked Guin, starting to feel anxious.

"Oh, you know, me and Philip, and Lancelot and Owen, and… just a few of our close friends. So, you okay flying home that Monday evening and then flying back to Sanibel that Saturday? Of course, you're welcome to stay as long as you like, I just—"

"That's fine, Mother," Guin interrupted. "Go ahead and book the flights. Just get me aisle seats if you can and try not to book me on that flight that gets in around midnight."

"Will do. Oh, I'm so happy you will be home with us."

"Actually," said Guin, "I was thinking of staying with Lance and Owen, at least part of the time."

Silence.

"Mom, you there?"

"I'm still here," she said, sighing audibly. "Stay where you like. At least let me take you shopping while you're home."

"I'm not twelve, mom. I don't need you to buy me clothes."

"I know you are not twelve. I just thought it would be fun to have a girls' day out. It's been so long."

"Fine, mom. Whatever. Look, I've got to go. Send me the e-ticket once you've purchased it."

"I will! Bye dear. See you soon!"

"Bye mom."

Guin ended the call. What had she just agreed to?

Guin was busy at her desk, doing research for her Thanksgiving roundup, when she heard her phone buzzing.

She opened the drawer and pulled it out. It was Craig.

"Hello?" she said, hoping the call hadn't gone into voicemail.

"Hey, am I catching you at a bad time?"

"No," said Guin. "You meet with Mr. and Mrs. Simms?"

"I did."

"And?"

"Let's just say they weren't terribly fond of the late Veronica Swales."

"Do tell."

"Not much to tell. They didn't think the young woman was good enough for their only son. Pretty typical."

Guin rolled her eyes.

"Did they give a reason for their disapproval?"

"Does it matter?"

"Not really. Just curious. They have a daughter, yes?"

"Yes. She's five years older than Billy and just had her first kid."

"Does she work in the business?"

"She did, until she had William Simms III. Cute kid."

"They showed you photos?"

"There were photos all over their office. Kinda hard to miss. Good-looking family."

"Getting back to Veronica, did they know she was pregnant?"

"They claim they didn't, though they didn't seem surprised."

"Hmm…" said Guin. "So, do you think either of them could have killed Ronnie, or maybe hired someone to kill her?"

"I don't think either one of them would do the deed themselves. And if they hired someone it's highly unlikely they would have told him to leave the body at Mr. Simms's parents' place."

"Good point," said Guin.

She sighed.

"So, where does that leave us?"

"You get any more information out of the detective?"

"Not really," Guin said. "And I'm still waiting for that list of everyone who accessed the Simms place that weekend. You have any ideas?"

"I have a feeling that whoever did it was someone she knew, intimately."

"Agreed," said Guin. "And the person knew about Billy's grandparents' place being vacant—and had access to it."

As Guin said it, her mind flashed on the photo she had taken from Joey's Custard, of Ronnie with Billy and Jake. Jake had dated Ronnie in college and was best friends with Billy. And he had disappeared not long after Ronnie's body was found. Could he have killed her?

Suddenly, an image of Gillian popped into her head. Gillian thought she and Billy were soulmates, but Billy was still in love with Ronnie. Ronnie being pregnant with Billy's baby would definitely ruin her shot at getting with Billy. And she was big and strong enough to do her petite housemate some serious harm.

"What are you thinking?" Craig asked, interrupting Guin's stream of thought.

"Oh, sorry. I was thinking about Ronnie's housemate, Gillian. She was in love with Billy, and could have easily overpowered Ronnie, though I can't see her intentionally killing her housemate. And I still haven't ruled Billy and Jake out. Speaking of Billy, were you able to verify his whereabouts that weekend?"

"I was, to a certain degree."

"And?"

"He checked into his hotel late Saturday night."

"So he could have done it," said Guin. She had been

going back and forth on Billy.

"But he had dinner beforehand with a bunch of his college buddies," Craig continued. "So he would have had to have left Sanibel by four."

Guin frowned.

"They weren't just covering for him?"

"Doubtful. He paid for dinner on his credit card."

Guin sighed.

"That still leaves Jake and Gillian."

"And the baker," said Craig. "Don't forget, they found flour on Veronica's body."

"Yes, but she worked in a bakery, so…"

"Still. I'd go back and ask the baker and his wife what they were doing that evening," said Craig.

"Fine," said Guin. "I'll arrange a time to go back over there."

"You want me to go with you? I don't like the idea of you questioning them by yourself."

"You think they're going to throw me in the oven?"

"Hey, you can never be too careful."

"I'll be fine, Craig."

"Just do me a favor and let me know when you go over there, just in case."

"Fine," said Guin. "When I get off the phone with you I'll call over there and find out when Jean-Luc has a minute. Then I'll send you a text. Okay?"

"Okay," said Craig.

"Oh, and you'll never guess what I'm doing this Saturday morning."

"What?"

"I'm going fishing!"

"I'm sorry. I think we have a bad connection. I thought I heard you say you were going fishing this weekend."

"Ha ha. Very funny."

"So, what brought on this sudden urge to go fishing? I thought you hated fishing."

"I never said I hated fishing."

"Uh-huh," said Craig.

"The detective invited me to go. One of his foursome cancelled, and he wanted to know if I was available. I guess none of his other buddies could go."

"Uh-huh," said Craig.

"What does that mean?" asked Guin, becoming annoyed.

"Nothing. So, who you going out with?"

"Captain Al."

"Well, I hope you have a good time."

"Me too. So, you have plans for the weekend?"

"Just the usual: poker game Friday night. Then going to do some fishing. And Betty and I are going to a concert over in Fort Myers Saturday night."

"That sounds nice," said Guin. "Oh, I'm almost forgot. Any news about Jake Longley?"

"As far as I know there's still no sign of him."

"I hope he's okay. Well, I should get going."

"Me too," said Craig. "Just Guin?"

"Yes?"

"Be careful."

"Aren't I always?"

Craig didn't respond.

They said goodbye and ended the call. Guin then called over to the bakery.

"Bonjour, Jean-Luc's!" came a cheery, distinctly non-French female voice.

"Bonjour," said Guin. "Is Jean-Luc there?"

"He's in back. Who should I say is calling?"

"Tell him Guinivere Jones."

"That's an unusual name. Is it English?" the woman asked.

"It is," replied Guin, praying the woman wouldn't ask her more questions.

"I'll just go see if Monsieur Fournier is available," said the woman, mispronouncing his name.

Guin sighed and waited.

A couple minutes later the woman came back on the line.

"I'm sorry, he's busy right now. Can he phone you later?"

"That's fine," said Guin.

She gave the woman her number. Then they said goodbye and hung up.

CHAPTER 39

Jean-Luc phoned her back a couple of hours later. Guin told him she was working on an article for Thanksgiving, which wasn't a lie, and asked if he had a few minutes to chat with her, in person. He suggested she stop by the bakery the following afternoon, after they had closed. Guin said that would be fine. The bakery was on the way to Ris's place. She would interview Jean-Luc, albeit about Veronica and Jake, not Thanksgiving, then continue on to Fort Myers Beach. She sent Craig a text, letting him know she'd be meeting Jean-Luc at the bakery the next day around four. Then she went back to working on her articles.

She took a break a little after six, retrieving her phone from the drawer and checking her messages.

Craig had sent her a text with the thumbs up emoji. She smiled.

There was also a text from her brother.

"I hear you'll be joining us for Turkey Day! You need a place to crash?"

"Can I stay with you and Owen, at least part of the time?" she replied.

"Of course!" came the response, a few seconds later.

"Thx," Guin wrote back. "We can discuss later."

"NP," replied Lance, followed by several x's and o's.

Guin smiled. It would be fun to hang out with him and

Owen. If she could just get through the actual day without wanting to throttle her mother.

Speaking of throttling, her mind immediately flashed on Veronica Swales. She shivered. While she might get annoyed with her mother, she would never actually strangle her, though…

She checked her other messages. There were a couple from Shelly, asking if Guin wanted to drive to Naples with her that Sunday.

"Sure," Guin wrote her back.

There was also a message from Ris.

"Thinking of you," he had written, followed by the emoji blowing a kiss.

Guin smiled and sent the same emoji back to him. She would miss him this weekend. She had thought for a minute about going with him up to Panama City, but the idea of spending all day in the car, then sitting around waiting for him to complete the Ironman, then hanging out with a zombie for the next 24 hours, then having to drive eight hours back to Sanibel, sounded like a weekend in hell.

As she was staring out at the trees, her phone started ringing. She glanced down but didn't recognize the number. Normally, she would have let it ring, but for some reason she answered.

"Guin Jones," she said, using her professional voice.

"Ms. Jones?"

"Speaking."

"It's Jake."

At first it didn't click.

"Jake Longley," the male voice continued.

"Oh my God! Jake! Are you okay? Where are you?"

"I'd rather not say."

"Are you okay?"

"I'll live."

"What happened to you?"

"Look, can we meet someplace?"

"Sure. Where? When?"

"You busy right now?"

Guin looked around. The cats were both asleep on her bed, as usual.

"Nope."

"Can you meet me at the Point Ybel Brewing Company?"

"Is that on the island?"

"No, it's in Fort Myers, right by Love Boat Ice Cream, on San Carlos Boulevard."

"Ah," said Guin. Everyone in the area knew about Love Boat, which also had an outpost on the island, over in Jerry's Plaza.

"What time?"

"How soon can you get there?"

Guin typed "Point Ybel Brewing" into her browser.

"Give me an hour. Will that work?"

"That's fine. See you in around an hour."

"Have you spoken with the police? They've been looking all over for you."

"No, not yet. I've been laying low."

Guin was about to ask another question but he interrupted her.

"Look, I've got to go. I'll see you at Point Ybel in an hour."

"Okay," Guin began, but he had already hung up.

Guin wasn't sure what to do. She paced around the bedroom, the cats eyeing her. Should she tell the detective Jake was okay? Call Craig?

"What would you do?" she asked her felines.

Fauna yawned.

"You're no help," Guin said, continuing to pace. As she did, her phone buzzed. She looked down at it. There was a new email. She swiped to see who it was from. Well, what do you know? It was from Ann Campbell. That was unexpected. Maybe she and Lenny were playing bridge tonight and he had mentioned the list again?

Guin went over to her computer and viewed the email on her monitor. There was no message, just an attachment. She double clicked to open it. It was a spreadsheet listing phone numbers in one column and then the date and time next to them. The spreadsheet wasn't labeled, but Guin assumed it must be the list of people who had accessed the lock box at the Simms house, which had one of those new lock boxes you accessed with an app on your phone.

Thank you, Lenny!

She wanted to examine the document, to see if she recognized any of the numbers, but she really needed to go, now, if she was to be on time to meet Jake at the brewery. And she needed to change, though she wasn't sure what appropriate brewery attire was.

She hurried over to her walk-in closet and threw on a pair of jeans and a nice top. Then she scooted into the bathroom and ran a comb through her hair and put on some lip gloss.

"Good enough," she said, examining her reflection.

She grabbed her bag and her keys and hurried to the front door, the cats following after her.

Fauna blocked her path and started to meow.

"Right, food."

Guin turned and headed into the kitchen. She grabbed the bag of cat food from the pantry and poured some kibble into their bowls.

"You happy now?" she asked the cats. Fauna glared up at her, then began to eat.

Guin sighed.

"I'll be back in a little while," she called from the front hall. "Please don't puke on anything while I'm gone!"

She ran down the stairs, opened the garage, and got in her Mini. She was about to pull out when she decided to give Craig a quick call.

"Everything okay?" he asked.

"I just got a call from Jake Longley."

"Is he okay?"

"I'm about to find out. I'm meeting him over at the Point Ybel Brewing Company in Fort Myers."

"You sure that's wise? You want me to meet you over there?"

"No. I'll be fine. And he told me to come alone. But thank you."

"I could sit at the other end of the bar. No one would know."

Guin smiled.

"Thanks, Craig, but really, I'll be fine. However, I do have something I could use your help with."

"Shoot."

"I'm going to forward you an email I just received from Ann Campbell. I'm pretty sure it's the list of phones that accessed the lock box over at the Simms place."

"I'll get right on it."

"Thanks. Okay, I've got to go. I'll check in with you later."

She ended the call and forwarded Ann's email. Then she started the car. She looked at the time. Ugh. She just hoped there wouldn't be too much traffic getting to the Causeway.

Guin arrived at the Point Ybel Brewing Company a little before seven-thirty. The place was dimly lit, and there was a good crowd. She just hoped she'd be able to find Jake. She made her way to the bar and got the attention of one of the bartenders, a friendly looking bear of man with a beard whose arms were covered in tattoos.

"Excuse me," she said, glancing around. "I'm looking for someone."

"Aren't we all. How can I help you?"

"Well, he's a guy, in his early twenties, has red hair, about medium height…"

She glanced around.

"You looking for Jake?"

It was another bartender, a woman around Jake's age, who had come over upon hearing Guin's description.

"Yes. Do you know where I can find him?" asked Guin.

"You Guin Jones?" asked the female bartender.

"That's me."

"Okay, come with me."

Guin looked over at the other bartender, who winked at her. Then she turned and followed his colleague to the other end of the bar. Seated all the way in the corner, nursing a beer, his head down, was Jake.

"Your friend's here," said the female barkeep.

"Thanks, Jo. You're the best," he said, looking up slightly.

Jo placed a hand on Jake's shoulder.

"Let me know if you need anything."

He smiled up at her and Guin could see his face. There were fading bruises everywhere. She sat down next to him.

"Who did that?"

"I'd love to know."

Guin waited for Jake to explain.

"I was working late over at the bakery Friday. I got in my car to head home, when just as I was getting on the Causeway, it started to act up."

He took a sip of beer.

"You want something?" he asked.

Guin didn't really, but she felt it would be rude not to order something.

"Hey, Jo!" Jake called.

Jo immediately came over.

"Everything okay?" she asked, looking from Jake to Guin.

"Yeah, everything's fine," said Jake. "Guin here just needs a beer."

"What'll it be?"

"Uh, what do you recommend?"

Jo described several beers they had on tap.

"I'll have a Sanibel Red Island Ale, please."

Jo made her way over to the nearest tap and pulled Guin an ale.

"Here you go," she said, depositing the mug in front of her."

"Thanks."

She took a sip.

"So, as you were saying…"

"So, I was driving over the Causeway and my car started acting strange, kind of stopping and starting."

Guin took another sip of her Sanibel Red. It was quite tasty.

"Then what?"

"I made it through the toll booths, but I decided to pull over. It was pretty dark out, but I didn't want to keep driving. Anyway, not a minute after I pulled over, this motorcycle pulled up behind me. At first the guy seemed friendly, asked if I was okay. I told him my car was acting funny. He volunteered to take a look, said he was a mechanic. I told him sure, not thinking anything about it.

"He popped the hood and shined the flashlight on his

phone around. I stood next to him. Nothing seemed wrong, though not that I would know. Then the guy makes this weird comment. Said he was sorry to hear about my friend. I said, What friend? He says, 'That pretty blonde you were seeing.'"

"Ronnie?" asked Guin.

"Who else could he have meant? So anyway, he's poking around under the hood and keeps talking about Ronnie. Says he heard she was seeing this French guy and that that must have been hard on me. I didn't say anything. But then he asks me, 'So, you think the French guy knocked her up?'

"I was pretty freaked out, but I tried to stay calm, said I had no idea what he was talking about. That's when he grabbed me. Told me to stop playing dumb. Said if I just answered his questions, he wouldn't hurt me.

"I told him I had no idea what he was talking about. That's when he punched me, hard, in the stomach."

Jake took another sip of his beer.

"Then what happened?" asked Guin.

"I doubled over. I was like, what the fuck, dude? What was that for? And then he hit me again. Totally winded me. He waited for me to get my breath back, then asked me again about 'the French guy' and Ronnie."

Guin sipped her beer and waited for him to go on.

"So then the guy grabs me by the collar and says, 'You gonna tell me or do I have to force it out of you?' And I said, 'Dude, I have no idea what the fuck you are talking about.' That's when he punched me in the face. I went down pretty hard. He was pretty angry. He dragged me behind the car, where no one could see us. Then he asked me again if Ronnie was getting it on with the French dude. I could barely think, let alone speak. He tossed me to the ground and kicked me. Pretty sure I lost consciousness then. Next thing I knew, I was coming to, behind my car, and he was gone.

"I was in really rough shape, but I somehow managed to make it across the way to the restaurant there. The hostess asked if she should call an ambulance. I guess I looked really bad. But I didn't want to go to the hospital. I just asked if I could use their phone."

"Who did you call? Where did you go? The police and the Fourniers have been trying to find you."

Jake gave a pained grin.

"I'd rather not say. A friend's."

He glanced down the bar and Guin followed his gaze. Jo the bartender was looking over at them. She was a petite brunette, slim and very toned from what Guin could see. Guin guessed she could more than hold her own in a fight. And judging from the way she was looking at them, Guin felt she would wrestle Guin to the floor if she did anything to Jake. Guin smiled at the thought, then turned her attention back to Jake.

"You have any idea who the guy was?"

Jake shook his head.

"Any idea why he was asking you those questions?"

Jake looked into his beer.

"I've been thinking about that the past week. It could have been some jealous guy Ronnie had flirted with. She was always flirting with guys, even when she was dating Billy."

"But why would he come after you? And why would he be asking if she was seeing a French guy?" asked Guin, though she had her suspicions.

Jake sighed. Waited a few seconds. Then spoke.

"The guy could have seen us together someplace. We would go to happy hour and to movies together."

"But why keep asking about 'a French guy'?"

Jake continued to stare into his beer.

Guin waited.

"I wasn't supposed to say anything."

"Ronnie's dead, Jake. If you know something…"

Jake sighed again.

"Ronnie was kind of seeing Jean-Luc."

"By *seeing* you mean…?" asked Guin.

"Yeah, I think so," said Jake. "Ronnie didn't give me all the details. She just went on about how incredibly sweet he was and how she loved his accent."

"Did anyone else know about her and Jean-Luc? Did Madame Fournier suspect something was up?"

Jake looked thoughtful.

"They kept it pretty professional at work, at least I thought so. Though when Jean-Luc got her that bracelet and she wore it to work…"

So Jean-Luc had been the one to give Ronnie that charm bracelet.

"She made a point of twisting her wrist and saying how she loved her new bracelet, right there in front of Madame Fournier. I thought she was crazy, but Madame Fournier just scowled and told her to take it off, that jewelry was not allowed to be worn while working in the kitchen. It was pretty ballsy of Ronnie, but she was like that."

"And when did she find out she was pregnant?" asked Guin.

"Just before she died. She hadn't been feeling well and bought one of those at-home pregnancy tests. She did it at the bakery, which I thought was kind of stupid, but she said she didn't want her housemates or Billy knowing about it."

"And?" asked Guin, though she already knew the answer.

"She was pregnant. She was actually pretty happy about it."

"Happy? Why?"

"I think she thought Billy would have to marry her, you know, do the right thing."

Guin raised her eyebrows.

"I thought they had broken up. And what about Jean-Luc?"

"I think Jean-Luc was kind of a fling. Billy was her one big love, or that's what she had told me. She told me the whole break up thing was mostly for his parents, that they would still get together on the sly. Billy's parents didn't approve of Ronnie."

"So I heard. Do you think she told Billy, about being pregnant?"

"She said she was going to. We actually had a big fight about it. I thought she should tell him right away, but she wanted to wait. I finally convinced her to tell him, but…"

"What happened?" asked Guin.

"She said she was going to meet him at his grandparents' place after work that Saturday. Billy was looking after the place. But Billy said she never showed. He said he waited there for half an hour, but he had to hit the road. He had some dinner thing up in Orlando. He said he texted her, but she never replied."

"So she didn't tell him about being pregnant?"

"No. At least I don't think so. She had told me she wanted to tell him in person."

"And she was sure the baby was Billy's?"

"You think it could have been Jean-Luc's?"

"You did say she and Jean-Luc were seeing each other. That might explain the biker."

"I don't know for sure if the two of them were actually, you know…"

"But you suspected."

Jake signaled for another beer, having drained the one in front of him.

"You okay?" Guin asked. Jake looked awfully pale, and those bruises gave his face a greenish cast.

"I'm fine. You should have seen me a few days ago. If it wasn't for—"

Jo slammed down a mug of beer in front of Jake. He gave her a sheepish grin.

"Thanks Jo."

She eyed Guin suspiciously, then went to help another patron.

Jake took a sip from the fresh mug.

"I guess maybe the baby could have been Jean-Luc's, but… Ronnie was convinced the baby was Billy's."

They sat side by side sipping their beers, not saying anything for several minutes. Guin went over Jake's story in her head. The answer to who killed Ronnie lay in there somewhere.

"You said she took the pregnancy test at the bakery?"

"Yes," replied Jake.

"And there's only one bathroom there?"

"Yeah," said Jake.

"Do you know what Ronnie did with the pregnancy test after she took it?"

"I assume she threw it in the garbage."

"And do you recall who was working at the bakery when Ronnie told you?"

"Just Jean-Luc and Madame Fournier."

"Could either of them have overheard you?"

Jake thought for several seconds.

"I suppose so. Now that I think about it, Madame Fournier told us to stop our yapping and get back to work."

"And that man who stopped, the biker who beat you up, would you be able to recognize him if you saw him again."

"Oh yeah," said Jake. "It was dark, but I'd remember those tattoos and that beard."

"So why didn't you go to the police with all this?" Guin asked.

Jake looked down and sighed.

"I had some weed in my car. I was worried the cops had found it and would arrest me, even though there was barely enough to roll a joint."

Interesting. No one had mentioned finding any weed in Jake's car. She wondered if the biker had taken it.

"Well, I appreciate you telling me all of this, Jake, but you should really talk to the police. Promise me you'll call Detective O'Loughlin at the Sanibel Police Department in the morning?"

"Sure, okay, if you think it will help."

"It will definitely help."

Guin got up to leave.

"You going?"

"Yeah, I'm not much of a drinker, and you've given me a lot to think about."

She threw some money on the bar.

"That should cover both our drinks."

"Thanks," said Jake, "but…"

"Have a goodnight, Jake. And tell Jo I said goodbye," she said, smiling at him.

Jake blushed.

Guin placed a hand gently on the young man's shoulder.

"Take care of yourself. And let me know if you need anything."

"Thanks," he said.

Guin waved goodbye to Jo and the bear of a bartender. As soon as she got outside, she grabbed her phone.

CHAPTER 40

"Sorry to call so late."

"Guin, it's not even nine o'clock," Craig replied. "We're not *that* old."

"Sorry," said Guin.

"And stop apologizing."

Guin was about to say "I'm sorry" but stopped herself.

"So what's up?"

"I just met with Jake Longley over at the Point Ybel Brewery. He's got some nasty bruises, but he's okay."

"Well, that's good to know. Where's he been?"

"Staying with a friend."

"What happened to him?"

"I'd rather not discuss it over the phone. I'm in a kind of public place," she said, looking around the parking lot.

"You want to come over here?"

"You sure it won't be an imposition?"

"Nah. Betty and I are usually up until at least ten."

"You sure? I'm about twenty minutes away."

"Come on over. I'll make sure Betty keeps her clothes on."

Guin could hear him chuckling and Betty asking him what was so funny.

"Thanks," said Guin. "I'll be there soon."

Guin made good time to Craig and Betty's and was standing in their kitchen.

"Can I get you something to drink or maybe to eat?" Craig asked. "We've got plenty of food in the fridge."

"Just a glass of water, thanks," said Guin.

He grabbed a glass from the cabinet and filled it with water from the refrigerator.

"Here you go," he said, handing her the glass.

"Thanks," Guin replied. "Where's Betty?"

"She's watching TV in the bedroom, one of those reality shows."

"Ah," said Guin.

"So, what did Mr. Longley have to say for himself?"

Guin then repeated what Jake had told her.

Craig whistled.

"That's quite a tale. Do you believe him?"

"Why shouldn't I?"

Craig scratched his head.

"Well, the bit about the biker roughing him up seems a little far-fetched. Or maybe he was meeting the biker about a drug deal and it went down wrong."

That hadn't occurred to Guin. Jake just didn't seem like the type to do or deal drugs. But what did she know?

"You say Jake said the guy was a mechanic?" asked Craig.

"Yes," said Guin.

"And that he had followed him across the Causeway?"

"That's what Jake thought, yes. Though he could have been parked nearby," said Guin, now that she thought about it. Though why would Jake lie?

"Tell you what. There are only two garages that do repairs on Sanibel. I'll go over to both of them tomorrow, see if either has a mechanic who fits the description Jake gave you. Shouldn't be too hard to find him, if he exists."

"That would be great, Craig. Thank you."

"No problem. I'm curious to know if Jake was telling the truth."

Guin yawned.

"Well, I should be on my way."

Craig smiled.

"Past your bedtime?"

Guin yawned again, then smiled.

"Almost."

They got up and Craig walked Guin to the door.

"Tell Betty I said hi."

"I will," said Craig.

"Oh!" she said, suddenly remembering the email she had sent to him earlier. "Did you get a chance to look at that email I sent you, of the phones that accessed the lock box at the Simms place that weekend?"

"Sorry. Afraid I haven't had a chance to take a look. I'll do it in the morning."

"No worries," said Guin. "I'll take a look too. Then we can compare notes."

She said goodbye again, then headed to the Mini. It was nearly nine forty-five. She debated whether to call the detective on his mobile or not. She settled for texting him, telling him she had located Jake and that Jake should be calling him in the morning. That done, she started the car and headed home.

The cats were there to greet Guin when she walked in the door. She bent down and stroked each one, eliciting loud purrs. Then she went into the kitchen. Even though it was late, she needed food, having not eaten anything at the brewery or at Craig's. She opened the refrigerator and grabbed the jar of peanut butter, some apricot jam, and the bag of multigrain bread and made herself a peanut butter and jelly sandwich, which she ate standing up.

Fauna gazed up at her, accusingly.

"What?" said Guin, chewing a bite of sandwich. "I'm hungry."

"Meow!" said Fauna.

Guin sighed and walked over to the food bowls. There was still food in them.

"You have food," said Guin.

"Meow!" said Fauna.

Guin rolled her eyes.

"Fine," she said, opening the fridge and grabbing the carton of milk. She went over to the cabinet and grabbed a little bowl. She poured a little milk into it and placed it on the floor. Fauna immediately went face down into the bowl, lapping up the milk. Guin smiled and took another bite of her sandwich.

As she was staring at Fauna, she heard her phone ringing. She had left it in her bag. She walked around the corner and retrieved it. It was the detective.

"Detective, to what do I owe this honor?"

"You texted me."

"Well, thank you for calling," she said, trying to disguise the fact she had a mouth full of peanut butter and jelly.

"You okay? You sound funny."

"Sorry," Guin replied, swallowing the bite of sandwich. "I'm just eating some PB and J."

"Oh," said the detective. "So what's this about you meeting with Jake Longley?"

Guin grinned.

"He phoned me earlier."

"And you didn't notify me?"

Guin had many responses to that question, none of them particularly polite, but she held her tongue.

"What did he have to say for himself?" asked the detective.

Guin continued to grin. Could it be she knew something the detective didn't? As if reading her mind, the detective spoke.

"You want a medal? Now are you going to tell me where you found Mr. Longley or am I going to have to go over there and arrest you?"

Guin imagined the detective coming over and handcuffing her. Then the scene took a decidedly unprofessional turn and she started to choke.

"You okay?" asked the detective.

Guin took a large sip of water.

"Sorry, some PB and J went down the wrong way. You were saying?"

The detective sighed.

"Just tell me what you found out about Jacob Longley."

"He'll tell you himself, tomorrow. I told him to phone you first thing."

Guin waited for the detective to say something.

"Fine," he said, finally. "But if I haven't heard from him by nine a.m., I'm sending a car to get you, and you will tell me everything you know about that young man."

Guin felt practically giddy. For once she was the one with the information.

"Yeah, yeah, yeah," said Guin dismissively. Despite his threat, she doubted the detective would actually send a police car to her place.

"Anything else you'd care to share?" asked the detective.

Guin thought for a minute.

"Nope. Anything you want to tell me?"

She waited several seconds for the detective to respond, but he did not.

"Well, goodnight, detective. Thanks for the call."

"Just do me a favor and try to stay out of trouble."

"Me, get into trouble?" Guin said, facetiously.

She could hear the detective sigh.

"Goodnight, Ms. Jones."

"Goodnight, detective."

She ended the call and finished her peanut butter and jelly sandwich. She smiled at the thought of knowing something the detective didn't, then yawned. Although she was tired, she needed to type everything Jake had told her. Then she could get ready for bed.

CHAPTER 41

Guin woke up Thursday morning feeling a little groggy. She rubbed her eyes and looked over at her clock. It was 6:30. She rolled over and closed her eyes, but it was too late. The cats already knew she was up and pounced.

"What do you two want?" she asked them, though she already knew.

She closed her eyes and pretended to be asleep, but the cats weren't buying it.

Flora tapped Guin's nose gently. Fauna was less delicate. She jumped on Guin's back.

"Ow!" said Guin.

Flora again pawed Guin's face. Guin sighed.

"Fine, I'll go feed you."

She made her way to the kitchen, the cats trotting after her. She gave them some canned cat food and refilled their water bowl. She thought about trying to go back to sleep, but she knew it was pointless. As soon as she got out of bed, her brain kicked into gear.

May as well make some coffee.

Her coffee made, she padded back to her bedroom and booted up her computer. She wanted to check out the numbers on the list that Ann Campbell had finally sent her. She waited for her computer to start up, then took a seat.

She opened the file and stared at the numbers. There

weren't that many. That wasn't surprising as the house hadn't officially been on the market at the time. And the list likely didn't include members of the Simms family, who all had keys. Though Billy said he had misplaced or lost his. Guin made a face.

Guin recognized Polly's phone number and she assumed a number that showed up several times was Ann Campbell's. There were only two other numbers. The first one had accessed the house at noon that Saturday. Guin cut and pasted it into her browser. It belonged to a prominent agent on Sanibel by the name of John Larson.

"John Larson," she said aloud. J. L. Could he be the mystery man?

She did a search for "John Larson." He was well known on Sanibel and Captiva. One of the top real estate agents. And he had a wife and three kids. It seemed unlikely he would be the killer, but she would need to check him out.

Guin sighed. Every time she thought she had narrowed down the list of suspects, it seemed to get longer.

There was just one number left. Per the list, it had accessed the lock box that Saturday evening. Guin cut and pasted it into her browser and hit "enter." She waited for the page to populate. She stared at the screen. Then clicked on a link. The number was registered to… Christina Fournier. Guin nearly spilled her coffee.

Don't jump to conclusions, she told herself. She now knew Madame Fournier was a real estate agent. And it was possible, because of her hours at the bakery, that she would show a house in the evening, after work. But something didn't seem right.

She glanced at the clock on her monitor. It was nearly seven-thirty. She sent Craig an email, telling him what she had found and asking him to call or text her after he visited the garages.

She glanced at the clock again, then out the window. It was still early, and the sky looked clear. She could go for a beach walk and be back in plenty of time to get in a full day of work. Her appointment at the bakery wasn't until four. Besides, a walk on the beach would help her organize her thoughts.

She threw on a pair of shorts and a t-shirt, pulled her hair into a ponytail, grabbed her beach bag and keys, and headed out the door.

It was a beautiful morning. Though to Guin, who had grown up in New York and had lived in New England most of her life, every morning on Sanibel was beautiful. She loved the warm weather and the endless sunshine. Heck, she didn't even mind when it rained.

She had decided to go over to Bowman's Beach, as it was the closest beach to the condo. The sun was just coming up. Perfect timing. She took a couple photos, to share on Instagram later, and headed down to the water.

As she stared down at the sand, looking for shells, her mind kept returning to what Jake had told her the night before and her discovery that Christina Fournier had been to the Simms house around the time that Veronica Swales was killed. It couldn't be a coincidence.

Think, Guin, think! she told herself.

Suddenly a furry object dashed past, scattering sand on her.

"Oh my! Sorry about that."

Guin looked up to see a woman, probably in her late sixties, holding two empty leashes. The woman looked quite apologetic. Guin turned to see two French bulldogs, one blue, one tan, chasing each other on the beach, looking as happy as could be. She smiled.

"Napoleon! Josephine! Come back here at once!" called the woman.

Guin let out a bark of laughter.

"I love the names!"

"My daughter named them. They're actually hers. I'm just dog sitting while she and her husband and the kids are on vacation."

"Very nice of you," said Guin, watching the dogs frolic at the edge of the water. "Aren't you worried they might run in?"

"Oh no," said the woman. "They don't really like water."

Guin wasn't so sure. They looked like they were having a grand old time.

"Napoleon! Josephine! Come here this instant!" she commanded.

The dogs looked up and immediately ran over to her, kicking up sand in their wake. Guin smiled as they came panting up to her, damp and sandy.

"Is it okay to pet them?" she asked.

"Oh yes," said the woman. "They're very friendly."

Guin let them sniff her hands. They seemed quite intrigued.

"They probably smell my cats," she explained.

She then petted them. They were very soft.

She stood up a couple minutes later.

"Well, thank you for stopping. They're lovely dogs."

The woman smiled.

"They love people."

She turned to the two dogs, whose tongues were hanging out.

"Josephine! Napoleon! March!"

She then headed down the beach, toward the parking lot, the two French bulldogs trotting after her. Guin smiled. If she didn't have the cats, she would seriously consider getting a French bulldog, if she could find one at one of the local shelters.

She continued down the beach a little way, her mind again going over the events of the past twenty-four hours. The more she thought about it, the more she was convinced that the Fourniers were behind Veronica Swales's death. She just wasn't sure yet which one had done it or if they had done it together.

Guin took a shower when she got back to the condo, then sat down in front of her computer to work on her other articles. However, she was finding it difficult to concentrate.

Finally, around noon, Craig called.

"Yes?" said Guin, as she picked up. She had been so eager for news she had left her phone out instead of tucking it in a drawer as she worked.

"I found him, Jake's mystery mechanic."

"Where? Does he work at one of the garages on the island?"

"Over at Smitty's. Of course, he denied having anything to do with Jake's disappearance. But your friend the detective and two of his officers showed up just as I was about to leave."

"Did the detective arrest him?"

"I don't know. He took him over to the police department to question him there."

"Were you able to find out anything?"

"Well, it may mean nothing. I'm still checking. But the mechanic's name is Declan O'Sullivan."

"So?" said Guin, not following.

"Like I said, it could just be a coincidence. O'Sullivan is a pretty common Irish last name. But the owner of the bakery, Christina Fournier, her maiden name is O'Sullivan.

Snap. Another piece of the puzzle just fell into place in Guin's mind.

"It can't be a coincidence," Guin said.

"Yeah, it seems unlikely, but I'm going to do a bit more digging. I have a buddy who'll know."

"You have lots of helpful buddies, don't you?" said Guin, smiling.

"In this business, it pays to be friendly," said Craig.

Guin thought she needed to make more of an effort to be friendly, though it was a lot easier on Sanibel than it was in New England or New York.

"Good work, Craig. I have some news, too."

"What's your news?"

"Pretty sure Christina Fournier visited the Simms place that Saturday night. I found her number on the lock box list. Of course, it could just be a coincidence. She is a real estate agent, and she works at the bakery during the day…"

"We seem to be uncovering a lot of coincidences," Craig said.

"Indeed. I'll find out more when I see Jean-Luc this afternoon."

"You want me to meet you over there? I don't like the idea of you being there all alone with them after what we've uncovered."

"I'll be fine."

"Just be careful. And call me, or better yet the police, if you need backup."

"Promise."

Craig then made Guin promise to call or text him after she left the bakery and said he would call the police himself if he hadn't heard from her by five. She rolled her eyes but said she would call or text him the moment she was done there. They then said their goodbyes and ended the call.

Guin shook her head. She knew Craig meant well, but

sometimes she felt he treated her like one of his granddaughters, when he should know by now she was perfectly capable of taking care of herself.

Which reminded her, she wanted to follow up with the detective, find out about this Declan O'Sullivan.

She called over to the Sanibel Police Department and was told the detective was busy. She asked if she could leave him a voicemail and was transferred. When she was done leaving her message she sent him a text, just to cover her bases.

The rest of the day seemed to drag by. She glanced at her phone. Three o'clock and still no word from the detective. She sighed. May as well leave him a voicemail on his mobile, too.

"Hi, this is Guin—Ms. Jones. I left a message for you over at the Sanibel Police Department earlier and sent you a text, but I didn't hear from you. I heard you took Declan O'Sullivan in for questioning. Did you find out anything? I'm heading over to the bakery to speak with Jean-Luc at four. I'll try you again later."

She then sent him another text, telling him to check his voicemail.

She stared at her computer, unable to concentrate, having typed only a few sentences.

"I give up," she said.

She changed into a pretty sundress, for her date with Ris later, and combed out her hair. Then she put on some mascara and lip gloss. Not too bad, she thought, looking at her reflection. She gave the cats a little food then headed out the door.

Guin arrived at the bakery a little before four. There were still a couple of customers in the shop. Madame Fournier was helping them. Guin smiled at her as she entered and Madame Fournier smiled back.

As soon as the customers left she turned to Guin.

"Can I help you, Ms. Jones?"

Guin looked at the pastry case. There was very little left, though she would have happily taken what was there.

"I have an appointment to see Jean-Luc at four. Is he in the back?"

"Oh, that's right," said Madame Fournier. "He mentioned you might be stopping by, something about a Thanksgiving article, wasn't it? We're offering all sorts of lovely pies and things for the holiday."

Guin had used the Thanksgiving article as a pretense.

She was about to say something when Jean-Luc appeared.

"Ah, Guinivere! So good to see you. And how lovely you look!"

He smiled at her, his eyes twinkling.

"Well, I have to run over to the bank," announced Madame Fournier. "So I'll just leave you two to it."

"*Au revoir, cherie*," said Jean-Luc as his wife brushed past him.

Guin watched her go and then heard the back door slam.

"Is this an okay time to talk?" she asked. "I'd actually like to speak with your wife, too, but…"

"You can speak with her later. Come, let's go into the back. There are some things in the oven I need to keep an eye on."

Guin involuntarily shivered at the mention of the oven, but she followed him to the back of the store, to where they prepared all of their baked goods.

"So, you are doing an article about Thanksgiving."

"Yes," said Guin, hesitatingly. "But first I need to ask you a couple questions."

"Of course!" said Jean-Luc.

"Was Veronica Swales working here the Saturday she died?"

Jean-Luc made a face.

"I am not sure," replied Jean-Luc. He looked pensive. "I think so, but I would need to check."

"Was Jake working here too?"

"No, he had off that Saturday."

"And you and Madame Fournier? Were you both working here that Saturday?"

"We work here every day," he replied.

"What did Veronica do, when she worked here?" Guin asked.

"Mostly she worked in front. She was very good with the customers, always getting them to buy more. But sometimes she would work with me in the back. She was very interested in how you make pastry and bread."

He smiled.

"Did you know Veronica was pregnant?"

His smile immediately faded.

"Veronica was pregnant?"

Jean-Luc seemed truly surprised. He mumbled something in French, which Guin couldn't understand, and ran a hand through his hair.

"You are sure of this?"

"Yes."

Jean-Luc seemed stunned by the news.

"Could it have been yours?" Guin asked softly.

"I don't know," he replied very quietly. "Christina and I, we were never able to have children."

So, he wasn't denying that he had slept with Veronica, even though Guin knew Billy Simms was almost definitely the father of the unborn child.

"So, you two *had* been seeing each other."

Jean-Luc sighed.

"*Oui.*"

Guin waited.

"She was so vivacious! Like a breath of fresh air. And so eager!"

"Were you in love with her?"

Jean-Luc sighed.

"Maybe. I do not know."

Guin looked at Jean-Luc. He was only a few years older than her and quite good looking in that Gallic/French way. Veronica wouldn't be the first young woman to fall for a man old enough to be her father, especially one who was good looking, could make heavenly pastries, and spoke with a French accent.

"Did you kill her?" asked Guin.

Jean-Luc was about to reply when Christina Fournier materialized, as if from thin air. Had she been lurking in the back the whole time, listening?

"Don't say anything!" she boomed.

"Christina, *cherie*!" said Jean-Luc, soothingly.

"Save it," replied his wife, giving him a look that would turn most men to stone.

"You know Veronica meant nothing to me. It was just, what do you Americans call it," he said, looking at Guin, "a mid-life crisis." He turned to face his wife. "I would never leave you."

"Just shut up already," snapped Madame Fournier, her Irish accent more pronounced.

"You didn't answer my question," Guin said to Jean-Luc, looking right at him.

"I would never harm Veronica," he replied.

Guin looked over at Madame Fournier and unconsciously took a step back.

"That little bitch ruined my life. I saw the way she looked at Jean-Luc. 'Is this the right way to knead the dough, Jean-Luc?'" she said in a falsetto voice, no doubt imitating Veronica. "Disgusting. She could have any man she wanted. Trying to seduce my husband right under my nose," Madame Fournier said with a sneer. "But I had her number, I did."

"Oh?" asked Guin, innocently.

"I knew she was pregnant. Overheard her and Jake talking. But if she thought a baby would get him to leave me, she had another thing coming."

She glared at Jean-Luc, who had opened his mouth to protest but quickly shut it again.

Guin stared at Christina Fournier.

"You killed her, didn't you?"

"It was an accident."

"An accident?"

"She was getting ready to leave. Going to meet that boyfriend of hers at his grandparents' house. The tart. I had overheard her talking to him on the phone earlier. Made me sick.

"I decided to confront her, about the baby. I had heard her and Jake talking about it the day before and found the pregnancy test in the garbage. I asked her if it was Jean-Luc's. She gave me this saucy look and said 'Maybe.'"

"Where was Jean-Luc?" asked Guin.

"Out making deliveries."

"What happened next?" asked Guin, unable to tear her eyes from Christina Fournier, who had grabbed the handle of a knife that had been resting on the table and was gripping it.

"I lunged at her. She kicked and screamed. Even pulled my hair, the little minx."

Madame Fournier looked lost in thought.

"Next thing I knew, she was slumped on the floor. I

thought she must have fainted. I yelled at her to get up, but she didn't."

"Why didn't you call an ambulance, or the police?" asked Guin.

Madame Fournier laughed.

"And tell them what?"

She had a point.

"Then what did you do?" asked Guin.

"I dragged her body out the back and threw her in the back seat of my car. Covered her with a tarp I kept in the trunk. Then I cleaned up the mess she'd made."

Guin looked down at Jean-Luc. He looked horrified.

"Then you drove over to the Simms place when it was getting dark and dumped her body in the spare room."

Madame Fournier looked at Guin.

"How'd you know that?" she asked.

"Your phone number was recorded on the lock box."

"Damn," she said. "And here I thought I was pretty clever. Well, you still have no proof."

"Oh, I have proof," said Guin, bluffing.

Christina lunged toward her, the knife from the table raised in her right hand.

Guin screamed and managed to swerve in the nick of time.

All of a sudden there was a commotion outside and the back door flung open.

"Freeze!" called a familiar voice.

Guin's heart nearly stopped. It was the detective, accompanied by Officer Pettit and Officer Rayburn.

"Drop the knife, Mrs. Fournier," ordered the detective.

The knife clattered to the floor.

"Cuff her," directed the detective.

Officer Rayburn came over and placed a set of handcuffs on Madame Fournier.

"Him too," said the detective, looking over at Jean-Luc.

"That won't be necessary," said Jean-Luc.

He hung his head, got up, and followed his wife and the two officers out the door.

"You okay?" asked the detective.

"Yeah," said Guin, though she was still in shock. "What are you doing here?"

"You left me several messages. When I didn't hear back from you, I started to get concerned. Then your friend Craig called saying he was worried about you. That you had gone over to the bakery and hadn't checked in with him."

"I told him I would call him when I was done here."

"Well, when he didn't hear from you..."

Guin glanced up at the clock. She had no idea what time it was and was stunned to learn it was almost five-thirty.

"I need to go," she said, getting up.

"Go where?" asked the detective.

"I have a date with Ris, Dr. Hartwick. He'll be worried if I'm late."

The detective stared at her.

"You're kidding, right? You're in no shape to drive, and I need you down at the police department."

"Can't it wait until first thing tomorrow? Surely you have enough evidence against them without me?"

Guin knew she should go with the detective, but what she really needed right then was a drink and Ris's strong, soothing arms around her, as pathetic, needy, and unfeminist as that sounded.

The detective rubbed his face with his hand.

"Please detective? Ris is competing in the Ironman Saturday and is leaving at dawn tomorrow. And he's expecting me for dinner at six-thirty."

She gave him a pleading look.

"Fine," said the detective. He did not look happy. "Be at

the police department at eight a.m. tomorrow. If you're late, I'm sending a patrol car to find you."

"Thank you, detective!"

She started to lean over to give him a kiss on the cheek but stopped herself.

"So, I'm free to go?"

"Go," said the detective.

Guin stopped at the back door.

"Aren't you coming?" she asked.

"I've got some work to do here first."

Guin stood there for a minute, looking at the detective. He was walking around the kitchen, making notes in his little book. Part of her wanted to cancel her date and stay. She shook her head and left.

CHAPTER 42

Guin unlocked the Mini and was about to open the door but stopped. Instead she reached into her bag and retrieved her phone.

"You okay?" came Craig's voice.

"Yes, thank you," Guin replied. "She did it, Craig. Though she claimed it was an accident."

"The wife?"

"Yeah," said Guin. "Look, I've got to go, but I'll follow up with you later."

"You at the police department?"

"No, I'm on my way to meet Ris. The detective kindly agreed to let me go. I'll go over there first thing tomorrow."

"Well, I'm glad you're okay. I was getting worried."

"I'm fine. I'll phone you tomorrow right after I'm done being interrogated by the detective." She smiled as she said it.

Craig grumbled something in response, then they ended the call.

As she drove to Fort Myers Beach, Guin had to remind herself to focus on the road, as her mind kept wandering back to what had just occurred at the bakery. Part of her wished she had remained with the detective and gone back to the police department with him.

She sighed.

A few minutes later she pulled into Ris's driveway.

His beach cottage really was lovely. A little too close to the neighbors, but the plants on either side helped shield it from prying eyes. He had had the place professionally landscaped when he moved in, but he had made sure it didn't look too manicured and that the landscaping company used mostly native plants.

The inside of the house was also very nice. Ris had hired a local interior designer known for her coastal chic decor—a friend of his ex-wife's whom he had dated. (And who was in the process of appealing a murder conviction. But that's another story.).

Guin stayed in her car for several minutes, looking at the cottage. Was she silly to want her own place when Ris had offered to share his with her? Granted, it wasn't on Sanibel, but it was pretty much perfect otherwise. It just wouldn't be hers.

She sighed again and quickly checked her phone. There was nothing that required her immediate attention.

She put away her phone and went to the front door.

Even though she had a key, she still felt funny about using it. She hesitated, then rang the doorbell.

Ris answered, looking effortlessly chic (and very fit) in his drawstring pants and polo shirt.

"You know you don't have to ring the doorbell," he said, smiling down at Guin.

"I know, but it still feels weird to just barge in," she replied.

"You would never be 'barging in,'" he said, taking her hand and pulling her to him.

He leaned down and gave her a kiss, which wound up lasting several minutes.

Guin finally pulled away, blushing.

"What will the neighbors think?" she asked.

Ris glanced around.

"No one can see, and I don't give a rip what the neighbors think."

He then pulled her back into his arms and kissed her again.

Guin giggled and swatted him playfully. When he acted this way, he made her feel like a teenage girl, instead of a divorced 41-year-old woman.

They walked into the main room.

"Mmm… something smells good, really good…"

Was that tomato sauce?

"I'm making pasta."

"I thought you were on a special diet."

"And now I'm carb loading."

"Ah," said Guin.

"Hope you don't mind."

"Me? Mind eating pasta? Never."

"I made meatballs too."

"Catch me. I think I'm going to faint," Guin said, placing a hand on her forehead.

"And bread."

"That does it. I'm moving in," said Guin.

Ris laughed.

"You know I'd like that," he said, looking at her.

Guin suddenly felt hot. She knew Ris wanted her to live with him, but she just wasn't ready.

"So, what time are you heading out tomorrow?" she asked, trying to change the subject.

"Five a.m."

"Ouch," said Guin. Though she knew he was usually up at five anyway. "You find anyone to go with you?"

"Actually, yes. Turns out one of my colleagues at FGCU is also competing."

"Oh, what's his name?" asked Guin.

"Dr. Penelope Adler."

"Ah," said Guin.

"She's in the biology department."

Guin made a mental note to do a Google search for Penelope Adler in the morning.

"Well, nice that you have someone to go with you." Though Guin could hear the falseness in her voice.

"You know there's always room for you, Guin, if you change your mind."

For a second, Guin thought about it. Then she shook her head.

"Can't. They just arrested the Fourniers."

Ris looked confused.

"They're the couple that own my favorite little bakery. The wife killed that young woman we found at the beach house, Veronica Swales."

Ris whistled.

"Yeah, I was there when the police came to arrest them."

Ris did not look amused.

"You okay?"

"Oh, I'm fine," Guin lied.

Ris did not look like he believed her.

"Really, I'm fine," she repeated, putting a hand on his arm and reaching up to give him a kiss on the cheek.

"See? Perfectly okay."

Just then a timer went off. Saved by the bell.

Ris walked back into the kitchen and turned the timer off. Then he opened the oven to remove the meatballs.

"They look good," said Guin.

"I hope so."

"Here, come taste the sauce," he said, lifting the lid of a pot.

"It smells amazing," said Guin, closing her eyes and breathing in the rich tomato scent.

He grabbed a spoon and dipped it into the sauce, then gently held it up to Guin's lips.

"Oh my God. That's amazing!" she said, opening her eyes.

Ris was smiling at her.

"I'm just going to warm up the bread. Then we can eat."

Dinner was delicious. Ris had made a big salad with his signature dressing. And the linguini with meatballs had been incredible.

"Are you part Italian?" Guin had asked him. "Because the only place I've had a sauce that good is either at an Italian restaurant or in Italy."

He had laughed and thanked her and told her that he was English, Irish, and German, though his ex-wife was part Italian, and he had gotten the recipe from her mother. Well, that explained it, thought Guin. Still, the fact that he could cook like that said volumes. And again she wondered if she was crazy not to accept his offer to live with him.

She helped him clear and clean the dishes, though he insisted he could handle it.

"Well, I should get going," said Guin, after they had finished cleaning up.

He grabbed her around the waist and held her.

"Must you go?" he asked, leaning down and kissing her.

She felt her legs go momentarily weak.

"You have an early morning…" she protested.

He continued to kiss her.

"I should really go," she said, pulling away.

"Stay," he whispered in her ear.

She looked up into his green-gray eyes. They looked like the sea after a storm. She was very tempted.

Suddenly the phone rang, breaking the spell. It rang

several times then stopped. Then it began ringing again.

"I'd better get that," he said.

"Hello?" he said, picking it up. "Hey Fiona. What's up?"

He held up a finger, indicating he'd just be a minute.

"Honey, hold on. I have Guin here."

He placed a hand over the phone and mouthed "It's Fiona."

"I know," Guin mouthed back, smiling.

She walked over to Ris, got up on her toes, and gave him a kiss on the cheek.

"Thanks for dinner," she whispered. "Call or text me when you get to Panama City tomorrow."

"Will do," he whispered back.

"Yes, honey. Sorry about that. Now what's the trouble?"

Guin gathered her bag and let herself out.

Saved by the bell, or phone, she thought.

She got in the Mini and headed home.

Guin had immediately Googled "Penelope Adler" when she got home. As Ris had said, she taught biology—and was an avid runner. She was also married with two children. Not that that meant anything. Plenty of married people with kids had affairs. Guin chided herself for being so suspicious. But ever since she had found out her ex-husband Art had cheated on her, with their hairdresser no less, she had become suspicious of all good-looking men.

She pulled on her nightshirt, brushed her teeth, and washed her face. Then she climbed into bed. It was after ten, but she wasn't tired. She had too much on her mind. She thought about taking half a sleeping pill, but she wanted to be alert for her meeting with the detective the next morning.

She closed her eyes and did several deep breathing exercises. Finally, after reading the birding book she had bought for just such occasions (it always made her sleepy) and doing another round of breathing exercises, she fell asleep, joining the cats who were snoozing away at the foot of her bed.

Guin arrived at the Sanibel Police Department promptly at eight the next morning and this time had brought her own coffee.

She announced herself at the window and was told the detective was expecting her. She then made her way back to the detective's office, telling the woman at the desk she knew the way.

"Ah, Ms. Jones," said the detective, standing up to greet her.

He was smiling, which was very uncharacteristic. And she was tempted to ask him if he had gotten laid, but she stopped herself.

"You're in a good mood," she said.

"What makes you say that?" asked the detective, still smiling.

"You're smiling," Guin replied. "You never smile."

"I do too smile," he said, no longer smiling.

"Rarely," said Guin, taking her usual seat.

The detective also sat.

"So, did you arrest them?"

"We let Mr. Fournier go, though we took his passport and told him not to leave the island."

"And Madame Fournier?"

The detective frowned.

"She's in custody."

"You arrest her?"

"Yes, though she claims it was an accident."

Guin snorted.

"You don't think so?"

"If you had seen the look on her face when she talked about that girl."

Guin made a face and shuddered.

"Well, that's her defense. She said the girl attacked her and she was just fighting back."

"Ha!" said Guin. "You've seen Christina Fournier and Veronica Swales. Do you really think that's what happened?"

"No, but it's not up to me to decide."

Guin had been leaning forward in her chair and now sat back.

"I know she strangled that girl. And I hope she pays for it."

The detective quirked his lips.

"And what about Jake's biker? Did you talk to him?"

"I did."

"And?"

"It would appear Mr. Longley may not have been making things up."

Guin gave the detective a questioning look.

"Mr. O'Sullivan does not have a sterling reputation."

"Drugs?"

"Among other things."

"So you're not going to arrest Jake?"

Guin waited for the detective to reply.

"No, Ms. Jones."

Guin breathed a sigh of relief.

The detective took out his notebook and pen and leaned forward.

"Now, tell me everything that happened from the moment you walked into Jean-Luc's yesterday…"

And she did.

CHAPTER 43

Guin recounted her conversation with Jean-Luc, as well as his wife's threats, and how Ronnie's body had wound up at the Simms place.

The detective listened to every word, jotting down notes, then thanked Guin for her time.

Guin asked him to keep her posted. She was going to ask him about their fishing expedition the next day, but the detective's phone had rung and he had asked her to see herself out.

"See you at Captain Al's dock tomorrow morning at seven," he had called to her as she was leaving. She gave him the thumbs up sign then left, closing the door behind her.

She texted Craig as soon as she had left the police department. He invited her over for a late breakfast. Betty had made a batch of her bran muffins. Guin accepted and headed over there, not having had breakfast before her meeting with the detective.

She arrived at Craig and Betty's place a few minutes later and was greeted warmly by both of them. Then Betty announced she was meeting her friends for their walk and left.

Craig invited her to have a seat at their dining table, and, over bran muffins and fruit salad, she repeated what she had told the detective.

"Nicely done, Ms. Jones," said Craig, smiling at her.

"You sound just like the detective," said Guin, grinning back at him. "So, what did Ginny say when you talked to her?"

Guin knew that Craig would contact her upon hearing the news.

"She was spitting mad we weren't able to wrap up the story earlier, so she could have run it in today's paper."

"Typical," said Guin, rolling her eyes. "But I assume you told her we would get her something this weekend."

"Of course," Craig replied.

"Well, no time like the present," said Guin, getting up. "Take me to your computer."

They spent the rest of the morning hashing out the story. A teaser would appear online later that day with both of their bylines, while the full story, or story to date, would run online that weekend. It was exhausting work, but both of them were used to short deadlines, and Guin was a fast typist. (As Guin didn't want to monopolize Craig's computer, they had agreed that Guin would finish the first draft of the piece at her place, then she would send it to Craig to edit before sending it to Ginny.)

That evening, as she lay in bed, she wondered how everyone involved would react to the news. It would certainly be a relief to the Simms family, and probably to Ann Campbell. But what about Veronica Swales's family? She had heard that they had been on island and had tried to contact them, but her efforts had been unsuccessful.

Finally, a little after ten-thirty, she fell asleep.

Her alarm went off at 6 a.m. the next morning. Worried she might oversleep, she set had set it for six, to give her enough time to dress and eat something before she had to be at the dock, which was less than ten minutes away.

She got up and made herself some coffee, giving the cats

some food and water as she waited for the French press to do its thing.

What does one wear to go fishing? she thought, staring into her closet. The day was not supposed to be too hot, and there was typically a breeze in Pine Island Sound. Probably best to wear a t-shirt and jeans and bring a light windbreaker, and maybe a sweatshirt.

She poured her coffee and nibbled on a protein bar. When she was done she headed back to her bedroom to finish getting ready.

She arrived at Captain Al's dock right at seven, bringing a large beach bag with her. She hadn't been sure what to bring, so she had brought along a towel, sunblock, bug spray, a sweatshirt, a pair of shorts, a water bottle, a small bag of nuts, a sun hat, and her camera, along with her purse.

"You know this is just a three-hour fishing trip," the detective had cracked when he saw her with her big beach bag.

"Remember what happened to the S.S. Minnow," Guin retorted.

"You got an evening dress in there, Ginger?" he replied, a smirk on his face.

"Ha," said Guin, though she was not amused. She had always fancied herself more Mary Ann than Ginger, despite the color of her hair.

The detective took her bag and helped her board Captain Al's boat.

Captain Al greeted her warmly.

"So, I hear you're taking up fishing."

"Not exactly," said Guin, looking over at the detective.

Just then two men appeared at the edge of the dock.

"Bill!" called out one of them, waving at the detective. He was carrying a 12-pack of beer.

Guin eyed the detective.

"Sometimes we get a little thirsty."

"Beer? At seven a.m.?"

The detective shrugged.

"Mike, TJ, allow me to present Ms. Guinivere Jones. Ms. Jones, Mike and TJ."

"Greetings," said Guin, extending her hand, which each man shook.

Guin had recognized Mike. He was the local medical examiner, or one of them. She didn't know the other man."

"You're that reporter," said Mike.

"Guilty," said Guin.

"She's the one who broke the Matenopoulos story and wrote about that guy getting killed this summer," Mike explained to TJ.

TJ looked unimpressed.

"You gents ready to shove off?" asked Captain Al.

"I sure am," said Mike. "How about you, Bill?"

"Ready, willing, and able," he replied.

TJ remained silent.

Guin felt like a third wheel. Make that a fourth wheel. Why had she agreed to go on this stupid fishing trip? Because the detective had asked her. That's why. She sighed.

"Everything okay, Ms. Jones?" the detective asked her, as they made their way into Pine Island Sound.

"I just don't understand why you asked me along. I feel like I'm intruding," said Guin, pouting a bit.

The detective gently placed a hand on Guin's arm, which surprised her.

"I invited you because I thought you might enjoy it."

"But you know I don't know how to fish."

"We'll teach you. Right boys?" the detective called.

"Sure," said Mike, smiling back at them.

"See," said the detective. But Guin did not see.

By the time they had returned to the dock a little before eleven, Guin was in a much better mood. True to their word, the men had coached Guin, and she had wound up catching several fish—and felt extraordinarily pleased with herself.

The detective helped her out of the boat.

"You have a good time?" he asked her, holding her hand.

"Surprisingly, yes," she said.

"See," the detective said, grinning.

"Not bad, Jones," said Mike, slapping her on the back.

TJ, who had barely spoken a word the entire trip, smiled at her.

"So, when are you coming fishing with me again," called Captain Al.

Guin looked over at the detective then back at Captain Al, shrugging.

"Craig better watch out or you'll be taking over his beat," he said, grinning up at her.

"Hardly," said Guin. "Craig's the fishing expert. I'm just a novice."

"Well, you go fishing with Bill here a few more times, and you'll be a pro," said Mike, grinning at the two of them.

They made their way back to their cars. Mike and TJ had driven over together and said their goodbyes, leaving the detective and Guin alone in the shaded lot. (Captain Al was busy doing something or other on his boat.)

"So, said the detective…"

"So…" said Guin.

She suddenly felt shy.

"Thanks for inviting me out."

"No problem," he replied.

"I hope I didn't harsh the guys' mellow."

"Oh no. I think they got a kick out of you. It's not every day they get to go fishing with a pretty lady."

Guin felt herself coloring slightly.

"Well, ah…" said the detective, shoving his hands in his pants.

"Can I make you some coffee?" Guin blurted out.

"Uh…" said the detective.

"I just got a batch of this special dark roast from Jimmy's Java. Haven't even opened the bag."

Guin knew the detective appreciated good coffee.

"Well, in that case," he said, smiling.

"Follow me, detective," she said.

She got into her purple Mini and headed slowly down the dirt road. As she made the turn onto Wulfert, she saw the detective following behind her and smiled.

EPILOGUE

Christina Fournier was arraigned the following week, charged with killing Veronica Swales and the attempted murder of Jacob Longley. Craig had been right about the biker and Christina Fournier being related. He was a cousin, hard up for cash. At first Declan had refused to say anything. However, when the district attorney offered him a deal for information, he immediately pointed the finger at his cousin (and ratted out a couple of his suppliers too).

As for Jean-Luc, he had closed the bakery temporarily and had contemplated closing the place for good. However, after pleas from his loyal clientele, Guin among them, and with Jake offering to go back to work there, he had reconsidered. Jake had even gotten his friend Jo, the pretty bartender, to go to work there too. It turned out she had a passion for baking and jumped at the chance to learn from a real French pastry chef. (When Jake had gently warned her to stay away from Jean-Luc, she had punched him on the arm and told him he was being silly.)

As for Ris, he finished all three legs of the Ironman in very respectable times for his age and felt quite pleased with himself. He had texted Guin late that Saturday to tell her, but she had already turned her phone off for the night and did not receive the message until the following morning, when she turned her phone back on.

They had arranged to have dinner that Tuesday evening at the Beach House in Fort Myers Beach, one of their favorite restaurants, located right on the water.

Guin hadn't seen Ris in days, so she took extra care to dress nicely, putting on her pretty blue mermaid dress, as she had nicknamed it, which brought out the blue in her eyes. She had even applied a little makeup and managed to tame her curly strawberry blonde hair.

She arrived at the restaurant a few minutes late, due to traffic, and ran up the steps to the hostess stand. She was greeted by Simone, who knew her and Ris well.

"He's waiting for you," said Simone, giving Guin a conspiratorial smile.

Guin suddenly felt a little nervous.

Simone led her to a corner table with a view out over the Gulf. It was dark, but the water was lit up from the gibbous moon and the lights around the restaurant and the ships anchored nearby. And you could see hundreds of stars dotting the sky.

Ris stood as Simone led Guin over. He took Guin's hands and leaned over to kiss her cheek, whispering, "You look beautiful," into her ear.

Guin could hear Simone audibly sigh.

"You don't look so bad yourself," she said, taking him in and smiling.

"Shall we?" he said.

Guin sat and he did also.

Guin noticed there was an ice bucket next to the table and raised her eyebrows. Ris gestured to someone and a minute later a young woman appeared with a bottle of Champagne. Guin opened her mouth to speak but swiftly closed it as the young woman deftly pulled the cork out of the bottle, barely making a sound.

Guin watched as she poured a little Champagne into two

flutes, smiled at the two of them, then placed the bottle back into the Champagne bucket.

Ris raised his glass and Guin followed suit.

"Are we celebrating something?" asked Guin.

"I hope so," Ris replied. "To us," he said, clinking his glass to hers and then taking a sip of the Champagne.

Guin took a healthy sip from her glass at the same time, then put the glass down.

"Guin," said Ris, taking her hand and looking into her eyes.

Guin felt unable to move.

"There's something very important I need to ask you."

To be continued…

Look for Book Four in the Sanibel Island Mystery series, *Bye Bye Birdy*, Summer 2019.

Acknowledgments

They say it takes a village to raise a child. In my case, it took an island—my "child" being this book series. The people of Sanibel Island, especially those in the shelling community, have been so supportive of me and the Sanibel Island Mystery series. Without them, there wouldn't be a book three. So I want to give a shout-out to the Shellinators, the Sanibel Shell Seekers, and the Sanibel-Captiva Shell Club. You guys rock, or shell.

I also want to thank all the stores on Sanibel that took a chance on this new author. Thank you to Rebecca and the staff at MacIntosh Books of Sanibel (and Brady the cat), Christian and the folks at Gene's Books, Melissa and Richard and the staff at Bailey's General Store, and Kari and the staff at Sanibel Moorings. Thank you so much for carrying my books.

I also want to thank my loyal first readers, Amanda and Diane, who have been with me from the start of this journey. Thanks for reading the books in manuscript form and helping to make them better.

Thank you to my incredibly talented and patient cover designer, Kristin Bryant. I particularly love this cover. And thank you to Polgarus Studio for making my books look as professional on the inside as they are on the outside.

Thank you to my cats for not throwing up on my laptop,

or my desk, or the bed, and for not threatening to sue (though in their case the descriptions are entirely accurate).

And a huge THANK YOU to my mother and stepfather, Sue and John, the best proofreaders/copyeditors a writer could have. Thank you for correcting my grammar, style, and punctuation, and for your continued support. (Any errors made on this page are entirely my fault.)

Lastly, thank you to my wonderful, supportive husband, Kenny, who has always believed in me.

About the Sanibel Island Mystery series

To learn more about the Sanibel Island Mystery series, visit the website at http://www.SanibelIslandMysteries.com and like the Sanibel Island Mysteries Facebook page at https://www.facebook.com/SanibelIslandMysteries/.

47580266R00214

Made in the USA
Columbia, SC
03 January 2019